PRAISE FOR
RACHAEL HERRON'S
WORK

"A poignant, profound ode to the enduring and redemptive power of love."
— Library Journal

"A celebration of the power of love to heal even the most broken of hearts."
- NYT Bestselling Author Susan Wiggs

"A heart-warming story of family, friendship and love in a town you'll never want to leave."
— Barbara Freethy, USA Today Bestseller

ALSO BY RACHAEL HERRON

FICTION:

STANDALONE NOVELS:

THE ONES WHO MATTER MOST
SPLINTERS OF LIGHT
PACK UP THE MOON

CYPRESS HOLLOW NOVELS 1-5:

HOW TO KNIT A LOVE SONG
HOW TO KNIT A HEART BACK HOME
WISHES & STITCHES
CORA'S HEART
FIONA'S FLAME

MEMOIR:

A LIFE IN STITCHES

The Darling Songbirds

by

RACHAEL HERRON

The Darling Songbirds / Rachael Herron. -- 1st ed.

ISBN: 1-940785-23-5
ISBN-13: 978-1-940785-23-3

DEDICATION

For Smiley's Schooner Saloon.
Keep pulling down those signs, Bolinas.

CHAPTER ONE

The saloon had always looked old-fashioned, but now it resembled a set in a ghost town. The boards creaked under Adele Darling's feet as if they hadn't been stepped on since women wore hoop skirts. Cobwebs on the porch slung themselves from top beams to bottom ones, and an old wagon wheel leaned against a hitching post in front. It was as if the sidewalk had been poured right around the post, and her Toyota hybrid looked completely wrong parked next to it. It should have been a horse.

The problem was that Adele wasn't in an old western, or a ghost town. Darling Bay was the sleepy gold-rush town her great-grandfather had given his name to.

The town she'd left for good a long time ago.

There was a hand-drawn sign that said: *Hours – 11 AM–2 AM*. She glanced at her cell phone. Almost noon, and the doors were locked. Awesome.

She knocked on the wood next to the iron screen door.

"That won't do you no good."

Adele spun. "Sorry?"

The exceedingly short woman standing on the step below her wore a long, oversized blue dress that hung on her like a sack. Somewhere in her mid-sixties, she had a well-creased face, like a crumpled envelope. A dozen or more necklaces dangled around her neck, crystals and quartz and what looked like actual feathers, on tarnished silver chains. Her short grey hair stuck up in spikes as if she'd just run her hands over it roughly, but her smile was wide. "He ain't here yet."

Adele wasn't sure who *he* was. "Okay . . ."

"But if you reach up above the door," the woman pointed, "yeah, right there. You're a tall one, ain't you? Grab that key for us, will you?"

It wasn't that Adele was tall at five foot five. It was more like the woman was eye level to her elbow. "Got it." Now that the key was in her hand, Adele had no idea what to do with it. It wasn't like she would just unlock the bar's front door. Would she?

She didn't have to make the decision. In a move so quick it surprised her, the woman snatched the key from her palm and unlocked the iron security door, swinging it wide open and barreling through the wooden half-door as if she owned the place, which Adele knew for a fact she didn't.

"Sometimes I gotta open up for him, you know?" The woman moved to the right and snapped on two light switches, and then headed for the bar. She was a low, fast-moving bowling ball in blue. "It's usually harder 'cause it's tough for me to reach that key. It's not like I mess with the till or nothin', I just help him out where I can."

Adele trailed behind the woman. This wasn't the situation she had imagined herself in when she'd awoken this morning. All she'd known four hours ago in her San Francisco hotel was that she had a long drive up the coast. When she got to Darling Bay, she figured she would plan her next move.

So she'd gotten in her rental car and headed north. Highway One wound through the redwoods, darting out to the rocky coast and back inland again. She'd stopped once to stretch her legs, and had stood cliff-side watching elephant seals slap themselves up and down the coarse sand. It took a bit more than three hours to get to Darling Bay, a long-enough drive to make her feel as far from Nashville as she'd ever felt.

She used to be used to this feeling. This used to be home.

And now she had exactly no idea what that meant.

"You want a drink, dearie?"

Adele blinked. "I'm sorry . . . Who are you?"

"Well, I suppose I could ask you the same thing."

That was fair. "I'm Adele Darling."

"Oh, my *God*. You *are*."

Crap. Adele should have just said her first name. What was she thinking? Nowhere else would her last name have raised more than a vaguely puzzled eyebrow. *Sounds familiar ... can't place it.* But not here.

The woman clutched at her pile of necklaces. "They didn't tell me that."

"Who?" Adele was feeling more confused by the second. "I don't think anyone knew I was coming."

"But they usually tell me everything." She held up a chain that had a pink piece of stone at the end and peered at it closely.

"Your necklaces tell you these things?" Adele kept her voice soft. Maybe it was better not to startle her.

The woman stared at Adele as if she were crazy. "Not my necklaces. My *dreams*."

"Ah."

"Of course, it's not like they're always right. Sometimes they tell me a storm is coming when all that's going to happen is I forget to take the kettle off the stove. Same thing." She waved her arms above her head. "Clouds of steam. Just in my kitchen. You see?"

Adele nodded carefully.

"Where are the other two?" The woman peered behind Adele as if she were somehow hiding her sisters.

"Not with me." Nothing could be truer. "I didn't get your name." Adele held out her hand.

The woman's shake was firm. "Norma."

"And you're the bartender?"

Norma laughed heartily, but she spread her palms on the top of the bar as if to negate her next statement. "Oh no, not me. You're a funny one. I'm just a drinker, from a long line of the same. Speaking of which, what can I make you?"

Not the bartender, then, but not *not* the bartender. "How about a Coke?"

"With rum? And can I read your tarot cards?" Norma asked hopefully.

"I'm good on both, thanks." It was a bit early to start pounding liquor. "So if you're not the bartender, and the saloon was supposed to open at eleven . . ."

"Oh, he'll be here."

"Who will?" This was beginning to feel like a game of Who's On First.

"Nate."

"Nate?"

"You don't know him?"

"I haven't been here in a while," Adele said. If a while meant eleven years. She'd been far away from Darling Bay, sometimes as far as a person could get. "*When* do you think he'll be here?"

Norma frowned and held one of her necklaces, looking upward as if the answer hung in the cobwebbed rafters. "Soon." Then she filled a glass with Coke and slid it towards Adele. "Here you go. Now, tell me everything. How're your sisters? You know, my dad – may he rest in peace – died before y'all got famous, but I always think he would have loved you. When *your* dad died, I asked my dad to bring him into heaven with a big ol' hug. Felt so bad for you young gals. Are you getting the band back together? You know we talk about you all the time. And those magazines, they stopped printing those stories about y'all, and that's a good thing, but we never believed a word they said anyway. How's the little one? Lana?"

The back of Adele's throat itched. "Fine." She had no idea how Lana was since she never answered Adele's phone calls. The ache of it was dull and familiar. "Do you mind if I have a look around? While I wait for Nate?"

"Sure, sure." Norma bobbed up and down behind the bar, spinning into action. Tomato juice, sliced celery, vodka. "A Bloody Mary doesn't just appear out of nowhere. Gotta work at it." She frowned and looked upward again. "Unless you stare into the mirror, you know? And say those words? I'm not gonna do *that*. Okay. There." She added a dash of Tabasco. "Mine isn't as good as Nate's, but I'm getting there. Just gotta keep working on it."

Adele wandered towards the rear of the saloon. It was just as she remembered it, dark and dusty, smelling of splintered wood and spilled beer. The old jukebox glowed neon blue and green in the far right corner. Next to it was a skinny ATM that had been added since she was last here. To the left of that ran the long bar all the way to the back wall. How many buckets of ice had Adele hauled out of the old storeroom? The girls had loved being there in the saloon, still under-age, helping Uncle Hugh with stocking and refilling in the afternoons. They'd begged to be allowed to stay as late as they could, listening to the music, not leaving until Sheriff Tate came in after his shift and raised his eyebrows at the little girls doing their homework in the far left corner on the big, scarred wooden table.

The table was still there. Adele touched the top of it, feeling the ridges with her fingertips. People still carved their initials into it, using penknives and ballpoint pens. They didn't cut deeply (out of respect, perhaps – surely they would have dug more deeply into a tree) and the well-worn initials looped over each other, years and years of couples who had loved and lost and loved again. When Adele and her sisters had done their math homework here, they'd had to make sure their notepads were under their papers, or their pencils would stab through into the table's scars.

Somewhere on the table were their initials, too. All three of them, *AD + MD + LD. Adele and Molly and Lana.* Hidden now somewhere, buried by the map of other letters.

Adele realized she was humming and closed her throat. She heard the refrain of "You'll Never Leave" in her mind. Then she wandered back towards the front door. To the right was the stage. Just a couple of feet higher than the floor, it was made of the same old wood and, if she remembered right, just as rickety. Impulsively, she jumped up onto it, stretching her arms wide. A light snapped on above her head, and she grinned in delight. Even when they were kids, Uncle Hugh had kept that motion-activated light there, and they'd loved the way it had shone down on them like a spotlight.

"Sing us a song!" called Norma from the other side of the saloon.

Oh, hell, no. Adele swallowed her grin and raised a hand. "Maybe later." Or maybe never.

The old pool table stood in the same spot it always had. Adele could imagine a tsunami sweeping in and taking out the Golden Spike, carrying away the saloon and the café and the old hotel – the whole town of Darling Bay itself – but that pool table, as heavy as sin and older than Eve's apple, would stay right there, right where it had always been meant to sit. At some point over the years, the felt playing top had been repaired. Chalks, the old square kind, were lined up on the rail, and a half-dozen cue sticks leaned drunkenly against the short inner wall.

Adele could almost hear the crack of the balls. Molly had been their ringer, always willing to bat her eyes innocently at whatever guy thought it would be fun to show off his pool prowess to teenage girls. Molly would run the table, stick the guy's money in her pocket, and then ask Uncle Hugh for a round of root beer floats for her and her sisters.

Molly. She wanted Molly here.

She pulled out her cell phone. *Remember the root beer floats?*

Holding her phone in her hand in case the text actually managed to soar out to the cruise ship somewhere on the ocean, Adele used her other hand to lift up the bench seat in the front window alcove. There they were, all the board games they'd spent so much time with. She'd be willing to bet that the Monopoly set was still missing all the Get Out of Jail Free cards. (Sheriff Tate had gotten his feelings hurt one night when he'd been on a particularly expensive Monopoly losing streak.) And the Sorry! game . . . She pulled it out and lifted the lid. Yep, there they were. Each piece had little teeth marks at the top, marching all the way around. The blue piece was missing the round knobby top altogether.

While Adele raced around the board, passing her sisters with a cheery "Sorry!', Lana would get so mad she'd chew the pieces, leaving her tooth marks behind, or in the case of the blue one, biting the top right off.

Adele glanced left. Norma was looking into her Bloody Mary as if it were telling a fortune, so Adele quietly slipped the headless blue piece into her jeans pocket. From the layers of dust inside the bench seat, no one would miss the piece anytime soon.

She looked out the side alcove window. Across the middle parking lot stood the old café. Funny, she'd assumed it would be still be open, that Hugh's employees would still be running it. But it was shuttered and dark, an unbearable sense of loneliness coming from the ripped awning. She looked right, up to the slight rise behind the saloon and café. That was the hotel, the third old building that she'd called home every summer of her youth. It was where she would sleep tonight. She yearned for that, for this already-long day to speed up until she could just lie down, close her eyes, and breathe in the ocean-scented air.

The phone – the real one that hung on the bar's back wall – jangled. Adele jumped. Norma grabbed it without hesitation. "Golden Spike, this is Norma!"

There was a pause. "Yeah." She grinned. "Right again. You bet. I'll keep 'er running, boss. Yeah. Okay. And hey? I forgot to tell you I need a raise." She slammed the phone down with a hoot of laughter. "That was him!" She looked at Adele as if suddenly surprised to see her. "Oh! I should have told him you were here."

"No, that's okay. I'll see him when he gets here."

"So I guess *you're* the boss around here now." Norma was obviously startled by the thought, her grey eyebrows shooting higher. "Of course you are. Oooh." Her drink wrapped tightly in her hand, she leaned forward from her saloon stool. "You should tell him to hire me. I wouldn't drink all the booze, I *swear* I wouldn't." But there was a twinkle behind her expression that said the opposite was true, and that they both knew it.

CHAPTER TWO

Nate shouldn't have answered his cell phone that morning, but he was a sucker for a blonde. Especially if the blonde happened to be ninety-one and living on the boat he'd sold her five months earlier. Ruthann Suthers had asked, "Does it matter, dear, if my extension cord in the kitchen smokes a little?" Nate thought of the electrical fire at the hotel, and told her to call 911. She said, "I already did. They said it was okay, but they shut off my power." Nate had sighed and spent the next two hours crawling around the baseboards in the boat's mess. He'd installed three new surge protectors, and he'd tested each outlet. By the time he'd finished, he'd bruised a knuckle and ripped his favorite Merle Haggard T-shirt.

And he was late.

At least Norma had been at the bar to open up. Unless a wandering tourist or two showed up, she'd probably be the only customer until three, anyway.

He parked his truck in front of the post office. Getting out, he pulled his Charlie's Feed and Seed ball cap on backward. What he really needed was another shower. Maybe he could bribe Norma with a couple more drinks off her tab to stay a little longer while he cleaned up. He took the two shallow steps up off street level with one long jump.

Inside the saloon it was dim compared to the bright morning sunlight. Norma grinned at him from her regular bar stool. "Boss!"

"You keeping out the riffraff?" Too late, he noticed that someone else *was* in the saloon, way over by the bench full of board games. "Whoops." Not even a tourist – a pretty tourist, at that – wanted to be called riffraff.

"Nah, they're getting in. And hey, guess who it is."

He looked again. The woman was standing straighter now, pretending not to hear them. She kept her eyes out the side alcove window as if there was something more than just the old, closed Golden Spike Café across the parking lot to look at. And she wasn't just pretty. From this angle, she was a sight closer to beautiful. God, who did she remind him of? She must have driven up from the city or something. Some model, waiting for her photographer to shoot her on the beach. He'd seen it plenty of times before, pretty girls thinking it would be good to get shots of themselves in the water, or leaning against the high cliffs down at Fenton's Cove, not realizing that the fog bank usually made it not only a shoot in bad light, but also a shoot where they'd freeze their dang nipples off. If they stayed till October, maybe. That's when the sun came out around here, after the summer tourists had given up all hope and left. But this woman, with her honeyed hair and that perfect long nose, those lips that were quirking into something that looked like it was close to a smile, she'd be shivering in her two-piece soon enough.

"Howdy," he said politely. If his ball cap had been forward-facing, he would have touched the brim, but as it was he left his arms at his sides.

She turned to face him, and in that motion his heart dropped to the old floorboards and went right through, straight down to the dust and packed earth below, not stopping until it hit the world's molten core.

Adele Darling. Out of freaking *nowhere.*

CHAPTER THREE

Adele had never seen anyone go from "exhausted" to "ready to fight" so fast. She may have seen it on the television, watching boxing shows with old boyfriends. But not in real life.

The man – Nate, obviously – was wearing a baseball cap backward, and it didn't look like he'd shaved in at least a day or two. His eyes were stone-colored – a weathered grey-blue – and his skin was tan, as if he spent time outside pounding things furiously with hammers or maybe just those bare fists of his that were clenched at his side. He wore a ragged black T-shirt with what was probably once a picture of Merle Haggard (she couldn't fault his taste) but was now almost unrecognizable under a layer of dirt. His jeans, wide at the thighs and ripped at the left knee, were streaked with what looked like oil.

And he seemed pissed as hell.

"Howdy," she said back. As she did, she realized her mouth hadn't shaped that word since she and her sisters had quit singing. It used to be their thing. Their brand. Up onstage, a round of happy *Howdys* from all three girls, leaving the stage later with *Thanks, y'all!* Sure, all the country singers had done it, but they'd meant it. They'd been raised on the music they sang, and a heartfelt howdy was no small thing.

But now she wished she could take it back, along with her hand, which she'd already impulsively stuck out towards the man.

She didn't, though.

And, eventually, he took it. His hand was dry and wide. At least it seemed he'd washed *that* part of himself.

"I'm Adele Darling," she said.

"I know."

She took a quick breath. "That's not the reaction I usually get."

"Really." He sounded like he didn't believe her.

It was true, though. Before Norma had sort of recognized her, it had been months. Maybe, now that she thought about it, even a year or more. "What's your name?" She shouldn't have had to ask, and it was funny how it made her feel to do so – like she was standing on the wrong foot, about to topple over.

"Nate Houston."

What a country name. If she'd met a fellow songwriter with that handle, she would have known he'd made it up. Most songwriters" real names were Mark and Steve and Joe, but when they crossed into Nashville's city limits, they changed themselves into Rascals and Coles. Nate Houston, with its Texas-town last name, was a home run of a songwriter name. Not that he would know that, or care.

"You're the bartender."

He dropped her hand like she'd burned him. "Yep."

He was a sight better looking than the last bartender Adele remembered. Donna had been an institution at the Golden Spike, with her flaming red hair that came from a bottle and an attitude that came from the same place, different shelf. She was legendary for not only being able to drink all the customers under the table but for storing her upper teeth in highball glasses and then forgetting where they were. More than once she'd poured a Gin Fizz with a side of denture.

Adele smiled in a way she hoped was unthreatening. "Tell me more?"

He shrugged, like he was trying to shake himself into a more casual appearance. "Just that. Bartender, handyman, your general gofer. I helped your uncle out with near about everything around here. Sorry, by the way. About your loss."

The words sounded forced, as if he wasn't that sorry at all.

"How long have you been working here?" Adele tried to stay in one place, keeping her feet still. What she wanted to do was shuffle sideways, maybe get out of his solid-granite stare, but she wouldn't give this alarming person the satisfaction. She needed his help, needed him to be on her side. It wouldn't do to lose the one guy who knew how this place worked.

"Long time."

"Oh, yeah?" Why had her uncle hired this guy? Had they been close? At the mention of Uncle Hugh, she didn't even see the man twitch. Maybe there hadn't been much love lost for his employer? Although she had no idea who wouldn't love Uncle Hugh. He'd been such a big personality, trumpeting and blustering and always, always, loving.

Adele looked at Nate closer. He didn't look familiar. She would have recognized him if he'd been around when they had lived in town, right? There's no way she could forget a guy with shoulders like that, even if he had a face (and maybe the personality) of a chisel. "I left eleven years ago."

"Yeah."

"Ah." She wobbled. "When did you come to town?"

"Ten and a half." He shifted his weight. "Years."

The man made taciturn look chatty. Adele glanced towards Norma, but apart from watching them with big, interested eyes, she just stirred her celery stick in her now-very-low drink. "Seems like we missed each other."

"We sure did."

And he sounded so pleased about that.

"Look," Adele said, "I'm glad you're here. I just need the lay of the land."

"So you can sell."

Well, of course. It wasn't like she was going to stay and run this place, and her sisters were in the wind. Molly could barely find her phone often enough to text back, and Lana didn't answer her phone, ever. For some reason, though, Adele was suddenly loath to admit this to the man. "Of course. But I need more info on the property. You understand."

"Oh, I understand." His eyes said something else. And it wasn't a very polite word.

Why did he seem so angry with her? Like this was some kind of power struggle? Well, two could play this game, whatever it was. Hadn't she been the champion at every board game ever made? Sure, Molly had run the pool table (probably still could), but Lana hadn't bitten the top off the Sorry! piece because she'd been furious about winning. No, Adele always won the board games. She touched the broken piece in her pocket again, reassuringly sharp. "So it looks like the place could use a little clean-up."

Satisfyingly, she could almost hear his teeth clenching. A muscle jumped in his jaw. "You're probably right."

"Maybe I could help?"

"You had a look out the back yet?"

"No." She hadn't even gotten as far as the storeroom yet, let alone the outside patio that led up to the old hotel. "Maybe you can show me?"

This, at least, seemed to please the man. He dipped his head. "I would *love* to show you around.'

CHAPTER FOUR

H ot damn, would he ever show her around. A
lot could happen in eleven years. A lot could
go wrong. "Let's get started."

"Great." Her voice was cheerful. Light.

Let's see how long that would last. "Watch your step
here," he said, slamming open the door to the storeroom.
"That second step broke a while ago, but we found that
the brick works just fine for balance, if you're careful."
And if you didn't step on the left side of it, which would
pitch you right off. He didn't need to mention that. It
would be a simple fix, one that would take less than an
hour – the step just needed a couple of new boards.
That's why Hugh had put it off, and why Nate had, too.
There were always more pressing things needing to be
done when the saloon wasn't open, and there weren't
enough hours in the day to fix the old place up.

"Gotcha."

He waved his arm down the row of boxes. "Mostly drinks and mixes. Some paper products." The only light was a bare bulb hanging directly overhead, low enough that he'd learned to duck when he moved through the room quickly.

"Oh, yeah." Her voice was soft, and she was looking at the ice machine with what could only be called reverence, as if it were something beautiful, instead of a dented piece of steel machinery that worked most days *except* the hottest ones.

"Ice machine. Only sometimes it just turns into an ice bucket. Not ideal."

Her face didn't change. Her smile actually pitched upward, and she ran her hand along the side of it. "Wow."

She was easily impressed.

Adele laughed. "This was our job when we were just kids. We got the ice for Uncle Hugh." She pressed her fingers to her cheeks. "Silly, huh? We loved it. He made us feel so important. Somehow we thought that without us, he wouldn't have made it."

That was closer to the truth than she knew, Nate would bet, and anger slid up his spine like a hot blade again. "Yeah. Anyway." He led them through the storeroom's side door into the courtyard.

"Oh, *my*." Her voice was just a breath behind him.

Nate crossed his arms and tried to see the space as if he hadn't seen it in years. He squinted. Yeah, it was all right. Five years ago, he'd talked Hugh into letting him build an arbor over the small yard. He'd trained jasmine and a couple of grapevines over it, and now it was shaded most of the year. In the spring it was a sweet-smelling heaven, and in the summer tourists loved grabbing at the grapes that grew green and slightly sour overhead. Six picnic tables sat lined up, three by two, and some afternoons the whole patio would fill up with tourists and locals alike, drinking beer and shooting the breeze.

It was fall now, September. Early enough that the fog still hung on most of the day, and late enough that the tourists had packed up their tents and RVs and had trucked on home to wherever they came from so Kiddie Jr. could go back to school.

It was Friday, so it would be busy later. But aside from Norma and maybe Parrot Freddy – another of his favorite customers, a man who went nowhere without at least one of his two parrots on his shoulders – it would be quiet till early evening.

And now that was proving to be a good thing. He was glad the courtyard was deserted. And he was glad it was still light. Even he could admit that when the fairy lights came on, it looked magical out here.

She didn't need to see that.

"I love all that ivy along the fence. It's wonderful. Like a secret garden. I don't remember it being there."

"Yeah. I gotta rip that out. Wharf rats love it."

"Of course." Adele blinked. "The grapes!" She grabbed at one and popped it in her mouth.

Her gasp and instant frown told Nate that the grapes were still sour. He gave her props for continuing to chew. Lots of people just spat them out onto the ground. "And up we go." Nate took the back path at a quick clip, throwing open the low gate with a snap. "You haven't been here since the fire, right?"

He heard her heels skid in the gravel as she put her brakes on. "The *fire?*"

He *knew* Hugh hadn't told the girls about it. The old man had always wanted his nieces to think nothing had changed, that the Golden Spike trio, its saloon and café with the hotel on the rise behind it, was still running the way it had back in the day, years ago, before everything started to crumble. "Yeah. I thought you might not know." He curled his fingers behind him, still not turning. "Let's get this over with."

The path wound through head-high greenery, up a steep slope to the rooms in back. "Watch your step," he said again, even though he probably didn't have to. The girls would have run up and down this path probably hundreds of times, maybe thousands. The path was the same, but everything else had changed. Forming an upside-down U shape, there were four rooms to the left, four straight ahead, and four on the left. Long porches ran the length of the building, in front of each door. There used to be porch swings, too, one between each room, but only two were safe enough to sit in anymore.

At least the garden still looked pretty. Overgrown, but full of roses.

"What happened?"

What hadn't? Nate took the quick right that led up to the porch for rooms nine through twelve. "It's not as bad as it sounds." A bald-faced lie. It was bad. He wanted – needed – her to see that for herself. He felt her behind him, so close that if she'd reached forward, she could have grabbed his shirt.

Lord, he hoped she didn't do that.

Up the steps, then onto the long porch. "Go ahead," Nate said. He pointed at the door to room ten.

"It's not locked?"

"City girl now, huh? No, there's no reason for it to be locked."

She pushed open the door. "Oh." She pushed it a little farther. "Oh, no."

The room was bathed in cerulean light, the blue of the tarps that flapped in the wind overhead. This room had been the nicest one – a huge antique sleigh bed in pride of place, with a matching dresser and long table. There had been a red velvet couch, and two comfy old armchairs had sat in front of the fireplace. The wallpaper had been deep green, and the pictures on the walls had been of the rocks and the ocean, hung in gilt-edged frames.

Now there was nothing but the stained green carpet, the smell of the sea, and the constant *flap flap flap* of the tarps above.

"We moved the furniture to a storage place on Route 119. All of it is pretty heavily smoke damaged, but there's a company who said they could get most of it out if we were willing to pay them all the money in Hugh's bank account." Which wasn't much. He hoped like hell she *knew* it wasn't much.

Adele stepped farther inside. She spread her arms, palms out, and looked up. Her face was light blue under the tarp's glow, and she looked like a frozen angel for a minute. Was she listening? Praying? She turned, drawing her hands in front of her stomach. "Tell me what happened?"

"The fire department said it was electrical. We knew we had upgrades to do, but Hugh kept putting it off, and I didn't think it was as bad as it was." Guilt twisted in his gut again, for the thousandth time. He'd checked the wiring, twice. He'd climbed up in the attic, and he'd drilled a couple of holes. The wires had looked okay. Old, yeah. But okay. He hadn't seen any fraying, and when he tested them with the voltmeter, everything had seemed all right. "It started in a wall in room nine, and went right up into the roof. Lost most of that." He craned his neck. "As you can see."

"When?"

He thought. "It was summer. God, a year ago now. Maybe fourteen months?"

"Fourteen *months.*"

Nate shrugged. "Well, yeah. Time flies." He'd been working on getting reclaimed lumber to start the beam work, but time kept slipping away on other more urgent projects.

"It's not . . . so bad, I guess? Wouldn't take much to fix it, right?"

Was she high? Yeah, they could have fixed it, if Hugh had had any money at all, which he hadn't, by the end. If Hugh had just sold to Nate, Nate would have been able to get a loan to cover at least some of the repairs. But as it was, he had to leave his money in the bank in the *hopes* Hugh would someday sell to him, instead of investing it in the property like he wanted to. "It would take a lot, believe me."

She looked up again. "What about when it rains?"

What did she think the tarps were for? "This is California. El Niño aside, it doesn't rain."

"What about the insurance?"

He rubbed the back of his neck. "Yeah. About that." Couldn't they get into this later? Like, over whiskey? Nate, who hardly ever drank – who had a very good reason *not* to drink – suddenly wanted a Jameson. Neat. Maybe a double.

Adele's eyes blazed a light blue heat that had nothing to do with the tarps over her head. "He was either insured or not. And since he was running a business and I'm sure that there are municipal codes about these kinds of things, even in Darling Bay, he must have been insured."

"You'd think that, right?"

"Oh, God."

"He'd let it lapse. After Gus Treat's bus ran into the corner of the saloon —"

"Seriously?"

"Don't worry, he wasn't hurt. But we had to prop up the western wall with braces and it took Dexter's construction company a month to get around to finishing the work. The insurance premium doubled. Hugh was just taking a while. To figure it all out."

"So it burned. While he had no insurance."

Nate clapped his hands, causing her to jump. He felt only mildly guilty. "Now she's got it. Shall we move on?"

She tapped her nose as if she were considering it for a moment. "Okay," she said finally. "Wait. Is room eleven like this, too?"

"Nine, eleven and twelve. All four of them. Exactly the same, except that room twelve still has a working bathroom."

"Wow."

"Yep."

Adele attempted a smile. It quivered. "It's just a lot to take in. Fixable, of course. I'm sure. What about the other rooms?"

Fixable his ass. He'd been *trying* to fix this shit for a long time now. "Room four had a flood about a year ago. There's some mold damage in the bathroom we've been — I mean, Hugh had been waiting to repair that until the roof got fixed on the other side."

"Mold damage."

"It got into rooms two and three, too. And room six has some termite problems."

"Some?"

"Okay, a lot. In the front walls. We're assuming that's gotten into rooms five, seven and eight, but we haven't gotten Dexter to check yet. We didn't really want to know."

"Sure." She stood on the porch next to him, her eyes closed briefly. She looked just like she had on the covers of their albums, just as young. She had to be over thirty now, maybe thirty-three? How did she pull off looking dewy and fresh and sweet when, he, at thirty-five, felt like his bones had too many miles put on them, too fast?

Then she said, "What about room one? That was always my favorite anyway."

"That's mine."

"Really?"

What, it shouldn't be his? "In exchange for working here. It comes out of my salary." It wasn't like he'd been ripping Hugh off, but he'd be damned if he would prove that to her.

"Of course, I understand."

She didn't. She didn't understand anything. Not yet. "So, next –"

"But where do the guests stay?"

He looked at her face carefully, to see if she was serious. "We don't have guests. We haven't had any in a long time." He felt his scowl form and didn't try to wipe it off. "You really don't know anything about the business anymore, do you?"

"No guests at all?"

"No."

"But how . . . ?"

Nate leaned back against a post and rubbed the tense spot between his shoulder blades. He probably looked like a bear scratching his back on a tree, but he didn't care. "How did he stay in business? Yeah, that's a question I've been trying to help him with for years." It was why he'd been working with the bank for more than a year. It was why he'd sold his boat to Ruthann. He'd been so damn *close* to buying the property – so close he could almost feel the deed in his hand. Hugh had almost – *almost* – given up hoping that his nieces would come back to Darling Bay and take over the property.

"And I saw – the café is closed, too?"

"Has been for years. Had to bring it up to a new code, and he never had the cash for that, either."

"Everything is fixable."

"Wait till you see the fryer."

"Let me guess. Grease fire?"

"Two."

"So we . . ."

"You and your sisters own a dump."

"Whoa." Adele's face was pale, her eyes even brighter blue. The fog, just beginning to dissipate into wisps over the garden, revealed a blue sky that was just the same color. "Entropy is a bitch, huh?"

It startled him enough that he laughed. He couldn't help it. So often he'd had the same thought, trying to keep up with the run-down place with little cash and no time to do half the things he had on his daily to-do list.

"What about the apartment over the saloon? Hugh's place?"

Even though Nate had gone into this tour to burst the hometown girl's foolish bubble, not even he was looking forward to this part. "It's still there."

"Can we go see it?"

"You sure?"

"Why?" She shot him a suspicious glance. "Did it burn up too?"

"No . . ."

"Oh, God, was that where he died?"

"No!" Hugh had dropped dead of a massive coronary right where he would have wanted, behind the varnished bar top pulling drinks while a pretty local gal (Sally Williams) sang onstage. He hadn't been breathing by the time Nate got to him, thirty seconds after Norma screamed. Even with CPR and the ambulance and Tox Ellis putting on the shock paddles and hauling Hugh to the hospital where they tried another couple of times, he'd never opened his eyes again. "But it's where he lived, and that was bad enough."

Adele shook her head, her hair flowing around her face like a shampoo commercial. Did she know it did that? Yeah, sure, she did. She had to know exactly the effect her looks had on people. Especially on men.

Nate took a deep breath, resolving not to stare at her for one more second. He would barely glance at her. Maybe then he wouldn't notice how her breasts held up her shirt just right.

"Come on," she said. "It can't be that bad. I mean, he was always a collector, right?"

"Collector. Huh." Nate didn't want her to see it. He hadn't wanted anyone to. Before the lender came for the appraisal, he'd been going to hire a couple of guys and clean it out in one fell swoop. He'd tried to start on it one afternoon himself, but it had been too much. Just way too much. "That's a nice way to put it. He wasn't a collector anymore." *Just tell her, Houston. A hoarder is more like it.*

"Show me?"

"You sure? I don't think you know what you're getting into."

She lifted her hands up then let them drop. "It's why I'm here."

"Okay. But remember I didn't think we should do this." He wanted it to be on the record. "I think you should just hire a crew to go in and clean. The Post brothers, they've done this kind of work before."

Adele walked past him, so close the skin of her wrist almost brushed his. He pulled his arm back sharply.

"It can't be as bad as what I'm imagining now," she said.

CHAPTER FIVE

U ncle Hugh's apartment, accessed by a steep set of stairs on the side of the main saloon building, looked okay on the outside. Sure, there were empty boxes and bags of recycling on the rear porch, but there was a picnic table that matched the ones downstairs in the patio garden, and a grill that looked like it had gotten regular use.

Nate trailed behind her on the way up. It had been obvious he'd almost enjoyed showing her how bad the hotel had become. When she'd spun in place under the tarps and met his gaze, he'd had a challenge locked behind his eyes.

But he seemed miserable now.

"Is it unlocked, too?"

"No. That I keep locked. Just in case."

"In case what?"

He cleared his throat with a rumble. "I don't know. God, in case some kid thinks it's fun to break into a dead man's apartment and dies from some kind of environmental hazard. Here."

Nate held the key out to her. He didn't even want to open the door himself. Adele felt a shiver of fear run under her skin, but she took it.

"Okay. Here goes."

"I'll just sit out here, 'kay?"

"Oh, no!" Adele spun and grabbed his wrist. It was warm and wide, and felt somehow electric. Embarrassed, she dropped it, fast. "I'm not going in without backup. Please?"

He sighed, but then nodded.

She opened the door.

And it was, really, beyond imagination.

The door opened into the kitchen, but no one entering would ever have guessed that was what it was. Everything that made it a kitchen was invisible, up to and including the refrigerator. The room was full of newspaper, so full that Adele's first thought was how heavy that much paper must be. Was it even safe to stand here? Were they in danger of dropping through, into the saloon below? That would be a pretty bad way to die. And her sisters would be so mad at her.

"Holy Tanya Tucker."

Behind her, Nate snorted. She wasn't really sure how he managed it, since she herself was trying hard not to breathe. The room didn't smell rotten, exactly – it was different. As if the paper had gotten wet at some point and started to mold. It was mustily sweet and entirely unbearable.

A narrow path was cut through the piles that in some places rose above her head.

"I don't understand. Where did he even get this many newspapers? Every *Darling Bay Gazette* ever printed, all the issues combined, wouldn't add up to this many." She ran out of breath and took an extra, rapid one. "I don't see – is there even a stove in here? There used to be a stove." Adele made herself take a step or two into the room. She pushed down the wings of panic that beat in her chest.

"Yeah, it's under there still. I shut off the gas up here a year or two ago, when I realized he was putting the papers on top of the stove. The pilot light made it too dangerous. He mostly ate outside at the grill. Are you claustrophobic?"

"No."

"Good."

"But I might be soon."

"Yee-ah. That happens in here." Nate's voice was different now, less aggressive.

"Should I keep going?"

"I don't think so."

That was obvious. "Is it like this all the way through?"

"Each room is a little different. This is the paper room."

"Oh, God." Adele went forward to the doorway. To the right used to be a small bedroom where Hugh had always slept, and to the left was the bigger bedroom. When they were girls, their mom and dad would sleep in the parlor at the front of the apartment, and the girls would pile together in the king-sized bed in the bigger room.

Now, Hugh's room, its door stuck permanently open, was full of . . . she couldn't even work it out at first. "What is all of that?"

"Buoys."

"Pardon?" From floor to ceiling, the room was packed with shapes that didn't make any sense. Most were round, like mannequin heads, but there were no faces. The windows were completely covered by them, so the only light that came in was from the doorway she stood in. "I don't understand."

"From the water. Old ones. He liked the glass floats best, but those don't wash up that often. He'd get really excited about those. These are mostly the plastic kind; some are styrofoam."

"So that smell . . ."

"I think it's seaweed. And other gunk."

But the way Adele remembered seaweed, it smelled good. It smelled green and salty, strewn on the tide-worn sand. This smelled rotten and sour.

"He didn't clean them before he threw them in here. Didn't think they needed it."

"I don't – what was he going to *do* with them all?"

Nate yanked off his ball cap, revealing a head of thick wavy brown hair, smashed half-flat. He ran his hand over his face then through his hair, standing it straight up. Then he jerked the cap back on, brim-side forward this time. "I must have asked him a million times. Sometimes he would say they were for a boat. Sometimes he would claim he was going to sell the glass ones on eBay. But he never did. The room pretty much filled up a couple of years ago, and since then he just kept shoving them in." Nate spoke over Adele's shoulder. He was so close to her that if she'd stepped backward, she would have run smack dab into him.

Instead, she straightened her shoulders and locked her knees so they wouldn't lurch. "This doesn't make sense. He collected beer cans, I remember that." Recalling that brought sense to the other smells, though, the under-scent of yeast and brine. "Those are in another room. Am I right?"

He pointed behind him, into the room she used to sleep in with her sisters. It was full of paper bags, piled to her chest height. Each bag was overflowing with flattened cans. "He started crushing them, at least. Before that, they wouldn't fit at all."

"He always said he was going to recycle them."

"These were the ones that wouldn't fit into his bin every week. He was going to bag them and take them in for cash, but as far as I know, he never even made one run."

"He wasn't a hoarder when we left."

"He wasn't one when I met him. But he sure as hell turned into one."

Adele had seen enough TV shows on hoarding to know the mental disorder could be triggered by trauma. Uncle Hugh's brother – her father – had died. Would that have been enough to do it? They'd been close . . .

And the girls themselves had scattered after that. None of them had ever come home to Darling Bay. Adele hadn't come because she thought it would make her too sad; to be back in the place she'd been so happy, without her mother, without her father, without her sisters who meant so much to her that every second without them hurt.

What if that *had* done it? What if by staying away they'd made their uncle actually sick?

The very thought made her nauseated, and the apartment's smell was such an assault Adele wondered if she were going to throw up. She couldn't – there was no place to do so. And if she started, she doubted she'd be able to easily stop. What had crawled into those cans and died over the years? So many things could have gotten in and grown or reproduced.

"What's in the parlor? Oh, no. Not beer bottles?"

"I told him I'd put him in a home if he carried up the empty glass from the saloon. The floor wouldn't have held. I think he finally believed me about that. The parlor's full of books."

"Well."

"They smell less, anyway. Still heavy, though, and I'm worried about what could have crawled in under them. Bugs, mice, rats –"

"Ugh. What about the bathroom?" She'd seen the television shows. She knew what hoarders did to bathrooms.

"It's not as bad as you'd think. That's his magazine room, and the claw foot tub has been too overflowing with them for years, but his shower and toilet are clean enough. He tried." Nate paused, sticking his hands into his pockets as if he were nervous he'd touch something by accident.

"This is *not* trying." This was nothing but failing. On every single level. How was it possible that she and her sisters hadn't known how bad it had gotten?

"I think he tried hard, actually. He tried his ass off. I told him that if I came up to find he couldn't use his toilet I was going to tell the zoning board. I came in once a month to make sure." Nate covered his face with his hand, then spoke around it. "Can we get out of here now, please?"

"Out." As soon as she said it, she wanted to climb over him, to kick and flail her way to the door, screaming all the way. "Oh, sweet Loretta, yes. *Out.*"

They stood on the patio. Adele pinched her nose and breathed through her mouth, two long steadying breaths. "How could this have happened to him?"

Instead of answering, Nate said, "Loretta?"

"Loretta Lynn." Of course.

Nate seemed to accept this. He rolled his neck and then shrugged. "He was old. No family to take care of him. Probably more common than we think."

Sudden tears, fast and unwelcome, pressed against the backs of her eyes. "Don't you dare." Uncle Hugh had still had family. Yes, they'd left. Everything had broken. They'd just been trying to put their lives back together ever since. "He didn't say he needed us. Not once."

"He didn't ask you to visit?"

"Of course he did. He loved us. He wanted to see us. But we were . . . God, we were always so busy." *So sad.* Her voice broke. "He didn't say he needed us."

Nate's voice was suddenly too loud, as if he'd been holding it back till now. "And what was he supposed to do? He was too proud to admit he needed help, and besides, most days he didn't think he did. You should have been here the day that I told him it wasn't *normal* that a grown man slept on top of an old couch, wrapped in a sleeping bag. It was like it hadn't occurred to him. That day, I thought he was going to cry, you know that?"

"But –"

"But he didn't. He just laughed it off, the way he laughed everything else off, and he pulled another drink for someone he loved downstairs and he told his stories, and you girls never came home. He'd lost everything over the years, everything but the saloon, and he held on to it, to share that at least with you, and none of you ever came. Not one of you." Nate yanked at the latch of the porch umbrella, folding it halfway down and then springing it back up again, locking it in place.

Grief warred with anger in Adele's chest. Uncle Hugh was gone. They'd all blown it. They knew it. They'd never get a chance to apologize. But this guy had no right. "You know what?"

He fiddled with the umbrella latch. His scowl was deep, a long furrow creased across his brow. "Yeah?" It was a dare. He *wanted* her to come at him, she could feel it.

And his anger diluted hers, suddenly. He was correct. He was totally right. "We should have come."

"Huh?"

"You're right. That's all." She raised a shoulder and let it drop, hoping some of the tension would leave her neck. "Lord. I guess I need to find a place to stay tonight."

She saw it hit him. "You thought you'd stay here tonight? In the hotel."

"Kind of. I thought . . ."

"You were going to stay in there." Nate pointed back towards the open door to Hugh's apartment.

"It's where we always stayed. I just made the mistake of thinking that . . ." *That things wouldn't change.* "That he still had a spare bed."

"To be fair, he probably does."

Adele laughed in spite of herself. "I bet you're right. It's in there somewhere." She shuddered. "Can you *imagine?*"

He shook his head, hard. "Look. I'm sorry."

"You did nothing wrong. Nothing at all."

She let herself sit on the bench of the picnic table. Exhaustion flooded her, mixing with the guilt, creating a toxic, enervating sludge in her veins.

"You must be tired. It's a long drive."

"It's fine. Does Miss Clarkson still rent out rooms?"

Nate swung a leg over the opposite bench like it was a tiny horse. "Not since she got busted for renting them out by the hour."

"Ouch. In sweet little Darling Bay?"

"Every place has its dirty secrets, even here."

Adele looked back towards the apartment door. How many times had she and her sisters run in and out, letting the screen door slap closed behind them? Uncle Hugh would roar at them, a happy bear pretending (and failing) to be angry. They would just giggle and run faster. Hugh and Dad would sit right here. It was a different porch table they'd sat around then, a round one. Now it was rectangular. Dad was gone, eleven years now. Uncle Hugh was gone. Her sisters were far away, and Darling Bay had changed so much she'd gotten lost coming into town, ending up going the wrong direction on a one-way street for half a block. Luckily, it was still a sleepy town, and one old farmer in a beat-up pick-up had honked at her to let her know, waving kindly at her as she did a panicked three-point turn.

Nate cleared his throat. "Want a beer?"

She laughed. "No, thanks. I think the sun's nowhere near the yardarm, whatever that means."

"Hey, I run a saloon. No judgment. And look, you can still stay here."

She looked around the upper patio. "Where? Half the place has no roof, the other half is falling apart."

"My room. Last one standing."

"No."

"I'll grab a bag and clear out for you. I just put clean sheets on the bed today."

"No way," she said. "I'm not kicking you out of your home."

Nate shifted and planted his hands on his knees. "I'm sorry, who owns the property now?"

"That doesn't make it my home." Home was Nashville. Wasn't it? The thought was so confusing it swept everything out of her mind except a blind feeling of dread.

"I've got a boat." Again he didn't meet her eyes. "Down at the marina. A sleep-aboard. I'll head there for a few days, while we get things sorted here."

We. A muscle unkinked in her neck. "Are you sure?"

"Yep." He stood, unfolding to his full height. His shoulders were so wide they blocked the sun's glare.

CHAPTER SIX

As much as their mother's death had been foreseen – the terrifying chemo, the useless radiation, the longer goodbyes that meant everything and helped nothing – their father's death hadn't. Tommy Darling, healthy and in his prime, dropped dead of a massive heart attack.

The Darling Songbirds had been in New York, prepping for Madison Square Garden, the first stop on their biggest-ever tour. They'd booked forty-two shows around the globe, every single one sold out. The girls weren't opening for anyone, not anymore. They didn't need a bigger bill as a draw. No guest spots by Carrie Underwood. No Garth Brooks popping on stage to help them out.

This was it.

And their dad had very strong feelings about how the girls had made it. "Your mama got to heaven, and she started singing. Up there, they listen better than they do down here, and they started asking her what she knew about music, and she started pullin' those strings, and that's why we are where we are today."

We. He'd always said *we* when talking about the Songbirds. The tabloids had accused the sisters of being daddy's darlings, of living for his dreams, but even in that they'd gotten it wrong. All four of them, the girls and Tommy, they'd always done it for Mama, for Tommy's darling Katie, the songbird who'd been too sad to find her voice, the original Darling girl who'd lost her life before she had a chance to see her baby birds truly fly. The tabloids pulled the metaphors along as far as they could (babies with no mother in the nest, Katie flying to heaven alone) but the truth was that the girls had never been lonely, not once, not until Tommy got that look of surprise while standing on the stage being built at Madison Square Garden. He'd had a mike in one hand and a cup of Dunkin" Donuts coffee in the other. He dropped the coffee and that's what Adele remembered most from that moment – the way the coffee splashed across the stage and then back up, onto her cowboy boots and up her sisters" jeans. They'd all laughed a little at their father, a known klutz.

Then he'd fallen, and he hadn't gotten up.

The next night, Adele had made them go onstage.

No one else was there to do it. They'd never bothered to hire a stage manager – their father had been their stage manager since they'd first won that family band contest at the Tennessee State Fair. Sure, they had reps and two agents, and they had a production crew *and* a stage crew who were the best in the business. But both their parents were gone. That made Adele the oldest.

"I can't," Molly had gasped around sobs that morning. "I won't."

"Lana? You know we have to."

Lana had just shaken her head and parted the curtains of the sterile hotel room on the thirty-sixth floor that looked down at Times Square. Lana hadn't cried yet, and Adele knew she wouldn't, not for weeks. Maybe months.

"Come on," Adele said. "He would want us to."

"Don't you dare," said Molly. "He *wouldn't*."

Adele heard the air conditioning kick a notch higher, which didn't make sense, since she was freezing. They all were. She could see the goosebumps on Molly's arms, and Lana's shoulders were hunched forward as she stared out the window. "This is what he worked for."

"We all worked for it." Lana shrugged. "Now he's dead."

"So we give up?"

Lana rounded on her, the drapes scudding closed like heavy clouds. "He died *yesterday*. Give us a fucking break."

"We don't get one of those."

"Oh?" Lana's eyebrows were high. "The show must go on? You're going to push that shit on us? Now?"

Adele's legs felt hollow. "You bet your ass it does."

"Let us bury the man."

"It's too late to refund eighteen thousand people. We could have pulled the plug yesterday, but not today."

Lana's face was white except for the two red spots high on her cheeks. "Did you actually just say "pull the plug"?"

Wrong words, they were all the wrong words. "Forty-two cities. Ten weeks. We can do this. Daddy put this all together – he's never been more excited about anything, ever. You know that. We get up there tonight, we show the world we're stronger than they ever knew. We sing for him. We sing for Mama. They're together for the first time in six years. Tonight they can watch our show together – you think that's not the one thing they'd both want?"

The thing was, Adele believed her own words. So did her sisters – she could see it. Molly turned over on the hotel couch, her shoulders shaking. Lana stormed out of the room muttering something about the vending machine.

That night, they went onstage. The normally dazzling lights were brighter than ever, and reporters with their press badges were packed so tightly against the edges of the stage Adele thought they must be holding it up. They were all there, waiting for them to fail. For the girls to fall apart in front of God and everyone else.

And they did exactly that.

Molly fainted, collapsing in the middle of "Wait Till Your Father Gets Home". On a stage where everything was vibrating with noise, even with her back turned as she sang stage left, Adele felt the thunk of it travel up her legs. There, right where their father had fallen, lay Molly, bleeding from the head.

Lana – who had been slow and sluggish for the last hour, as if high on something – dropped her mike and rushed forward. Molly was coughing then, her lids fluttering. Lana held Molly's head in her lap as the flashbulbs beat against their skin.

And Adele kept singing.

It was unforgivable.

Wait till your father gets home, just a little longer now.

I swear to the moon above, he'll be home soon, my love.

She knew – later – she should have shut down the show. Three words: "Cut the sound." Those three words would have killed the show – and the tour – as dead as their father.

Idiotically, she'd thought she could still fix it. Molly would stand, and Lana and she would hold their sister up and finish the final lines together. *He'll be home soon, my love.*

But they didn't. She sang the last line as two paramedics in blue raced across the stage. The lighting wobbled, and for an impossible moment, Adele tried to remember what the next song was.

Then she knew: the show was over. The tour was done, before it even really started.

"We're sorry." She apologized to the world. She didn't know until later how much those few sentences had destroyed her sisters. They were played on national media, over and over: Molly flat on the stage, Lana darkly furious, Adele *apologizing*. She should have been *hiding* them, folding them under her wings, protecting them. Instead, she'd shoved them onstage, and in doing so, she'd broken their wings, snapping each one. The Darling Songbirds were done. "We're so sorry," she said.

Adele heard people in the audience crying. She touched her ear jack but heard nothing but a low whistle. A reporter at her knee shouted something at her. He had tears streaming down his face, and Adele couldn't quite figure out why.

The chime of Adele's phone lifted her out of the memory, or the dream. She'd lain down to nap, and now she was panting, sweat dripping at her hairline. She was confused for a moment until she remembered where she was – in the bartender's borrowed bed. Light was still coming in through the parted curtains, but just barely – she could see pink and orange in the sunset-lit clouds.

The chime was a text from Molly. Finally. *Root beer floats? I only liked Coke floats.*

Adele smiled. That was right. *Oh, yeah.*

Remember when I was on that diet when I was fifteen? And I only liked Diet Coke floats?

With sherbet, because it was low-fat.

Disgusting. How's it going there?

Also disgusting.

??

Adele fell backward on the bed, holding the phone above her, trying to ignore that the whole room smelled like Nate – like woodchips and soap and something spicy, like cloves.

This whole place is awful. The hotel is wrecked. Fire, mold, termites, ruin. Basically every single plague of the Bible has landed between rooms two through twelve.

Seriously?

And Uncle Hugh was a hoarder. Again, she wondered if they'd triggered that change. Guilt tasted like acid at the back of her throat. No point in sharing the worry with Molly, though. *I'm going to have to hire a backhoe to dig his apartment out. The café looks like it's been closed so long we might have been its last customers. The saloon is open, but barely.*

Shit.

Yeah.

Well, if anyone can fix it, it's you.

Adele felt a weariness settle into the base of her bones. *I guess.*

Where are you staying, then?

The bartender's room is the only good one.

You kicked out the bartender?

He offered!

Is he hot?

Adele's thumbs hovered over the phone's keyboard. She shouldn't answer it truthfully, that the guy could make the polar ice caps melt just by hitting them with that dark stone-colored smolder.

OMG I knew it.

I didn't say anything!

You paused. That's all you needed to do. What's he like?

Oh, Molly. Always on the lookout for love, and finding it more often than not. She just didn't pick the right ones. Ever. *He's rude. Ugly. Super old.*

Bull.

She looked around the room. It had only taken Nate a few minutes to pack a duffel bag of jeans and shirts and whatever it was in the small bathroom that smelled like cloves. He'd only taken one of the two guitars with him. He'd left a Martin, an old one, that she was dying to try. She'd propped her own guitar up in its case next to it.

Let's leave it at this: his name is Nate and he plays guitar.

You're doomed.

Adele laughed. *You like the bad boys, not me. Speaking of which, how's Rick?*

An asshole, like all the others. I'm off men forever.

For a week. How long are you on board this time? Adele didn't even know where her sister was, which ocean she was currently in. Her whereabouts changed so fast, it didn't even warrant keeping up on it anymore. One week Molly would be in Alaska, watching icebergs calve, the next, she'd be pulling in to port in Puerto Rico, dispensing eating advice to people who would nod agreeably and then ignore her completely, hitting up the buffet tables like they were about to starve to death.

Molly said being a dietician on a cruise ship was like being an abstinence counselor at an orgy.

A week. We hit Sicily and then head to Greece.

I hate you.

You should. It's not snowbirds this time – it's some singles hook-up thing. Younger and cuter.

Adele couldn't even imagine the trouble Molly could get up to on a cruise like that. *Use protection.*

Oh, stop. What time is it there?

8 pm. I think. After Nate had handed over his room key, Adele had looked around the room for something to do. Usually that something was easy to find, even in a hotel room. Adele could always find something to clean, to straighten. The amount of satisfaction she got from making pictures hang perfectly straight was almost physical. Once, in a room in Miami, the air conditioner had stopped working, and she'd fixed it with just a bobby pin and some Scotch tape.

But Nate's room was perfectly clean. It was orderly, too, but only because he didn't seem to have many possessions. He had an old PC laptop on top of the small desk, and the guitars. In the drawer next to the bed was a single pair of earplugs, still in plastic wrap.

Who was this guy?

Adele had given up trying to figure it out and had gone down to the marina and hiked out to the headland to say hello to Darling Bay. It had been a family tradition when she was little, back when both her mother and father were alive. If Mama was feeling bright enough, they'd hike all the way out, all five of them, her father carrying little Lana, her mother picking flowers and leading them singing old country tunes, Johnny Cash being her favorite. When they got to the point where the cliff jutted out and the wind blew stronger than anywhere else, where they could see the whole town, they stopped. They all waved hello. *That's the town your great-grandfather built. Look at it now, all twinkly and perfect.*

The memories had made her heart ache, but sweetly.

Still following Darling tradition, she'd gotten a burger at Roper's, sitting outside and watching the seagulls fight with the fishermen coming in with their catches. With a full belly, she'd come back and collapsed onto room one's creaky old bed (she tried not to imagine the way Nate might have made it creak). She'd napped almost a full three hours.

Her phone pinged in her hand again. *You have to go down to the saloon.*

She texted back, *And do what?*

Have a beer with the cute guitar player.

I should be working. This isn't a vacation.

Right now? Come on. When is your next song due?

Adele touched the tip of her nose. Molly was a human lie detector. *Not for a month.*

Plenty of time for you to sell the place and plenty of time for you to have fun.

Not that much fun.

I meant in the sack.

I know what you meant.

Doing the dirty. Gettin' busy. Knocking boots. Get it on.

Adele felt her cheeks heat as she tried not to laugh. She wanted to say, "I love you. I miss you. I need you here with me." But she and her sisters were careful not to talk like that. It hurt too much. *We're not all like you, Molly.*

More's the pity, too. Hey, I've got a client in a sec. Go get 'em, tiger.

Xo.

U too.

Adele sat up. She looked down at the black shirt that was stained from where she'd dropped mayonnaise on it from her burger. Should she change? No. It was just the saloon she'd grown up in. She shouldn't care what she was wearing.

But then she swapped the dirty black shirt for a clean white one and ran a comb through her hair, cursing herself as she did. Come on. Concern for her appearance didn't mean anything except that she was courteous to others.

That's what she told herself, anyway. She couldn't quite figure out an excuse for why she felt compelled to slick on the pink lip gloss that one record exec had told her made her look like an angel about to fall, so she just pressed her lips together and stopped trying to come up with one.

CHAPTER SEVEN

S o. When were you planning on telling me?"
Hank Coffee sat at the saloon, twirling a coaster
between his fingers.

Nate frowned and slid a Mountain Dew down to
Angela Murphy who didn't drink but liked hearing
Parrot Freddy's travel stories as much as she liked
stroking Ethel's vibrant wing. "Telling you what?"

"About the girl."

"What girl?"

Hank snorted. "I'm halfway tempted to keep going
with this, to see how long you'll pretend you don't know
what I'm talking about, but I have this weird feeling you
could keep it going way longer than I would find
amusing."

"Possibly."

"So?"

Nate raised one eyebrow and remained quiet.

"Okay, I have to say it, huh? Fine. But you're totally buying my next beer."

"Sure." Hank never had more than one anyway. And Nate wasn't going to say it.

"Adele Darling."

Funny, her name had always gotten to him. When Hugh had talked about his nieces, the Darling Songbirds, Nate had always thought Adele's name was the prettiest. The most songbird-like. Turns out he was right. He didn't need to see the other ones in person to know that she had to be the easiest on the eye out of the defunct group. That fall of honey hair, those eyes that looked bedroom-ready even when she was just standing there, asking questions he didn't want to answer.

"What about her?"

Hank slapped his coaster on his knee. "I knew it!"

"You don't know crap."

"She's back in town to take over the saloon."

"No way." It was a knee-jerk response. She was in town to sell. She had to be.

"Then what? Are her sisters coming?"

"I didn't ask her family's itinerary." Nate lifted a hand at Mack, the drummer in the band.

Hank twisted, looking behind him, as if hoping to find Adele there. "But that's what she's doing, right?"

"She said something about selling it."

"Oh, man." Hank leaned forward. "Did you tell her you were going to buy it?"

"She's grieving, man. I just showed her around." Hank was right, though. It should have been the first damn thing out of his mouth. *Hugh promised me I could buy the place. You gonna honor that?*

"Loser. She still as pretty as she always was?"

Nate ducked his head to look over Hank's shoulder. "Be careful that Samantha doesn't hear you ask that, buddy."

"Ah. Sam's good. She knows there's no woman prettier than her in the whole damn world." Hank grinned.

Hank and Samantha were the happiest couple he knew, and it seemed genuine. Highly irritating, too. Hank and Nate were close, had been since Hank had been on the paramedic crew that transported Nate's mother to the hospital after one of several overdoses. But no matter how close they could claim to be, Hank and Samantha were each other's favorites, in all things. Just plain annoying. "She coming?"

Hank nodded. "She'll be here soon. You didn't answer my question about the Darling girl."

"She's all right, I guess."

"Yeah?"

"Fine. If you like that kind of thing."

Something happened to Hank's face, as if he knew a joke that Nate didn't know the punch line to yet. "What kind of thing is that? Brown hair, blue eyes? Pretty as a picture?"

Nate shook his head, trying to rid his head of the image of Adele's face when she'd first seen the courtyard and how pretty it was. She'd lit up, just like the strings of white lights that were illuminated out there now. "Nah, her hair's not brown, it's more like . . . not quite blonde, more like *dirt*-colored, like the last inch of a warm Hefeweizen someone left in a pint glass."

Hank snorted. "Yeah?"

"And her eyes, they're not really that blue."

"Mmm?"

"More like a foggy day kind of blue." He'd seen them change color, as she'd looked first at the courtyard and then into Hugh's disaster zone. "No. More like smog. Dirty-blue."

"You say dirty about her a lot."

"Well." Nate shrugged. "If the shoe fits."

"Dirty?"

The voice was Adele's, and it came – horrifyingly – from behind him. It was too late to save himself, and he knew it.

Adele's eyes snapped (her gorgeous, wisteria eyes – nothing like dirty blue anything), but something like a smile was fighting her mouth. She hit his upper arm with her fist. It was softer than a real punch, but harder than a play tap.

"I have dirty beer hair? *Smog?*"

She didn't. She'd done something to it – maybe just combed it out – so that it flowed over her shoulders in soft waves. Her white T-shirt clung to her curves, and

Nate had to actively counsel himself to remove his eyes from the vee of the fabric. "I like Hefeweizen," he said weakly. "And, um, pollution gets a bad rap. Why are you sneaking in the back, anyway? No one does that."

"Hey," said Hank. "Isn't this your new boss, Nate? The one you were telling me about? The slave driver who's going to ruin everything, right?"

"*Dude*," started Nate, but then Adele was around him and on the other side of the saloon, wrapping her arms around Hank.

"There you are," she said, kissing him on the cheek.

Nate felt some kind of jealousy spark, an empty lighter clicking uselessly.

"You're even prettier now, you know that? Exactly the opposite of what Nate was just telling me."

"Hey!"

But Adele just laughed. "Where's Samantha? Congrats on finally getting your girl, by the way. I loved the Facebook posts of the wedding, and I'm so sorry I wasn't there. I can't believe you really dressed up in your big duct tape head to walk down the aisle." Sam taught self-defense and Hank was one of her padded instructors on his days off from the fire department.

"I can't believe the first thing my brand-new wife did was kick me in the crotch!" Hank laughed happily. "She's coming down as soon as she closes the studio. Should be soon. With both of our schedules, we haven't had a Friday night date in a while. We're going to watch Dust

& Rusty play and maybe I'll make you shoot some pool with us."

"Molly was the shark, not me."

"I seem to remember you weren't bad."

Adele bit her bottom lip, and Nate wondered if that lip gloss he couldn't stop staring at was a controlled substance. "That was a long time ago. We were all so young then."

Hank laughed. "I still remember your favorite drink from when you were what, twenty-one?"

Her voice was soft. "I was twenty-two when we left."

"Yeah. Then. It was that horrible Clamato stuff, poured in a Bud."

"That's the most embarrassing thing anyone's ever said about me, and the tabloids have rumored that I've been kidnapped by sex-trafficking aliens." Her gaze flickered to Nate, and he felt his stomach jump.

He probably just hadn't eaten in a while. That was it. He grabbed a bag of salt and vinegar chips, the least popular of the bags he sold. He didn't like them much, either, but maybe they'd settle this case of nerves he was feeling. He chewed and then said, "Can I get you a drink?" He felt, rather than saw, the chip fly out of his mouth and land on the saloon. Smooth.

Hank guffawed, but Adele pretended not to notice. "Sure. How about a Hefeweizen?"

"Well, what do you know?" Nate grabbed a pint glass. "Those just happen to be on the house tonight."

"What a stunning coincidence," said Adele. She pulled up a bar stool and sat, leaning comfortably against Hank.

"So y'all know each other," said Nate, adding stupid to his repertoire of clumsy and verbally challenged.

"Small town," said Adele. She and Hank shared a private smile. "I just never held a candle to his dream girl."

No way. Her and Hank? How many times had Hank and Nate sat around listening to Hugh talk about his perfect songbird nieces, and Hank had never said a word to Nate? What the hell was that about?

"I'm going to go grab some glasses. Holler if anyone needs me." It was an excuse. At least once a night, usually more, he had to do a sweep of the saloon and of the outdoor courtyard, picking up pint glass empties and dumping them into a bus tub. It was still early enough that he hadn't even come close to running out yet. He'd be lucky if he came back with more than three glasses, total. But he had to get away.

"Hey, Rich. How's it going? No, you're not done with that? I hear you. Gladys? You need me to grab that?"

Gladys held on to the dribble left in her glass and glared at him. "Still drinking. Hey, is that a Darling girl over there?"

"You never know." Nate hoped he could get away with just that, but Gladys's fingers grabbed his shirt, crab-like and sharp.

"I do know. She's here now? Missed the funeral, didn't she? All of 'em did. That one's Adele?"

"Didn't really notice," he lied. "Maybe a refill on that?"

Gladys let go of him. "Oh, that'd be good. Thanks, sugar. Get the gossip for us, huh?"

"You bet." *Never.*

The funeral. Had it really been necessary for her to mention that? Nate's mood dropped just thinking of the day. A rare summer storm had swept in the morning they'd put Hugh in the Darling Bay cemetery, and instead of being a short and warm rain shower, it had been cold and dark. Completely appropriate, under the circumstances. The weather had grieved like Nate had. Thunder had rocked the bay, and lightning had started a couple of vegetation fires in the valley, so that two entire fire companies who'd been in attendance had to race away before it was over. Hugh would have gotten such a kick out of them being at the service – he'd always loved the fire department's drum and piper corps. He would have thought it was funny as hell that Earl Cornejo had to stop bagpiping right in the middle of "Amazing Grace" to run out to the fire engine, but Nate hadn't thought it was humorous at all. It had broken his heart, really. It had been the first time he'd cried in public since his mother had struck him across the face in a grocery store when he was five, knocking him backward into the shopping carts. He had learned from her not to cry, that life was too hard to give in to it.

And Hugh had been the one to teach him that life was too good not to give in to laughter.

"How about you, Randy? Ready to let that glass go? No? Okay." Nate hurried past the end of the bar, trying to shut his ears to whatever Hank and Adele were talking about – not hard when the Darling Songbirds" second album seemed to be playing all the way through at full volume. Whoever had cued that up on the jukebox either had a good sense of humor or no tact at all. Nate would bet on the latter.

He eyed the front – no new customers. With perfect timing, Dixie made her way through the swinging half-door. Thank God. She was technically his second bartender on Friday and Saturday nights. She covered him when he took breaks or played with the band. He gave her a long distant salute, and she returned it with a snap.

Nate escaped through the storeroom and out the side door to the back courtyard. With any luck, no one had seen him leave. With a little more luck, no one would look for him for a while. It felt like a lot, all of a sudden. Adele, back in town. Hugh, gone forever. He wanted to breathe the night air by himself for a few long seconds before he had to get onstage.

It wasn't until he was sitting on the first long bench that he remembered the last time he'd sat out here.

CHAPTER EIGHT

Nate and Hugh had sat out on the saloon's back courtyard a million – maybe more – times, under the twinkling lights of the white strands and the stars above, both. Hugh had sometimes lit his battered old pipe, but Nate was fine sitting on one of the benches with open hands, just looking up. The night before Hugh had died, they'd had a surprisingly quiet Thursday night, and the saloon was completely empty at ten o'clock. They'd sat out there, watching the stars blink at them – no fog, so cool they'd both needed their jeans jackets.

As if Hugh had known he was on the way out, he'd said something that hadn't made sense until later. "Hey, kid. I know you want this place."

"Yeah," Nate had said, smiling upward. He did. Ever since he'd been able to talk Mariah at the bank into believing he was a good bet. Well, he'd had to sell his boat to Ruthann to bring his points all the way and have the cash for the down payment, but it had been the right thing to do – he could feel it. The money was there, ready. He could buy the place as soon as Hugh told him he could have it.

"Keep fighting for it." Hugh had said he would sell and then changed his mind an hour later so many times that Nate wasn't going to believe it until the deed was in his hand. Hugh kept thinking the girls might come back. Claim their inheritance. But everyone knew the Darling Songbirds had flown away forever. Otherwise they would have come home sooner.

"You want me to keep fighting you for the place? Okay, then. But don't tell me you didn't ask for a battle, old man."

"I mean it, Nate. No joke. If I'm not around. Do what you have to do."

Had Hugh known? Had he felt, even then, that his life was drawing to a close? Had he foreseen Adele coming back to town in order to sell the one thing that Nate held important? If so, why hadn't Hugh just sold it to him? None of it felt fair, but that wasn't news. Nate had learned a long time ago that life didn't play by the rulebook.

And now he'd lied to Adele about still having the boat. What was he supposed to do, suggest they share the small room? His neck (and something else, something lower) heated at the thought. He'd just toss

76

his sleeping bag in room twelve where the bathroom still worked. It'd be fine, even without a roof overhead. Like camping.

Nate collected the six ashtrays that rested on top of the picnic tables, stacking them to bring inside to wash. Then he realized they were all clean and unused, so he set them out again. There was absolutely no reason for him to be out here in the twinkle-lighted dark; this was just him running away. But hell. What was the harm in that?

"It's prettier out here than it ever was." Adele's voice was soft behind him. "I love the lights, how they sparkle through the grapevines."

Was she going to make this a habit? Sneaking up behind him and sending goosebumps up and down his spine? If so, Nate didn't like it. "Yeah. Thanks." He looked over her shoulder. "Do I have a customer?"

"I don't think so," she said. "And there's someone bartending now. Short brown curls?"

He didn't have to tell her anything about how he ran the bar until she actually asked. "Yeah, well, I should get back in there." He could smell Adele's perfume, light as a butterfly's wing and sweet as jasmine, and his head did a dizzy reel. He slid his right hand into his front pocket and gripped his mother's two-month sobriety chip, just long enough to settle his head. *Too bad she never got her three-month chip.*

Women. He'd believed in his mother too many times.

Hugh had believed in his Darling Songbirds way too many times.

"Wait —"

But Nate was fast, moving around the last table and through the storeroom, back into the saloon before she could finish what she was saying.

Scrug was almost finished setting up the amp onstage, and Mack was checking the microphones. "One, two, can y'all hear me?"

There were a couple of new customers seated at the saloon, but Dixie had them well in hand, whipping up some frothy concoction while telling them a joke at the same time. Adele took her seat next to Hank at the saloon. She looked at him expectantly. "So, tell me about the band."

Hank hooted. "Yeah, Nate, tell her about the band."

"Shut up."

Adele sat forward eagerly. "Are you in it? I saw your guitars. I really wanted to play your Martin, but I didn't dare touch it. It looks like an antique."

He wasn't going to get out of this, was he? This was the way his night was going to go. The owner of the Golden Spike was going to watch its bartender play guitar on a broken-down stage in a podunk town, and that bartender was just going to have to take it. "It's as old as I am, maybe older."

"Must be worth a fortune." Her voice was soft, but he could clearly hear her through the noise in the saloon.

"It's a piece of crap." The Martin had been his mother's beater guitar, given to her by the man he'd suspected but never confirmed was his father, and it had always been passed around to the drunkest person in the room. It was the guitar that could take a lickin', and it wasn't worth more than a couple of hundred dollars, despite its age and provenance. "Plays for shit. Sounds terrible."

"Why do you keep it, then?"

Sentimental reasons wasn't a good answer. *Same reason I keep her chip in my pocket.* "Might need firewood someday."

Hank said, "Don't let him fool you. Nate could make a neckless guitar sound great."

"You're good, huh?"

Her smile looked real, and it made Nate itch. "I guess I don't suck that much."

The door swung open, and Samantha walked in. Thank God for small mercies. "Hey, Hank, look who's here."

Hank lit up like someone put a quarter in him. "There's my girl." Samantha laughed and kissed him roundly. Nate watched, a little embarrassed, but unable to look away from their happiness, like it was a car wreck, only the exact opposite. A collision that ended in joy.

He met Adele's eye, and then wished he hadn't. There was something in her gaze, something soft and wistful, and there was nothing he could do about that – nothing he *wanted* to do.

So he drew a pint of Samantha's favorite beer and slid it across the bar. "Hey. Sam. When you come up from air, look who's here."

Samantha and Hank pulled apart, both blushing. Or maybe they had both just overheated. "Sorry." Samantha turned to Adele. "Oh!"

They hugged quickly.

"It's been a long time," said Adele.

"So long. I loved your third album. It was the soundtrack of my life for a while."

"Thanks," said Adele.

"Do you get this wherever you go?"

"No way. In every town except Darling Bay, no one knows me from Eve. Wait. I take that back. A couple of weeks ago I was recognized, and it was very exciting but then I realized she thought I was Lorelei Gilmore from the *Gilmore Girls* and I'm obviously not, and both of us ended up very embarrassed."

Samantha laughed. "Did you have a cup of coffee in your hand?"

"I did. That's where the resemblance began and ended."

"No, I can see it." Samantha wrinkled her nose. "Totally. You've got that vibe. And hey, look, Nate looks like Luke Danes, doesn't he?" She nudged Hank in the side. "Don't you think?"

"I will never admit that I watch that show with you."

Samantha nodded solemnly. "Then I will never tell anyone that you're the one who bought the DVDs in the first place."

Nate leaned forward, hands on the bar. "I have no idea what you're talking about, but this staring at me thing has to stop, so somebody change the subject, for the love of God."

Adele came to his aid. "When does your band go on?"

"Not for at least three or four hours," said Nate. Maybe she would give up and go to bed. Immediately.

And just like that, he imagined her in his bed. Under his sheets. What did Adele wear to sleep? A white camisole? A red nightie? Nothing at all?

Mack gave a howl from the stage while beating on the drum's high hat.

Nate jumped. "Or now. Maybe we could go on now."

Adele's grin was huge. "Excellent."

For the first time in more years than he could count, Nate felt a surge of stage fright.

He hated it.

CHAPTER NINE

Adele couldn't remember the last time she'd just watched a band play for fun. A band in which she had no investment, made up of members to whom she had no ties. She hadn't written the song for the lead singer. She hadn't introduced one of the members to her old publicist, and no one was trying to ride her now-threadbare coat-tails. Nashville was huge and bright, a tinseltown honky-tonk. Darling Bay was sleepy and Adele already knew the band would be done by eleven. The city noise ordinance had always been respected – Darling Bay liked its peace and quiet.

Adele had nothing to do in the saloon, no job at all. She was just there, watching a country band play for an old wooden bar full of people. Okay, maybe *full* wasn't the word – there were a dozen, at most fifteen people – surely more would show up later? It was Friday night, after all. The few who were there, though, were singing along to the songs they obviously knew and loved. They were good songs, too. On the surface, they were lightweight, standard country fare, but each song had a second hard punch on the way back. *The bottle leaves me lost, empty, untrue, and baby, it still don't act as bad as you.* The songs were original – she knew that much. She would have known if they were covers.

There were only three members in Dust & Rusty. Samantha pointed at the drummer. "That's Mack." He was a skinny man with dark sunglasses, full-sleeve tattoos and a thick dark moustache. "He looks a little scary but he's actually a third-grade teacher."

Mack grimaced furiously and hit a double-stroke roll.

"He looks like he could eat a live chicken."

"Well, he *has* chickens, so I guess that's possible, but he treats them all like his babies, so I kind of doubt it. He raises Buff Orpingtons and helps out with the chicken section of 4H. Don't ask him about egg production unless you want your ear bent right off your head. He never shuts up about them. And that guy there, the bass player, that's Scrug Watson. He's a strawberry farmer, got a place about four miles out of town."

Scrug didn't look anything like a farmer from his neck down. He wore a grey suit and a button-down shirt so white it gleamed almost blue under the spotlight. A wide burgundy tie was tacked in place, and his black wingtips shone. But from the neck up, he was all agriculture –

wide, wind-burned cheeks, eyebrows blond from the sun, and a red John Deere baseball cap.

They were good. They had a clean traditional sound, Scrug doing most of the singing with Nate and Mack backing him on tight harmonies. Their third song was about a pick-up truck and a blonde, and while they were the ultimate country song clichés, something about the tune worked. She was impressed. Scrug could really sing. Mack could really drum.

Nate could play, yes. He played damn well, but beyond that, no one on God's green earth should be *allowed* to have that much natural charisma. Adele couldn't tear her gaze away from him. Onstage, under the bright light, his scowl turned less cranky and more sexy. He wore a blue T-shirt and jeans that fit his long legs just right. He'd been good-looking enough in the backward-facing baseball cap he'd worn earlier, but he was completely devastating in the beat-up brown cowboy hat that he wore now. When he tilted his head to glance at the fretboard, shadows leaped along his strong, broad jaw. The way his left hand skated up and down the strings made something in the pit of Adele's stomach twist. He kept those loose legs that the good players had, his knees slightly bent, his jeans tight over his thighs.

He made playing look easy, and Adele knew from years with her own guitar that the things he was doing were anything but. *Damn.*

She needed another drink. Or a water. Or maybe just a break from staring at the guitarist. What was she, eighteen?

At the bar, she ordered a sparkling water from Dixie, the woman with the short brown curls. She was pretty, built like a sexy fire hydrant – short but curvy, the slants of her body exaggerated. She wore a tight black low-cut top that showed off her cleavage, and her lower curves meandered out of the hem of her jeans shorts.

"We seem to be fresh out of the sparkling stuff, sorry. I got soda water or Coke."

"Soda water. Twist of lime?"

Dixie nodded and when she turned back with the drink, she said, "You know we never have the sparkling stuff. Right?"

"Uncle Hugh was always a stick-in-the-mud when it came to mixology."

Dixie snorted. "Mixo-what? You know, one night a guy came in here and tried to tell Hugh his Old-Fashioned recipe was wrong, that he needed to heat the sugar cube before dropping it in."

Adele could only imagine. Hugh had a big heart and a short fuse. "And?"

"He made it just like he always did, ignoring the asshole as he whined, then carried it to him around the bar. He was seated right where you are now. Hugh held it over his head, and the best part was the guy just looked upward, like he had no idea what was coming next."

"He dumped it."

Dixie grinned. "All over him. The guy threatened to sue him for the damage to his clothes, and that's when Hugh threw him and his three friends out. Physically. You know how he could roar into grizzly bear mode? That version of Hugh came out to play. I swear the guy was almost sobbing. We laughed for weeks over that one."

Adele squeezed the lime into the soda water. "You could insult him just about any way you wanted to, but you couldn't insult the way he ran the bar."

Dixie nodded in satisfaction. "Exactly right. Hey. My sincere condolences to you. I can't imagine what it must be like to be back without him here to greet you."

Was there a concealed barb in the words? A cloaked judgment for not getting there in time?

But nothing seemed to hide behind Dixie's words, nothing except clear and rather heart-twisting sympathy in her eyes. For the first time since pulling into town Adele felt like crying, felt the heat behind her eyes that told her if she didn't do something and quick, she'd be blubbering in the saloon she'd practically grown up in.

She glugged some of the soda water, grateful for its coldness. "So, how long did you work for him?"

"Me? Not that long. The last year and a half, I think."

Adele pushed her hair back and looked over her shoulder at the band. They were playing a sweet ballad about when to call your sweetheart and what you should call her when you did, and Nate took a short solo on the chorus. His voice was strong, his words clearly enunciated. Gravel lined his low voice, and he was perfectly on pitch.

His voice was so good it was almost annoying, and his playing was even better.

She hadn't expected this.

With a little more effort than it should have taken, Adele turned back to Dixie. "Yeah? What brought you here?"

"What else? Love."

"Always a good reason to go somewhere," said Adele.

"Not always the best reason to stay, though."

"Mmm." Adele sneaked another look over her shoulder at Nate. She couldn't help saying, "He's good. He's really good."

"Yeah. I hear that a lot from women on your side of the bar."

Adele started. "Really?"

Laughing, Dixie pulled a beer for a guy in an improbable corduroy blazer and then came back. "Yeah. You know. He gets a lot of that *What's a guy like you doing in a place like this?*"

Adele nodded. She could see that. And she couldn't help wondering how he answered.

Samantha and Hank were slow-dancing on the small floor occupied by a few other couples. Samantha's head was on Hank's shoulder, and they moved like they were listening less to the music than to each other's bodies.

Did Nate ever slow-dance like that with anyone? Was there a girl he regularly danced with?

"Hey, I just have to say –" Dixie leaned over the bar, displaying even more friendly cleavage. "Your first album? That one was my favorite. Everyone liked *Take It Slow on the Curves* best, but the first one, even with its rough production, that one got me through some rough times, you know? Oh, man." Dixie clapped a red-nailed hand over her mouth. "I shouldn'ta said that. I love the production on it. I didn't mean it the way it sounded, I swear."

"The production on that one *was* rough. We did it in our parents" garage with equipment we borrowed from a college kid who lived down the block. When we first recorded it, we didn't even have a band name. It wasn't till we came to Darling Bay that summer that Uncle Hugh came up with it."

Dixie nodded, looking satisfied. "He never stopped bragging that the name had been his idea."

"The Darling Songbirds" was fine for what they were back then. But now it was as old-fashioned as the town itself. Earlier, when that old album had been playing on the jukebox, Adele had had to swallow the urge to sing along with "Honey and Honky-tonk'. She hadn't performed with her sisters in eleven years, but she could sing those songs in her sleep.

The slow song ended. Nate stepped out of the light. Hank and Samantha came off the floor. Samantha said something to Dixie in a low voice that Adele couldn't hear, and both the women laughed. It wasn't about her, was it? Fresh nerves jumped through her.

Hank held his hand out to Adele. "Dance with me while they gab?"

With relief, Adele said, "Love to." As long as it had been since she'd hung out in a country saloon simply listening to music for the fun of it, it had been even longer since she'd danced on a bare-wood floor.

The next song was a two-step. Adele had forgotten how reliable a dancer Hank was. He had the rhythm, and what he lacked in panache he made up with sheer good-heartedness. When the band broke into a slower song in three-quarter time next, he held on to her and they moved into waltz steps. "You're the same guy," said Adele, "only happy. You didn't used to be that."

"You only knew me when I was hung up on a certain girl."

Adele laughed. "You *mooned* over Samantha, and she never saw you. I totally remember that. You were the most sentimental thing I ever met. But if you haven't noticed, these days that certain girl seems pretty hung up on you, too."

"Yep," said Hank simply. "We're happy."

Adele, unable to help herself, glanced at the three men onstage. Nate had a slight grin, and he was looking down at his guitar as if it were the love of his life, and maybe it was. "I'm so glad."

"What about you? Did you cart a man along with you into town, or is he coming along behind you?"

"No man," Adele said lightly as Hank wheeled her carefully around an elderly couple who were dancing with a steady but glacial pace. "Just me."

"I thought I read that you were hooked up with that singer."

"I was in Nashville. I'm a songwriter. Singers happen."

"Hey, now." Hank pulled away and looked at her. "You okay?"

How was it possible to feel these two ways at the same time? She was so *happy* to be here, to be dancing with Hank on the wooden floor she'd loved sliding across in socks when she was a kid and the bar was empty. At the same time, she was devastated that she'd missed saying goodbye to her uncle. "I'm okay."

She glanced again at Nate. And for one second, as he strummed a D minor 7th, he smiled at her. Their gaze tangled, and she lost her breath, and then Hank was turning her again, and she had to look into his face to stay steady on her feet.

"What are you going to do about Nate?"

"What?" Did it show that much? Was she really that obvious? She used to be smoother than that when she was checking someone out in a dark bar, but it *had* been a long time.

"Keep him? Fire him? Are you selling the place?"

"Oh. That."

"Because you should sell to him, you know."

"Sorry?"

"I'm glad you're back – don't get me wrong – I really am. But Nate loves this place, and he tried so hard to buy it off your uncle. I hate that he didn't get the chance, and now he might not get to."

"He wants to buy it?"

"He's been saving for years. I know the bank loan came through again more than a year ago, but Hugh was in one of his phases where he thought he might redo everything here and start over. You know how he was."

Bigger than life. Adele's father had always said his brother could talk a whore into saying the rosary. "Why does he want it? And if he wants it, why didn't Uncle Hugh just sell to him?"

"Not really sure. From a couple of things Nate has said, I think Hugh might have been using this place as bait."

"For us." But they'd never come.

Hank gave a quick nod. "Maybe. I just hope you think about giving Nate a chance."

Adele was suddenly suspicious. "Did he put you up to this?" Nashville had been like this. There was always someone ready to sweep you off your feet so they could try to get what they thought they needed from you. But she hadn't expected that kind of thing here.

"Of course not. I'm just curious for his sake. He's a good friend, and I don't want him to go anywhere."

"I haven't actually talked it out with my sisters – not yet – but we obviously can't keep this place."

"Yeah."

Hank pushed her into another spin, and she landed against him with a more solid thud than she'd planned. "It's a wreck," she said.

"Totally."

"Trashed."

"He showed you the rooms?"

"What's not burned out is dry rotted."

"Yep." Hank nodded amenably.

"And this saloon is as run-down as they get."

"Surprised the boards aren't dropping us to the dirt below right now." Hank gave a satisfied stomp with his boot.

"And the café is defunct."

"Has been for years. Old and moldy."

"But the coffee. Remember, people came from miles around just to get a cup to go? And the barbecued oysters, still fresh from the water every Saturday? And those fries? I've literally dreamed about those fries."

"Too much for him to take care of. He couldn't possibly do it all himself."

For a moment Adele forgot they were talking about her uncle and looked again at Nate. His fingers were moving fast and smooth on the strings, but his body stayed still, those long legs of his slightly bent. Ready to catch that guitar if it fell. Or a woman.

"So you and your sisters . . ."

Adele almost stumbled. "Yeah. We'd never be able to fix this place up." Even as she said the words, she felt herself fighting against them in her mind. Fixing? What *couldn't* she fix, when it came right down to it? Her whole job had been fixing. People wrote songs, and they paid her to fix them, to make them better. It was good, dependable money.

And she was great at it. She fixed her friends" love lives, cushioning the blows of bad break-ups and setting them up with people who were better for them. She fixed the things that broke in her old apartment (the toaster, the washing machine), perennially pissing off her ex-boyfriend, who thought that if he couldn't fix a pipe (and he couldn't) that they should hire a plumber instead of letting her work on it.

"Not many people would be able to set a ship like this to rights. It's already basically sunk," said Hank. The song slowed to a close, and Hank gave her one last spin before drawing her back. "Good crowd tonight, though. His band really gets them in."

It took a moment for Adele to realize he was serious. He thought the dozen people in the bar listening was a good turn-out.

He gave a short bow and winked. "Don't underestimate Nate. He's the real deal."

Adele gave a silly, awkward curtsy. They clapped for the band.

Nate ducked his head and stepped backward, giving the spotlight to Scrug.

And even though she tried – she really tried – Adele couldn't help the fact that her eyes still strained to see him through the darkness.

CHAPTER TEN

Adele didn't think she'd ever kicked so much in her life. She woke in Nate's borrowed bed – no, the hotel's bed – with her legs aching as if she'd been running all night. The mattress was too thin. Or too old. Or maybe it was too firm. Her broken sleep surely didn't have anything to do with its normal occupant, and the way she'd kept waking up with Nate's image walking through her dreams. No.

She thought with longing of her old bed in Nashville. It had been just right: a queen, soft on top but firm underneath.

She'd sold it along with almost everything else she owned, which, after the huge garage sale she'd had before leaving Nashville, wasn't all that much. She still had four boxes of Darling Songbird memorabilia, and her mother's hutch, the one she'd carted along with her no matter where she'd moved. All the rest of Adele's possessions had fit in a tiny storage unit, with room to spare.

If only she'd gotten the messages about Uncle Hugh in time.

She knew it didn't sound plausible, and if she'd been to a funeral to which no family member showed up, she wouldn't believe a single excuse. There wasn't a good-enough justification in the world.

But that was the truth – she *hadn't* been home to get the first crushing message from the coroner (apparently he and Uncle Hugh had been fishing buddies, and the coroner's voice had cracked as he spoke to her voicemail). She *still* hadn't been home when the second message landed from a man with a low voice who said, "I need to know if your uncle wanted a memorial, and if he did, what kind, 'cause I have no clue what would be best." He'd left a number but not a name.

She'd been absolutely unreachable, and God, how she wished she hadn't been. For the previous six months, she'd been dating a race car driver, Mitch, who was blond and funny and good in bed. They were equally semi-famous. Neither of them minded when they went out to dinner and people tilted their heads but couldn't *quite* figure out who they were. It wasn't until they hit the second mile of a fourteen-day backpacking trip in Cumberland Gap that she'd also realized he was a very bad planner. And he wasn't much of an actual hiker, either. Adele had been training since Mitch had invited her to come along. She'd been hiking with cans of soup in her backpack on Mitch's race days, and she'd been studying how to find water. She'd bought the smallest, most portable water purifier on the market. She read *Wild* and had seen the movie, too.

Less than an hour into the hike (right after they'd left cell range), Mitch had had a panic attack and decided he couldn't figure out what to do next. She'd had to take over the route planning and redo his poor plans from paper maps. At five days in, they'd crossed a major road, and Mitch, plagued by blisters as big as strawberries because he hadn't done a day's worth of training, hitched a ride back to the city. Adele had waved him off with an acute rush of relief, and then she'd continued to walk the rest of the planned eleven days. It had been grueling, and during one particularly extended lightning storm, terrifying. But she'd been happy when she came home, alone. She'd opened her apartment door, glad no one was with her. She could have the first shower. The first lie-down on the living room floor.

She'd opened her mail, and she'd found the eviction notice. Her apartment in Nashville, the place she'd lived for the last ten years, was half an old Victorian, and the owner had sold the building in order to make it into a doctor's office.

Then she'd listened to her voice messages, and found that at some point while she'd been sleeping by herself under the stars, while she'd been writing songs on the trail and singing them to herself over and over so she'd remember them until she pulled out her notebook, her uncle had been dying. And then he'd been buried. No one had Molly's or Lana's contact info, just hers, so none of them – not one – had been there to represent the Darling family.

And there was nothing she could do about it. She couldn't fix it. Nothing could make that kind of wrong right. It wasn't planned and it wasn't malicious. Adele and Molly had been talking about going to Darling Bay for the last couple of years. Lana had sent Molly a postcard that said she might visit Uncle Hugh on her way to Baja, but it turned out she'd gone to Alaska, instead. Adele would lay money on both her sisters being scared of going to Darling Bay, scared of being in town for the first time without their father there with them. Unbearable, really, how much sadness she'd always felt when she thought of Darling Bay.

None of it had gone the way it should have, and there was nothing Adele could do about it now.

So she'd held the garage sale and put the rest of her things into storage. She'd handed in her keys and gotten back her deposit. She'd bought a plane ticket and hired a car and now here she was. And surprisingly, being there wasn't as heartbreaking as she'd imagined it would be. Every corner, every nook of the space held a memory or two. But it felt good to be here, where the air smelled right.

Even if she was homeless.

Funny, she hadn't thought about that word before.

She owned no bed at all, especially not her perfect, lost-forever-now bed. She hoped it was giving the woman who'd bought it – a new-to-town songwriter who'd had the same excited look on her face that Adele had once had – the best dreams possible.

Adele twisted in the bed again, trying to unwind the crick in her neck. If this had been an actual hotel room currently being rented, she would have been tempted to write a review of it, telling future customers to avoid room one if possible.

Reviews.

Adele hadn't even *thought* to check them until that moment, which didn't make any sense. She was addicted to reviews. Something about them soothed her. When she couldn't sleep at home in Nashville, she sometimes brought up luggage sites on her phone and read the reviews of suitcases. It wasn't that she needed a new suitcase (she had a favorite that she owned and loved). It was more that she loved finding out what other people were lying in bed thinking about when *they* couldn't sleep (because who else would leave luggage reviews?). For every bag, someone wrote that the quality of the zipper could be improved. Someone else always thought the pockets were too small, and for every review that said that, there were three other people who thought the pockets were too big. The wheels spun too freely or they were too tight on their axles.

Everyone had a way to make things better. It was a truism wherever she went. People had opinions and they wanted to be heard.

She pulled her cell off the nightstand and opened Yelp. *The Golden Spike, Darling Bay.* The wi-fi connection dropped and rebooted itself twice, and both times, Adele logged back in quickly, skimming the reviews as quickly as she could before she lost connection again.

Holy crap. It barely had two of five stars. That was *bad.* If she'd been a tourist driving up the coast, she would have seen that and would have kept skimming, not even bothering to read why it had earned such low reviews. Her finger would have kept flicking the screen until something with more stars made a click seem worthwhile.

A tightness low in her gut, she opened the page.

Dirty.

Old.

Grimy.

Grubby.

Café – CLOSED.

Hotel – CLOSED.

Saloon – Not worth the time it takes to get a watered-down vodka tonic.

Keep driving.

I was scared I might get stabbed in this place.

Full of locals who look like they might be missing important teeth.

That wasn't true – Adele bristled and rolled on to her other side, wanting to give Rellie1 a piece of her mind. The locals were cowboys, ranchers and fishermen. They might be working class, but that just made them better. Stronger. It was a vibrant, tightly knit community. They weren't inbred, for Godsakes.

If I could give this zero stars, I would. Beer was warm. They said they had a problem with something and they were waiting on a part, but that's not a good answer. My boyfriend said his shot of whiskey was good, but I didn't like the way it tasted – so yuck. Since I can't leave less than one star and because my boyfriend isn't on Yelp, I'll say that the bartender was hot. Like dirty-hot, all growly and flannel-shirted and hot but only because his package is probably so big it's getting squished by those tight Wranglers, you know? Maybe worth one star. No, definitely. I'd go back just for him. But not for the warm beer.

Did Nate read online reviews? Somehow she doubted it, and a mischievous part of her wanted to show him that review, just to watch his face go darker.

But then they'd both be thinking about his package. His big package.

The sheets were making her too hot, and she pushed them off. She needed a shower. Then she'd find out if the bagel place was still making them fresh every morning.

Then . . .

She had no idea what would follow next. Technically, she would need to contact the bank, she supposed. And Uncle Hugh's lawyer. Figure out how to sell the property. Lord, what if it was worth so little that it didn't make sense to sell?

A strange feeling shot through her, electric and sharp. It took her a moment to figure out what it was.

It was hope – just a little chip of it, but still brilliant and strange.

CHAPTER ELEVEN

It wasn't until after Nate had struck his knuckles against her door (*his* door) that he realized Adele might still be asleep. It was only nine in the morning, after all. He'd been awake for hours – the floor in room twelve was harder than he'd thought it would be, even with a camping pad under his sleeping bag. It hadn't crossed his mind that she might not be awake. But she might be jet-lagged. Maybe she was a late sleeper anyway.

But he'd already knocked. He couldn't undo the sound. So he stood and waited. He flipped his mother's sobriety chip up once and caught it, slapping it on the back of his hand, like he was settling a bet.

You better hope she's dressed, Houston.

And then he took that hope back, just for one sweet second.

He leaned against the wooden post. He would give her thirty more seconds, then he'd assume she'd gone for a walk. Her rental car was still parked in front of the bar, but Darling Bay was so small that didn't really mean anything.

Just to be safe, he gave her a full minute. Then he let himself in. Slowly. He didn't like the woman, but he had no desire to give her a heart attack in case she actually hadn't heard him. "Hello?"

Nothing. The bed was empty, the sheets so chaotically arranged it looked like she'd spent the whole night spinning. With someone? Or alone? After all, she was from here. Kind of. "Hello? Adele?"

Crap. The door to the bathroom was closed, and he could hear the shower running.

Fast. He'd just be quick as lightning, grab what he needed, and then get out again. Next to the bed, that's where he'd left it . . .

"What the *hell* are you doing in here?"

Nate came up with a shout. "Whoa! Library book! I'm sorry!"

But he wasn't. Really, he knew he should have been. But Adele was wrapped in one of the old skimpy hotel towels, wearing nothing else but a furious expression. Nate forgot how to swallow.

"You might be aware of this already, but this is *not the library.*"

"No!" He ducked to look under the bed and there it was, his library book on artificial fishing lures. "This is due! Today!"

Her eyes widened, her fist clutching the top of the towel tightly. "That's the lamest excuse I've ever heard."

"No, really. It's due today, and this is new. There were two people on the waiting list for it, and Mrs. Purcell made me promise I'd return it on time."

"Are you *eleven*? Do you need a dime for your overdue charge if you get it back late? Because there's some change right there next to the TV. Grab ten cents on your way out!"

"I'm sorry for scaring you." He was, truly. "I thought you were out. Or I absolutely would have waited."

"You were snooping."

Nate hadn't even thought of doing that – now he wished he had. That would have made sense. But no, like the biggest dork in the whole world, he had actually just wanted to grab his library book. He backed up. "So sorry, again."

"The TV?"

"Huh?"

"It doesn't work."

"Oh, yeah. I know. It hasn't, not since we cut off the cable."

"Uncle Hugh loved cable, though." Adele pushed her long hair off her shoulder. It was dry, and the shower was still running, so presumably she'd been about to drop the towel on the floor. Lord give a man strength.

"He was the one who asked me to turn it off. Up here in the rooms, anyway. We have it going to the TV in the saloon, for sports."

"Why did he do that?"

Nate didn't say anything. Couldn't she figure it out?

"Well?"

God, she was irritating. Gorgeous, but what a pain. "He couldn't afford it. Why keep cable going to unoccupied rooms?"

Adele looked at the floor, her hand still gripping the towel tightly over her breasts. "Yeah. Okay."

The towel was short enough that it parted high on her thigh, and Nate forgot how to breathe for a second.

"Do you want to see his grave?" It wasn't what he'd planned on asking her when he saw her. He'd wanted to show her his business plan, impress her with his ideas for the property, then get her the hell out of Dodge.

She took a quick breath in, an audible sip of air. Maybe, if they were both having trouble breathing, there was a problem. Maybe he should install a carbon monoxide detector. He hadn't worried about it for himself, but better safe than sorry, and God knew the air was the only thing that hadn't gone bad around here.

"Yes."

In the split second it had taken her to lick her lips, he'd forgotten what he'd just asked her. *Hugh's grave.* That was it.

She jerked a thumb over her shoulder. "I'll just . . ." Her eyes were the same blue as the wisteria that draped over the low hotel porch railings, the wisteria his mother had planted. How had he called Adele's eyes dirty-blue?

"Yeah." Nate thumped the cover of the book with his palm. "I'll wait for you downstairs. In the bar. I have to open at eleven but we'll have time."

He almost tripped on his way down the gravel path to the saloon. He walked the path a dozen times a day, and he couldn't even trust his own balance now? That woman was throwing him. The less time he spent with her, the better.

Yet he'd just offered to show her Hugh's grave.

Behind the bar, he poured himself a cup of coffee, made in Hugh's ancient coffee machine. He drank too fast and it burned his tongue. Was his whole day going to be like this?

Fine, whatever, the day could go to hell as long as he got the one thing done that he needed to today: he had to get her to agree to sell to him. He was ready to say – to do – anything to extract that from her. He could be sweet as the valley's clover honey. He could be charming as old Myra Tenbottom on a bender.

He'd do what he had to do.

CHAPTER TWELVE

The sun felt good on the top of Adele's head as she left her room and headed for the parking lot. She'd dressed hoping for early fall sun: a thin black button-down shirt and a short jean skirt. Black sandals with straps and a wedge heel. The way Nate's gaze swept her body made her feel even warmer than the sunshine did.

Maybe the warmth was affecting Nate for the better, too. He smiled and opened the door of his truck for her. He didn't look surprised that she had her guitar with her – he just took it from her and gently laid it in the space behind the front seats.

And he didn't ask why she had it with her. That was nice. Adele didn't think she could tell him without crying, and she did *not* want to cry this early in the day.

He turned on the local country station and both of them hummed along to an old Willie Nelson song. They could have been any couple headed out for morning coffee.

The thought was jarring. Adele stopped humming and ran her finger along the side of the seat, playing with a sharp place where the vinyl was cracked.

She tried desperately not to notice how wide his hands were on the steering wheel. How he had shaved but had missed a bit just under his jawline. She pretended to herself that she didn't feel an insane urge to touch that spot. To kiss it.

Sweet Tammy Wynette, she was being ridiculous.

"Here we are." They were the first words he'd said on the drive. Adele still hadn't said any.

She scrambled out, carrying her guitar with one hand and pulling on her red cowboy hat with the other, glad she'd brought both.

Adele had always thought the Darling Bay cemetery was surprisingly cheerful. Far from being a spooky place of haunts and regrets, it was bright and green and open, full of rolling rises easily climbed in a dozen paces. Ornate marble crypts were on the right of the huge gate, and to the left were the old, almost-unreadable, simpler markers of the pioneers that had first been in the valley, before the town had a name. A vineyard ran along the edges of the graveyard, and the grape leaves were just starting to brown, announcing fall's swift approach.

It was gorgeous. Happy, even.

But Adele had lost her equanimity on the drive somewhere, and she held the handle of the guitar case so tight her fingers ached.

"This way." Nate pointed up a path.

Hummingbirds buzzed them as they walked, flirting with the air and the flowers around them. One solitary hawk circled high above. It cried once, a lonely sound that carried. Why was it crying? For a mate? From anger? From dizzy happiness or from sorrow?

Nate followed her gaze. "Saw one of those pick up a squirrel once. Tail whopped all over the place, even way up in the sky."

"Sounds like it might not have worked out well for the squirrel."

"I dunno. It eventually got dropped. Maybe it got a good bite in before it died."

"I hope so." Adele took a moment to imagine a huge pair of claws swooping out of nowhere to pick her up and cart her into the air. From up there, she'd have a view of all of Darling Bay. She'd be able to see the marina and Fenton's Cove, not to mention the Golden Spike. But she'd be so busy punching the huge raptor that pulled her up that she wouldn't be able to enjoy it. "Poor squirrel." Was it the imaginary squirrel that was upsetting her so much or was it the fact that she was about to come face to face with her uncle's grave? Adele took a deep breath and clenched her teeth.

"You all right?"

Of course she wasn't. But still, it was a kind thing to ask. She unlocked her jaw. "Sure."

"Okay."

Nate swung ahead of her, his long legs easy, his arms loose. The back of his black shirt advertised a feed company in Fortuna, emblazoned with a picture of a longhorn behind a short white fence. Instead of the battered cowboy hat he'd worn last night in the saloon, he wore his Charlie's Feed and Seed ball cap backward again, so the logo faced her as she followed behind him. How was it possible that he seemed like such a cowboy when he wasn't wearing a cowboy hat? Was it his walk? The way his legs ate up the distance as if there were a horse below him?

It was a good thing he liked his ball cap so much. The world didn't need him looking any better than he did. It was already a sin against nature that the back of his jeans looked that good. Nate wasn't overweight, not even a little bit, but he wasn't skinny, either. He was tall and broad and strong, even from the back. The Yelp review was right – he filled out his Wranglers so well he could appear in a billboard ad for them. Women would make a mad rush to buy them for their men in the vain hope that their asses would look the same.

That was *not* the right thing to be thinking while walking behind the man in a graveyard.

He spoke over his shoulder. "You want to hear about the memorial service?"

Of *course* she did.

And the thought of him telling her about it made her want to run across the graveyard and hop the low fence and just keep running, down the hills, to the water, where she'd start swimming and never stop till she reached Hawaii.

But she said, "Yes. Please."

He slowed so that she could catch up and walk next to him. "Did he ever talk to you girls about what he wanted? Or to your dad?"

"Not that I remember. He never said anything to you?"

"I guess it was another one of those things he just didn't want to think about."

"It seems there were a lot of those."

"Yeah. I called one of you – I can't remember which one. To ask. I just got a voicemail."

Funny, people had always gotten the three sisters mixed up, even though Adele didn't think they looked that much alike. "It was me."

Nate squinted sideways at her and kept walking. "Why didn't you call me back?"

"I wasn't home."

"For weeks?"

"Believe it or not, yeah." When she'd arrived home to discover the message, she'd called Molly and told her. Molly had become hysterical and had hung up, and Adele had spent the night wondering if she was okay. It turned out Molly had met up with the ship's purser-in-training and they'd gotten so drunk they'd reenacted the

Titanic scene on the prow of the ship. Not only was it lucky they hadn't lost their jobs, it was pretty fortunate Adele hadn't lost two members of her family that week.

Lana had never even had the courtesy to call Adele back. It was possible, Adele knew, that she'd changed her number, that she'd never received the message. Adele had sent her an email but it had bounced back, the address no longer good. She knew Molly would have told her, anyway.

So no, she hadn't bothered to call the stranger back who left a message asking about her uncle's wishes. It had been too late.

But she should have. She knew that. "Can I apologize to you now – and leave it at that?" Adele didn't expect it to work.

He was silent.

"Okay, then. I was off-grid, camping. When I came home, I found your message and an eviction notice. I packed up my entire life and came here as fast as I could, and it still took eight days to do it. I am sorry I didn't call you back. I should have."

He stayed quiet, but his pace slowed. Adele's heart dropped.

But then he said, "Accepted. If you threw in a thank you for handling all of it, that wouldn't be a bad thing."

"Thank you." She stopped, and he did, too. He shaded his eyes to look at her. "Really, Nate. Thank you."

"Yeah, well. I did the best I could." Something shimmered in the air between them. Adele felt her throat tighten.

"All right, then." Nate moved again, leaving the path and going up a low green rise.

Adele followed, careful not to step directly onto what looked like graves. "I'm pretty sure you did a better job than we would have. What did you end up doing?"

"We had a party."

"Perfect." A crow that was almost as big as a buzzard winged over her head. She felt the rush of air off its wing, and she flapped her arm at it. "What kind of party?"

"A big one."

"In the saloon?"

"Where else?"

"Open bar?"

Nate nodded and paused again, stopping under an oak tree. He looked at the crow that had perched on a huge limb above them. It cawed at them as if it were listing its complaints, one by one. "So open it hurt. A last hurrah worthy of the man. Liquor flowed like the Radiant River. Beer poured like the tide on a full moon."

"Ah, you're a poet." The surprise of it pleased her, warm as the sunlight on her arms.

He moved his jaw as if trying to loosen it. "Just a bartender. Pastor Jacobs did write a poem, though, and it was good. You should get a copy from him. The motorcycle gang from Radiant Valley roared by, in missing-man formation."

"I didn't know motorcycle gangs did that."

"Well, this gang is made up of eight sheep ranchers who decided to buy Harleys and ride on Sunday afternoons. They're called the Mutton Choppers, so it's not like they're very Sons of Anarchy or anything."

Adele smiled. "What else?"

Nate swung his arms and, in a surprise move, leaped for a narrow branch a good three feet over his head. He grabbed and swayed for a moment. Adele tried not to stare at the narrow band of skin that showed above where his jeans hung around his hips. She tried not to notice the muscles that cut into his lower abdomen, or the trail of darkness that led downward. And she *really* tried not to think about the liquid heat that rose inside her at the sight.

Ridiculous.

He dropped back to the dirt, slapping his hands against each other. He gestured farther up the small hill. "Almost there."

Adele cleared her throat. "Was there food?"

"Was there? Hell, yes. I hired Jones to bring the barbecue trailer out."

"Barbecue baby back ribs." Uncle Hugh's favorite food in the whole world.

"All you could eat. With potato salad and cilantro coleslaw and about a million cupcakes for dessert."

"That's a party, all right. People must have loved it."

"They loved him. I bet he'd given something to everyone in town by the time he died, whether it was a good listening ear, or a hug, or a drink on the house. Sometimes –" Nate broke off. "Did you know his last bartender? Donna?"

"Yeah. The one with the flaming red hair and the fake teeth. The drunk."

Nate winced. "Hugh kept her alive."

"I always wondered why he hired an alcoholic. Doesn't seem like it would be good for business, you know?"

"Business was second to him, I think. Taking care of people was first."

Uncle Hugh had always been kind to her and her sisters, filling their arms as they left with presents he'd been collecting for them during their stay – seashells and pieces of carved driftwood and Ziploc bags full of Jolly Ranchers and M&Ms. He'd hugged and kissed them, bragging about them in their hearing, making them feel special. Adele had never spent much time thinking about how he treated others. She should have, though. She added it to a laundry list of regrets that just seemed to be getting longer. "I took him for granted."

The look Nate gave her – of surprise and, perhaps, chagrin – shamed her. "Yeah," he said simply. "We all did. Okay, just up here."

"Was there music?"

"There was." His voice was hoarse.

"What music?" She shouldn't have asked. The answer might – no, it would – break her heart. But she had to know.

CHAPTER THIRTEEN

Nate didn't know whether to be angry with her or feel sorry for her. She obviously knew the answer to her question, or she wouldn't be pressing. Briefly, he considered lying. *We just had a big jam, an all-nighter, fifty people with guitars and fiddles, playing until the sun came up.*

But that wasn't the truth.

"The Darling Songbirds. All five albums."

She made a sound that was half-laugh, half-sob. "*Oh.*"

"I borrowed the PA system from the community center." He kept walking, keeping Adele just out of his line of sight, a foot or two behind him. He didn't want to know if she was crying, and he sure as hell didn't want to know if she *wasn't.* He raised his voice so she could hear him. "Crawled up on the roof and installed the speakers up there. So not only were y'all singing inside the saloon all afternoon, but everyone could hear you for blocks around." It had been lovely and had made his heart ache, being able to hear Hugh's favorite girls singing about love and loss even while he was grabbing six extra cases of napkins down the street at the Cash'n'Carry.

"We didn't sing, though." Her voice was small. "In person."

"No." What were the two of them *doing* here? Why had he offered to bring her? It was hard enough to grieve the man's passing in private, the pain still so raw it hurt like a grease burn, but to be at his grave with Adele – that just might be too much. His boots slowed.

Adele hurried then, and passed him. "Are we almost there?" Some women Nate had known held guitar cases like they were too heavy to carry far. Adele held hers like a musician, like the black soft case was just an extension of her body. It didn't slow her down.

"Yeah. That one."

But she'd already paused. He knew she saw the right one. The Darling Bay graveyard didn't receive that many new residents a year, especially now that so many people were choosing to be cremated. Nate didn't understand it himself. Why choose to burn your body and have to deal with the ashes (store them? toss them into the wind?) when you could just plant yourself in the dirt? Your whole body making the earth better, your molecules changing, spreading out, becoming the tree above, reaching for the light. He and Hugh had spent long hours talking about that. Nate had had no problem making that choice, at least, hearing Hugh's voice in his head. *Stick me in the ground. Don't worry about coming to visit, neither. I'll be busy, having a good old new time.*

The dirt of the grave was still dark and uneven. This wasn't one of those city graveyards where they covered a person with sod as soon as the widow turned her back – here, the caretakers (Willie and Wagoner Rayburn, who'd taken it over from their dad twenty years before) just let the grass cover over the graves in their own time. Sometimes weeds grew. A lot of the graves still had tenders, people who had loved the ones who were buried there. They came and pulled the weeds, and the nice thing was that they minded the other graves, too. It might take a while, but if Wagoner and Willie got a little slack (or spent too much time in the saloon with Norma and Parrot Freddy, which had always been a Rayburn trait), someone else in town would come back and pull out the mustard weed, planting pansies and marigolds.

"Oh. Look at it."

It would have been obvious to a stranger from out of town that the man buried here was beloved. The head of the grave was covered in bouquets of flowers. Some were dying – Nate would take those with them when they left – but some were still fresh. Mrs. Chumley, who grew the prettiest (and most award-winning, she never let you forget) dahlias in town had been here. Only true pillars of the community got one of her Crichton Honey dahlias planted upon death, only mayors and pastors and fire chiefs. Hugh's peach-colored prize-winner was already in the ground and well watered.

Adele dropped to her knees next to the flowers, her hand over her mouth. The guitar case fell, unnoticed, to the ground next to her. "Uncle Hugh." Her other hand reached to touch the stone.

Nate had gone traditional when he'd picked it out. No flashy marble, no syrupy saying. The stone was granite, deeply carved. It would stand against the weather, against the oceanic winter storms. It would be legible for hundreds of years. Nate liked that. He needed that.

Hugh Darling. He is remembered.

Adele looked up at him, her eyes suddenly blue-green instead of just sky blue. The change was as startling as the tears in those eyes. Somehow Nate hadn't imagined her crying, apparently because he was some kind of idiot. Of course she would cry.

His heart twisted in the middle of his chest like an old gnarled manzanita bush and his limbs froze into place as if the wood ran through his veins.

"This is so nice," she finally said, her eyes ocean-bright. "This is just perfect, Nate. Thank you."

Nate folded himself so that he kneeled next to her. He still couldn't speak.

The breeze, which had dropped as they'd walked up the hill, started again, and Nate could hear the ocean's low roar even here, at least a mile away from the waves. Adele shifted into a cross-legged position and folded her hands in her lap as if she were praying, but her eyes were open, fixed on the headstone. Her gaze was far away, and even though one tear traced its slow way down the side of the cheek closest to him, she had a small smile on her face, as if the memory was a sweet, cherished one.

After a few minutes, Nate wondered if he should leave her alone with her thoughts. He moved slightly, and in doing so, broke her reverie. Her eyes were clear blue again.

"I can –"

"No, stay." She touched his forearm lightly, and Nate caught his breath. He wanted to take her hand, to – to do something he wouldn't let himself do.

He just said, "Okay."

"Do you . . . I don't know if I should ask this."

"You can ask me anything." He ignored the part of his brain that pointed out they were words he normally didn't say to women.

"Do you know "Remember Me"?"

Of course he did. She'd be surprised, maybe, to know how very well he knew the Darling Songbirds" repertoire. Especially that one. Hugh's favorite. "Yeah."

"Can you play it for me?" She reached forward and pulled her guitar case along the grass towards her. "It's a good guitar. Maybe a little small for you. But I don't think –" Her voice broke and she covered her mouth with her hand again.

He waited.

"I don't think I can sing and play it alone. I've never sung it alone before."

"Of course." There was no other answer.

She was right, the guitar was small in his hands, but as he ran through the strings to check its tuning, its tone was as sweet as the Songbirds" voices themselves.

He strummed the simple chords, just G, C and D, and Adele sang next to him. The birds overhead quieted as if to listen. The wind dropped again, its soughing falling away.

Adele sang, and each word rang out simply and clearly, each word a bell, each one sung for Hugh. Those last two verses, they'd always gotten to Nate, and he felt a tug at the back of his throat as she sang them.

When the day is closing down,
When it's too dark to see,
When you think I'm not listening,
Just remember me.

When you doubt that I was here,
When you think you've lost the key,
Raise your glass again,
And just remember me.

As Adele's last word rolled down the hill towards the bay, Nate played the final chord as softly as he could.

Then she turned. She smiled at him. *Right* at him. Her gaze was sweeter than the song had been, and in that moment, Nate was struck by something terrible. This woman – the one who currently held one-third interest in the property he wanted to buy – was going to be nothing but trouble.

Honeyed, gloriously tuneful trouble – the very worst kind.

CHAPTER FOURTEEN

As they walked back towards his truck through the graveyard, Adele swallowed her embarrassment at making Nate play with her. He hadn't seemed to mind, after all. And he'd been good at it, too. Sure, it was a three-chord song (as so many of the good ones were), but he'd put the soft flourishes in the right places, letting the last chord fade out softly, like Adele herself did when she played it.

She could have played. She could have sung. But she knew trying to do both at the same time, and then singing alone, would have tossed her right into the middle of an ocean of grief. She didn't feel that buoyant lately.

"Give me a minute," said Nate. "I'll meet you at the truck."

Adele glanced back at him, but he was already striding westward away from her. His scowl had returned, and she wondered if that's what his face defaulted to when he wasn't trying to make it do something else.

At the pick-up, she popped the tailgate. From here, she could just see the southern tip of Darling Bay. The roof of the police station gleamed red, and through the sunlight, sparkling silver on the water, she could make out the newer pier. A sliver of the bay shined up at her. It winked, as if it knew a secret.

Nate had been so kind to her.

And, obviously, now he was visiting someone else in the graveyard. She wouldn't ask who it was, though she wanted to know. He'd let her have her grief, without prying. He'd done the one thing she'd asked him to, playing along on her guitar.

She watched a curl of smoke rise from the valley, where the grass on the hills was autumn-brown.

Home, sang her heart.

When Nate got back to the truck, his face was still stiff.

He started the engine with a roar. "Have you eaten?" He didn't look at her.

"I'm fine." As if to make a liar of her, Adele's stomach grumbled, so loud it was audible over the motor.

"Yeah. I can hear that." A few minutes later, he took the turn onto Lincoln smoothly, then onto First. He pulled in to the parking lot of Darling Dogs.

For a moment, Adele considered continuing to insist that she didn't need to eat, but damn, a hot dog from the best place in town sounded just about right. "Great. I'll buy."

"No need."

"In payment for the service." The last word came out too heavily, as if she was talking about the funeral. "Your guitar services, I mean." She shoved the sigh back into her chest and jumped out of the truck.

Chili-cheese dogs and Cokes in hand, they walked over to one of the small white plastic tables that edged the lot. They sat next to each other, facing the water. Adele was glad she could keep her gaze in front, on her food, on the boats, glad she didn't have to work on not looking at him, into those dark-denim eyes.

They were only half a block from the water. Two fishing boats chugged into port, moving slowly and heavily, as if their haul was good.

"I've been gone so long I don't even know what's in season."

"Sablefish and salmon. Probably. That's Dirk Whitey's boat."

"You know him?"

"I know everyone at the marina."

"Right, you have a boat." He'd said he was sleeping on board so she could sleep in his bed. "Which one is yours?"

He squinted. "Can't see it from here. Just a little fishing boat."

"You fish?"

It was as if she could almost see the tension leave his shoulders. His face relaxed. "Every chance I get."

Adele took a huge bite and closed her eyes to better enjoy it. Exactly the right bean-to-meat ratio.

Nate did the same.

After the red boat had docked and two men had jumped onto the pier, Adele's mouth was empty enough to speak. "My dad used to take us fishing when we were here. Never on a boat, though. He wasn't a fan, always got seasick. We would stand on the pier and nine times out of ten what I would pull up would be something like a string of seaweed or plastic bags. I was pretty good at getting my line caught on someone else's, too. The serious fishermen out there didn't like that much at all. But we had fun."

"Do you get seasick on boats?"

"You know, I'm not sure."

"How can you not know?"

She shrugged. "I think I inherited some of my dad's fear of the ocean from him, maybe. I just never find myself on the water."

"Hmm."

"You love it, though?"

He nodded. "My mom, she loved fishing. And boats."

"Did she have one?"

He gave a short laugh. "No."

Carefully, Adele said, "Is she still alive?"

"No." He stabbed a piece of hot dog with his plastic fork so hard she heard a tine snap.

It was obviously a sore subject, so she changed it. "You were really good last night."

His eyebrows flew upward and she felt her cheeks heat.

"I mean, onstage. You're an amazing guitarist."

"Thanks." Nate shoved a fry into his mouth.

"Really. Did you ever think about doing something with it?"

He frowned. "I am doing something with it. I'm in Dust & Rusty."

"I mean, professionally."

He shook his head.

"Who writes your songs?"

"I write most of them. Mack has two."

"They're good." She didn't say it lightly. They were so good she could fix them up and sell them for serious cash if he wanted her help. Adele reached in front of him to snake a fry out of the basket. They were salty and hot and greasy and just right. "You ever think about selling them?"

"The songs?"

He sounded so shocked she laughed. "Yeah."

"They're just country songs."

"Every country radio station in the nation subscribes to a service that guarantees them two new mega hits a week. That means there are a lot of songs that need to be written."

He palmed the top of his head, jerking back his ball cap an inch. "Those mega hits are crap."

"Most of them, yes. You could give them something good."

He took a long sip of his drink and then rattled the ice in the paper cup. "But I don't want to."

"Fair enough. Did you and Hugh ever talk about bringing bigger bands in?"

"No."

He was a man of few words, wasn't he? Adele felt something spike in the back of her neck. Irritation, maybe, or frustration. "Why not?"

"Why bother?"

"Because it would bring in more money."

"That wasn't the end goal for Hugh."

The spike was definitely frustration. It went higher, into her forehead. "But he let everything go. When did the café close, exactly?"

Nate stared at the bobbing boat as if the answer could be found on board. "Five years? Six?"

"Why did he let it close?"

"It just wasn't . . ."

She jumped on his pause. "Wasn't making money? Is that it?"

"It's not that easy, Adele."

Was that the first time he'd said her name out loud? She liked how it sounded on his tongue. "Tell me how it isn't."

"It wasn't just the money. It was a hell of a lot of work. Even with me working full-time for him, it wasn't enough. I tried to take over the payroll, but Hugh insisted on being in charge of personnel. Staffing alone was a nightmare. The café meant four cooks, three waitresses, one prep cook and two busboys. The hotel meant an almost full-time receptionist, because in a beach town, someone's always calling. It meant a full-time maid and a part-time one on the weekends. When he let those things go, it was just him and me and the saloon. And that was just right for a long time." He popped another fry into his mouth. It seemed like his version of punctuation.

"Bringing in fun bands, popular local ones, bands that are going somewhere but are still low in their trajectory – that could really do something for the saloon."

"I'm sure you're right. It would do something."

Adele didn't understand why his words sounded so loaded. "What about trying it out?"

"Look." He leaned forward, and the lightweight table skidded away from them more than an inch, kicking gravel as it went. He yanked it back, grabbing her drink as it wobbled, setting it carefully in front of her. "I'm just not sure what you're after here."

"I'm just tossing out ideas – that's all."

He made a growling noise in the back of his throat, and the two small children who were running past their table gave him a sideways look, as if he were something dangerous. "Ideas for what? For who?"

Maybe he *was* dangerous. That would explain the electricity that seemed to be crackling off his skin. "For the saloon."

Nate set his hot dog on the table slowly. Deliberately. "For whose saloon?"

Ah. That was it. "Okay. Hank told me you want to buy the place –"

"He what?" Nate's voice stayed quiet but the intensity of it made it feel like a roar.

"It's not like it's some big secret. It would have come up when my sisters and I sell, right?"

"Yep."

So much intensity packed into such a small word. Adele took a sip of her drink and wished she'd gotten a milkshake instead. It would be good to fight a straw. "What if I can help? You know. What if I can help you fix things while I'm here?"

A vein jumped in Nate's forehead. "What are you *talking* about?"

"I'm sorry, I'm not being clear." How could she be clear? She felt nothing but confusion. "We let Hugh down so many times – what if we had the chance to right that wrong?"

"He's dead. You can't fix dead."

Yeah, well, she knew that too well. How many times had she forced her mother to get a second, then a third, then a seventh opinion? The multiple myeloma that had killed her hadn't been fixable. If it had been, Adele would have done it, at any cost.

Nate stared at the water. "Are you selling or what?"

"We're selling. Of course we're selling. I just want to be sure we don't make a mistake."

"What? Like you'd take it all over? Nashville has the Bluebird and here we'd have the Darling Songbird Café?"

She spoke through gritted teeth. "No. It's the Golden Spike. Always has been." She didn't mention she didn't have a home to go back to. "We have no interest in the property."

He didn't appear to have heard her. "What, make it into a coastal Dollywood, is that it? Darlingwood?"

Would that actually be the worst thing that ever happened? "This is a sleepy town. Might do it some good to wake it up."

"Maybe we like sleepy."

"Maybe." She wiped her fingers with a napkin. She wondered if she had chili on her face and then decided she could live with it if she had to.

"Adele." Nate put on one of the fakest-looking smiles she'd ever seen. The corners of his mouth barely lifted and his eyes stayed dark. "I am . . . *glad* you've come to town. I know it's – hard – to have this kind of upset in your life. It must be tough."

"Why are you acting weird all of a sudden?"

His eyes widened. "I'm not acting weird. I'm just saying that I appreciate you're in a rough spot." The bizarro smile got bigger. "And I'm happy to help you out in whatever way I can."

"Is this you trying to charm me or something?"

Nate groaned and slumped into his chair.

"Aha! It is! Let me tell you something, bucko. You suck at it."

"I don't know why I even tried."

A tight spot in Adele's back loosened. "I know the place is important to you."

He gave a short nod.

"Want to tell me why?"

"Nope."

The same two children ran back the other way, both of them carrying red cartons of fries, their mother chasing behind them.

"Want to do it anyway?"

Nate looked up into the sky with such a look of concern that Adele followed his gaze in case something was falling towards them. Nothing was.

"I followed a woman here."

"Ah."

"She needed rescuing." He stuck his fork into the hot dog detritus and laid his palms flat on the white table. "I didn't get to do it. Then she died."

"Oh, sweet Patsy Cline, I'm sorry." The rescuer. Adele wondered if he'd always had to play that role or if it was something that had started as an adult.

"It's fine."

It obviously wasn't, but Adele got that. "And you stayed."

"Fell in love with the place."

"Darling Bay does that to you."

"I worked at the marina doing odd jobs until Hugh gave me the bartending job."

"Why did he do that?"

"What?"

She knew it was rude. She knew she shouldn't ask. It was wrong, and impolite and disrespectful. But the question burned inside her. Uncle Hugh had been a rescuer of people, too. There had been Old Stevo, the ancient hobo who rode the rails when he was sober enough to grab a freight car's handle. Uncle Hugh gave him money, even though he was well aware Old Stevo just spent it on tequila in whatever dusty town he landed after getting thrown out of his boxcar. Then there was the tiny, thin young man – what had his name been? Rodney. That was it. He had been a raging alcoholic since the time he was thirteen. Uncle Hugh gave him a broom to push half-heartedly around the property, and the spare key to the laundry room. Rodney had slept on the floor on his good nights. On his bad nights, he fought people and landed in jail for a few days. He'd died after stealing Hugh's old Pontiac and driving it off Piermans Bridge. And there was Donna, the drunk bartender. She'd been a sweetheart. She had a huge laugh and an enormous passion for high school football. She wasn't even a local, but could talk Darling Bay High School stats with the best of the old men. Adele remembered Uncle Hugh and her laughing, just the two of them in the bar. She just didn't remember many of her sober nights, not when Adele had been in town anyway.

Her uncle had loved the drinkers. The addicts. He had a track record of exactly zero when it came to saving them, but he'd never stopped collecting them, just like he collected the buoys and cans and magazines in his apartment.

So Adele asked the question, even though she knew she shouldn't. "Are you an alcoholic?"

CHAPTER FIFTEEN

W ell, that was a first. Nate had felt the question in people's eyes, sure. He'd seen it in their stares. One girlfriend thought he drank too much on a night when he'd had three beers. She'd broken up with him because of it. He'd just figured he'd been better off. Someone who worried that much might have driven him to drink just to prove a point. "Wow."

"Sorry. But I want to know."

"No one's ever asked me that before," he said.

"No?"

"No."

"Is that your answer?"

He barked a laugh. "I don't think you got the memo."

"Which is?"

He needed to stop noticing how her eyes reflected the sun and actually sparkled, like sunlight on waves. "That it's not polite to ask."

She squinched up her face in a comical scowl. "I forget about polite sometimes. And how people seem to think it's important."

"Overrated, really."

She nodded. "You haven't answered."

"I'm not an alcoholic," he said. God, it was refreshing to be asked, instead of just having everything he did be watched, measured against his bloodline. Once he'd been trying to fix a broken lathe in the arbor, holding a power drill over his head. The drill had slipped, falling on his eye and cheekbone. He'd needed two stitches just below his temple. For three weeks, as the bruising healed, townsfolk had avoided looking right at him. They used to look at his mom that way. That exact same way.

"Do alcoholics lie?"

He laughed again. Sitting next to Adele in the crisp ocean air felt like drinking ice-water after working outside all day. "It's their specialty, I happen to know. But I'm not lying. I think I'd know if I were a drunk by now."

"How old are you?"

"Thirty-five."

"And people know by then?"

"Dog with a bone, huh?"

She nodded, keeping her eyes on his. "I get that way sometimes."

"I see that. Yeah, I think I'd know." He paused, and then told her the truth, surprising himself. "I worry about it, though. In my head, I see it like a switch. On or off. Mine's off. I don't know what it would take to flip it on, though, so I'm careful."

"How?"

"Damn, lady."

"Sorry." But her smile didn't look sorry at all. "But how are you careful? I'm honestly just curious. You don't have to answer."

Astonishingly, he wanted to. He had a method, and he'd always known he'd worry if his method got hard to maintain, which so far, it hadn't ever done. Without touching it, he could feel the two-month chip burn in his front pocket. "I try not to drink when I'm upset. I never drink alone, although that would be easy to do, since I work in a damn bar. But I never have more than two drinks. And I never drink more than once a week."

"Lord. That's the way people drink at church in Nashville. I'm not sure that even counts as drinking at all."

He shrugged. "I sleep better at night knowing I'm not flipping that switch."

"Probably makes you a good bartender."

"I've heard drunk bartenders pour heavier. Get more tips." He hadn't just heard it – he'd seen it in action. The drunker his mother had gotten behind the bar, the more singles drinkers had slid her way. Tiny green apologies.

"What about you?" He'd never asked it of another person in his life, not even his mother. You didn't ask the obvious, after all. "Are *you* an alcoholic?" The answer was suddenly deeply important.

"Nope." Her voice was clear. "I fall asleep after two glasses of wine."

The relief tasted like honey in his mouth.

Adele drew her knees up and wrapped her arms around them. Side by side, they watched Dirk moving on the dock.

The silence was more comfortable than it should have been. Nate could have sat there all day, watching the boats wallow in, heavy with their loads. Three kids biked past, obviously thrilled it was the weekend, and then two older men he recognized from the city council meetings walked slowly by. They nodded at Nate and Adele. Nate nodded back. Adele did, too.

"So," Adele said, after they'd passed. "You take care of drunk people. That's what you do."

"Good God, woman. Are you a shrink now? Did Hugh forget to mention that to me?"

She shrugged. "Songwriter. You must know how it is. Songwriters, bartenders, therapists, aren't they all the same thing? You don't have to answer me. I know I'm pushing too much."

And he wouldn't. It wasn't like it had really been a question. Besides, what was the harm in it? Was anyone actually going to fault him for making sure Norma had gotten home safe after closing the saloon at night? There was that one time, when she'd left her front door open and a pot of water on the stove. If he hadn't checked because of the open door, her whole house could have burned down. And Parrot Freddy would forget to eat if someone didn't remind him to do it.

Instead of answering, he stood up. "You ready?" He bagged her empty paper tray with his and shoved them in the trash can next to the stand before walking towards his truck.

"Hey," she said from behind him. Her voice was tentative.

Nate opened her door for her. "You don't have to apologize."

"Okay . . . ?"

He realized she hadn't been about to. Damn it. Why did she tip him off balance so much? It couldn't just be the way she looked in that denim skirt, could it? Because she looked incredible, but plenty of pretty girls came through town, and lots of them ended up at the saloon for at least one drink. Plenty of them wore short skirts that showed off shapely calves. He was used to pretty.

She jumped in the truck, swinging herself up easily. Her rear end in that skirt swung right into the seat like she'd ridden shotgun with him a million times. Those long legs that ended at those strappy sandals distracted him so much he almost forgot which way to turn the key.

Yeah, she was *way* past pretty.

"I interrupted you back there," Nate said, as he turned onto Main.

"Oh. I was just going to ask something about the saloon." Now she sounded hesitant, for the first time.

"Go ahead."

"Do you ever host open-mike nights?"

"Nope." Nate couldn't think of anything worse. A bunch of locals with ukuleles and misplaced ambition didn't sound like his idea of a good time.

"They can be fun."

"I'm sure they can. If you like live karaoke that sucks. And songs that no one knows."

"Come on. Lots of people get their starts at open mikes."

"That's like saying lots of people become pro-baseball players after playing third base in Little League. Doesn't happen."

"Okay, even if no one is discovered, it can really pack people in. The people who want to play come in, they bring their families and friends."

"And *those* people bring their camcorders and get in the way while I'm just trying to sling drinks." Nate lifted one finger off the wheel as Skip Lemon passed them in the opposite direction in his perpetually clanging ice-cream truck.

"Camcorders? Really?" Her voice was amused. "So what you're saying is that you haven't had an open mike in the era of smart phones?"

He could give her that. "I'll admit it's been a while. Technology might change but people don't."

"Can I organize one?"

Nate gripped the wheel tighter. "At my bar?" Damn it. It was a kneejerk answer. It was, technically, *her* bar. It belonged to the Darling girls. It was no more his saloon because he worked there than the road was his because he paid taxes. "Shit."

"Yeah. At your bar."

It was nice of her. And he hated it. "Do whatever you want. It's yours, after all."

"I'm only thinking out loud."

"No," he said, turning too fast into the small sloped parking lot of the Golden Spike. His back wheels fishtailed. It was childish, but he liked the sound of it, a short, angry curse, one he couldn't say out loud. "That's fine."

"Nate –"

"Do what you want. Let me know how I can help." He put the truck in park and got out.

She was out and around the truck, back in his face in seconds. "I'm not trying to take over, I swear. I just want to help. You need more customers. I'm here for at least a couple or three weeks while we work all this out. I want to help fix what I can while I'm here."

And that was the quandary, exactly. The Spike was full of things that needed fixing, expensive things, problems he was dying to work on. By himself. He strode through the back courtyard, making for the rear door of the saloon. Sanctuary. "Don't need your help."

"Nate, wait."

He turned, giving her one last second. The sunlight brought out the honey color in her hair, making the top of it so light it was almost pewter. Her face was concerned. Like she wanted to fix him, too.

Her fingers laced together in front of her stomach. "Can I try?"

Nate couldn't tell her what to do with her property – that was thing. He felt a bolo tie of anger constrict around his throat. "Go ahead. You don't need my permission."

"But –"

Then, like the ass he was, he shut the door on whatever she was starting to say. She could say it to the courtyard grapevines, maybe sweeten them up a bit. He'd made them sour enough.

CHAPTER SIXTEEN

A dele figured that a couple of nights would give the town time to talk about an upcoming open mike night, and Wednesdays were, traditionally, a good night for them. Far enough from the weekend for people to get cabin fever, to want to get out. It had been that way in Nashville, and it would be the same here. She was sure of it.

While she waited for the bank's manager to get back in town to talk to her about the property, and while she avoided Nate (just the thought of him made her nervous), Adele hung "Open Mike at the Golden Spike" flyers. While doing so, she learned more about how the town had changed than she would have in a month of going to church.

She found out that Lily Dario had moved out of the taco truck (though she still used it on weekends at the beach) and had a real restaurant now, which was booming, lines out the door at night. "I can't believe you're back! How long will you stay? Can you come have a drink here tonight? Can you give me a few extra flyers to hand out? What if I can't get out of the restaurant in time to make it? Will you be playing, too? Are your sisters coming home? What time is it on?" The questions tumbled out of Lily so fast Adele didn't have to do more than answer the last one, pointing at the place on the flyer. "Seven. Wednesday night. I'd love to see you there if you can make it." She and Lily used to camp overnight at the beach when they could get away from their little sisters. Lily's hug smelled like corn flour and friendship.

She found out that John Skinner, the man who ran the pound, was as enthusiastic an accordionist as he was a dog rescuer. He put up two of the flyers and swore he would pass out more, then played her a reel while a pit bull puppy howled along adorably.

She found out that Skip's Ice Cream parlor had burned down. That one came as a shock. She couldn't count how many cones of bubblegum ice-cream she'd consumed over the years (Molly was peppermint; Lana was caramel vanilla). Almost every summer night their parents had bought them each a scoop and then they'd walked to the end of the pier and back. Okay, she and Molly had run to the end, racing every night to get the best place to stand – the tallest bench was the perfect place to lean over the edge and pretend you were flying. High school kids dove off it at night. It was rumored that a kid had once died doing it, hitting his head when a wave knocked him against a piling, but that was never confirmed, and no one seemed to know what kid it had been or what family it had come from, so it was most likely an urban legend like so many other Darling Bay stories. Lana had always walked behind them, with their parents, and after their mother had died, she'd walked with their father. It was because she was the baby, Adele and Molly thought. She'd been the last one to let go of holding their hands. Solitary Lana had been the one left behind in other things, too.

Seeing the boarded wreckage of the building made Adele's head hurt, an echo of pain that felt like the time she'd gotten three fillings at once at the dentist. When the Novocaine had worn off, only the ache had been left. She touched the windowsill. Other fingerprints had pressed at the burnt edge, and part of the wood crumbled under her touch.

Was the whole town falling apart? Deteriorating to fire or mold or simple old age? Would she leave and come back to find nothing? A Brigadoon that they'd dreamed up, once upon a time?

From behind her, a woman said, "One more block down, on the right."

Adele turned. It was Dixie, the curly-topped bartender from the Golden Spike. "Sorry?"

"Skip just moved instead of rebuilding. Insurance, you know. He has a bigger place now."

A sense of relief mixed with disappointment swept through her. Ice-cream could still be had. That was important in a town like this, obviously. What was a beach town without locally made ice-cream? But she was surprisingly sad that her childhood memory would never be relived. Even if she could actually get Molly and Lana here (something too impossible to let herself imagine), they would never stand in the same line they'd waited in as kids. She remembered that on hot September nights, the line could wrap to the corner and around the block. They would never run down the pier from the same place.

No matter where the ice-cream shop was, it couldn't bring everyone back. Period.

Adele tried to shake off the memories that had landed on her as heavily as a winter storm. "I'm glad to hear it."

Dixie dipped her head in the same direction. "Wanna?"

"What? Get ice-cream? What time is it?"

Dixie looked over her shoulder at the clock tower that stood above city hall. "Eleven thirty. But is there ever a *bad* time for ice-cream? Is there a five o'clock rule in place that I don't know about?" She raised her hands. "No, wait. If there is, I don't want to know about it. I want a butterscotch milkshake. Coming?"

Suddenly nothing sounded better. "Oh, yeah."

The new Skip's was bigger. Brighter. Better in possibly all ways. The old shop had just held a couple of tables pressed against the window – this one had at least fifteen, including one long one that could probably seat ten. Red fans turned lazily overhead, and all the accents were striped red and white, giving the impression that the whole place was made of peppermint. Molly would like this. Adele took out her phone while Dixie was ordering and took a quick photo. She sent it to Molly with the caption, *Come try the new Skip's.*

"And whatever she's having," said Dixie.

"Oh, no, I'll buy my own, don't worry about it."

"I insist. Welcome back."

Adele shouldn't let her pay; she knew that. Dixie couldn't be making much money at the saloon, working part-time. But she was momentarily confused, blinded by the *Welcome back* that she should protest. *I'm not staying. This is just temporary.*

But if Dixie had asked her where she was going next, she wouldn't have had an answer. So she just said, "Bubblegum. Thanks."

They sat at a table outside. Dixie stretched her legs out in front of her, sighing with what sounded like happiness. She sucked on her shake and then looked at Adele. "Well?"

"What?" Adele started.

"Are you always this jumpy?"

"No." Not quite true. Adele had been born the jumpy one. The worried one. But she was also the one who got things done, who fixed all the things, so she'd always felt justified in being a little jumpy. "Yes."

"Yeah, I thought so. What've you got there?"

Adele had set the folder of flyers on the table. Fresh excitement flew through her. "Open Mike night at the Spike! What do you think?"

Dixie laughed delightedly as she studied one. "Oh, my God. Why?"

Wasn't it obvious? "To bring in more people." She hadn't gone in to the saloon the night before, but she'd peeked in when she'd walked past. There had been three people sitting at the saloon, but apart from that, the entire place had been empty at nine pm. How on earth was Nate pulling in a pay check with no cash coming in? And *who* was writing his pay check? Probably him, right? Surely he had signature rights to the bank book. Which, really, could be a problem in and of itself. An unpleasant snake of distrust coiled in her belly – who was to say Nate wasn't the reason that the café and the hotel had closed?

She pictured him briefly – his trustworthy face. With those dark grey-blue eyes and that strong jaw, he was exactly the kind of guy a woman would be glad to see if her car was broken down on the side of the road. He would know how to wield a jack, and even though her dad had made sure Adele knew exactly how to pop a lug nut, she'd let him do it, just to watch his biceps strain (and, really, wasn't that part of feminism? Being willing to objectify men? Okay, that might be pushing the outer edge of her feminist theory seminar at college, but she was okay with that). Someone like Nate would have a spare bottle of water in the back of his truck for a radiator emergency. He'd have flares.

Flares. Just like the ones going off inside her as she imagined the way his arm muscles would look flexed and well defined, at the edges of his sleeves while he torqued a tire iron.

"Yeah," she said, as if convincing herself. "An open mike night at the saloon will pack them in."

"I don't know. Besides Dust & Rusty and the occasional gig by the Dukes of Buzzard, there's not that much music going on around here. Not since y'all left town." Dixie's voice sounded judgment free.

"Maybe that can change."

"Man, I can't *wait* to hear what Nate thinks about it."

"Why does everyone keep saying that?"

"Because he's Nate."

"What does that mean?"

Dixie leaned her head back, letting the sun bathe her face. "God, this feels good. It was such a cold, foggy summer." She slipped on a pair of black sunglasses. "You really don't know Nate at all?"

"I haven't been in town since before he got here. We left a long time ago."

"Ah."

There was something in Dixie's voice, something small but still very much there. "Did you two date? Oh!" Adele realized she might be being obtuse. Maybe she'd missed everything last night. "Are you dating now?"

"Oh, God, no. He's not my type."

The tall, good-looking, reticent half-surly type? Who didn't like that? Even Adele – who definitely wasn't looking for anything – could see Nate's inherent attractiveness. "Oh."

"Why? Is he your type?"

Adele stuttered something unintelligible before she realized Dixie was teasing her. In Nashville, she'd been spending so much time writing songs at the agency (mostly men) and with the Boot Scooters (all men) – she'd forgotten what it felt like to hang out with another woman. "Stop it."

"Hey, girl, I wouldn't fault you. He's a good guy."

"Seems like it." Adele paused. "Did you know that he wants to buy the place from me and my sisters?"

"He's been working on that for as long as I've known him. Are you going to sell?"

Why did people keep asking her that? There was no way for them to keep the place. It was impossible. She didn't want to answer, to go through all the impossible reasons again in her mind or out loud, so she spit out a piece of pink bubblegum. "I don't know why I get this flavor. I don't even really like chewing gum."

"Because it's fun."

"Fun."

"The most important thing in life."

Adele laughed. "You don't mean that."

"You think I don't? What's more important?"

Adele licked her ice-cream as she thought. There were so many things more important than fun. "Family. Friends. Health. Financial stability."

Dixie shook her head and her curls bounced. "None of those things are any good without fun."

"Financial stability is not fun. I mean, that's not what I would call it. But it's necessary."

"You kidding me? I'm one of those freaks who loves balancing her checkbook. Well, not my checkbook – I mean my debit card. That's fun to me. This here milkshake is my celebration for balancing it this morning. I know I can afford this." Dixie tilted her head to study Adele. "You know what?"

"What?"

She leaned forward and lowered her sunglasses, resting them on the tip of her nose. "You should sleep with Nate."

Adele choked on a piece of bubblegum. She coughed fruitlessly and felt her eyes start to water.

"Are you okay?"

She waved her hands in a universal *No problem* sign. She just had to cough. That was all. She tried contracting her stomach as hard as she could, and felt a little relief.

"Do you need the Heimlich?" Dixie half-stood, her arms spread as if Adele were about to trip instead of dying from lack of oxygen.

Adele shook her head, hard. It was *not* that bad. Was it? Briefly, Adele imagined her sisters at the funeral. *How did your sister die?*

Bubblegum.

What flavor?

Blue, Molly would say, choking back tears. When they pulled it out, it was blue.

It would be right up there with expiring on the toilet for embarrassing. Luckily, she'd be dead so she wouldn't care.

Then, just as black spots began to flicker at the edge of her vision, she coughed, and the gum flew out of her mouth. Funnily enough, it *was* blue. She had no idea what flavor it was supposed to be but it sure wasn't blueberry. She coughed and choked some more while Dixie patted her ineffectively on the back.

"Are you okay? Is it all out?"

"God," Adele choke-whispered, "I hope so."

"Was all that just because I told you to hook up with my boss? Aw, crap." Dixie clapped a hand over her mouth. "*You're* my boss now. I just told my boss to sleep with my other boss? That's messed up."

Adele could only cough more. She sipped her water and spluttered.

"Am I fired?"

Adele shook her head.

"Good. Because I'm standing by my assertion. As long as you don't fire me. You two should, like, *totally* get busy."

Finally able to string together more than one syllable at a time, Adele said, "Not gonna happen." And suddenly, she had a visceral stomach-flopping image of what Nate's mouth might look like wet. Very wet. Holy crap.

Dixie sucked at her straw. "Let me guess. You're the angel on your sisters" shoulders?"

Adele coughed again. "I can't keep up with you."

"Try. Are you their conscience? Because from what I've read about you, and from your songs, I think that might be it."

"Are you a psychiatrist in your other life?"

Dixie winked. "I have a couple of secrets in my past."

"Yeah. That's me." Adele rubbed at her throat with her hand and gave her melting cup of ice-cream a suspicious glance.

"Awesome. That means you're good enough at angel shit that you don't need one of those."

"Angel shit?"

Dixie waved her red nails in the air as if she were casting a spell. "All glitter, all the time. But trust me, it gets old, all that glitter on your shoulders piling up like sparkly dandruff. I'm going to be the devil."

"Pardon?"

"The devil on your shoulder. Or is one of your sisters already that for you?"

Molly was too sweet to be a devil. Lana would make a good one, but she hadn't been within a mile of Adele's shoulder in eleven years. Adele shook her head.

"Oh, goody." Dixie reached forward and pushed Adele's hair back. Through Adele's T-shirt, she tugged the top of her bra strap up. "I claim this spot, then."

"Um."

"Too late." Dixie let the strap slap back into place and then laughed.

CHAPTER SEVENTEEN

W hile Nate had been pretty sure the open mike night was up there with mayonnaise on peanut butter in terms of terrible ideas, he still felt bad for Adele.

She was learning it the hard way.

No one wanted to go to an open mike, except the people who wanted to show off. It was a fine thing to be held at the grade school, maybe. Some kind of fundraiser for a field trip, maybe. Send the kids of Darling Bay to the Monterey Bay Aquarium. Dads could sing old Hank Williams songs, and kids could make little bands and sing pop songs with censored swear words.

In the Golden Spike? Not so much.

Adele was bringing in looky-loos, that much was true. Half the Darling Bay Methodist Church senior center was here, all twelve of them sitting carefully in the old wooden chairs he'd had to drag out of the storage unit behind the parking lot. Six women were knitting, and two of the men were reading the paper in the dim light, holding the pages an inch from their eyes.

Roman Elmwood, the local boy scout leader, was there, doing a crossword while he waited.

Two of the waitresses from Caprese were in attendance, giggling, keeping a close eye on the three ranch hands who had come in from the Bar W. (How had Adele managed to get the word up to the ranches? Had she actually driven out and invited them?)

But it was quarter after seven. There was no one else coming. The church's senior citizens had each ordered a water (okay, old Bing Madson had ordered a rum and Coke, enduring the judgment of the church women's eyes. Those eyes were harsh. Bing was braver than Nate would have been. Maybe that's why men died before women – the weight of those heavy stares).

"See?"

She'd come out of nowhere, popping up just behind his elbow. Nate had always prided himself on being able to see the whole saloon at a glance, taking in who might start a fight while keeping his eye on the guy who was trying a little too hard to get a woman's phone number. But Adele kept coming in the back door quietly and startling him, and he didn't like it. Not one bit.

Now that he thought about it, why wasn't he hearing the creak of the storeroom when she came through it?

Ignoring her, he stepped around her and pushed the heavy door.

Nothing. It was silent.

"This used to squeak."

She grinned. "I oiled it!"

"You *what?* When?"

"Just now. It only took a second. I'm nervous." Adele twisted her fingers together. "I like to fix things when I'm nervous."

"Did it ever occur to you I *wanted* it to squeak?"

She laughed.

He didn't.

"You're *serious?*"

Nate nodded.

"But why?"

"I keep the bank bag back there, as well the extra bottles for the top shelf. That's a lot of potential loss."

Her cheeks were bright pink. "I would never have thought of that."

"Yeah." A *thank you* wouldn't kill him. He knew that. But he'd be damned if he'd say it. Was there even a way to make a door squeak again, once it stopped?

At least she was something good to look at. That helped, he supposed. She was wearing a red-and-white checkered western shirt with pink flowers embroidered on the shoulders. Her hair was loose around her face, curling at the ends. Her blue jeans were tight. Instead of cowboy boots, she was wearing shiny red heels with straps that went across her ankles. "I'm sorry," she said miserably.

"Whatever. I'll deal with it."

She rallied – he could see her doing it. "But see?"

"See what?"

She turned and gestured. "All these people!"

"There aren't many. And they're not buying." He felt like he was popping balloons as fast as she could blow them up.

"Even not buying much, I see a couple of drinks out there. Look at those cowboys. I bet you five dollars they'll buy those girls a drink within an hour."

Nate didn't doubt the truth of that. The women were getting gigglier and edging nearer the cowboy clump. "Yeah, but that's not the point. A few of my regulars aren't here."

"What, you think they're scared of a little music?"

"More like don't want to bothered by bad musicians. Maybe they just bought a bottle of vodka and are staying home tonight with their Wanda Jackson records." Nate had it on good authority that Parrot Freddy had done exactly that. He'd been mighty clear that he hadn't wanted either of his parrots to have to endure "a cacophonic clusterfuck."

Adele's color was still high, pink lighting the tops of her cheekbones. It didn't look like make-up, either, not like the waitresses over there. Nate knew all of them, had even dated Jessica Moniz once or twice. But there was just something about kissing a woman whose face left an oily tan-colored slick behind on his fingertips that Nate didn't enjoy.

Adele's face looked free from make-up, apart from that lip gloss that should be classified as a deadly weapon. She could kill a man wearing that stuff. It was good Nate's heart was strong and could remain unaffected.

"Don't worry," she said. "You'll be amazed at how much money the bar brings in tonight."

"It's not all about money, you know." It was about community. It was about the group of people he took care of. If Parrot Freddy wasn't in the saloon, Nate couldn't put a glass of water in front of him between each drink, could he? At home, Freddy was just going to chug the whole fifth and wake up tomorrow feeling like hell, dehydrated and weak. That wasn't good for his diabetes, either. Usually Nate could get a little cheese and peanuts in the guy (he bought and kept Fred's favorite, Monterey Jack, in the iced tea fridge, just for him). At nine, he reminded him to take his night-time meds. Who would do that for him tonight?

Three other regulars were missing from their bar stool line-up, three others who'd be nursing cases of beer and bottles of wine at home, where, if they needed assistance, no one would be there to help.

Norma, though, was here. Good old Norma. She was already dealing tarot cards out on top of the saloon with loud thunks, keeping a careful eye on the waitresses. She was good – within half an hour, Nate predicted each of the young women would be buying her a drink or two to read their fortunes. If she spaced them out right, she wouldn't have to buy more than her first drink tonight.

"Speaking of money."

Nate raised his eyebrows.

"I'll need to get the bank ledger from you soon. Maybe tomorrow?" Adele's voice was light, but she kept her eyes on her red shoes.

"Ah."

"That's –" She cleared her throat. "That's not a problem, is it? Does he still keep it in his office desk? I always loved those old folio-style books."

Had she even noticed she'd used the present tense? "He did. Yeah."

"Is the office unlocked?"

It felt like she was trying to steal money out of his wallet even though she had every right to ask. "No."

"Where do you keep the key?"

He reached into his pocket slowly and pulled out a key ring. "On my person."

"Of course."

"For safety." Even more slowly, he twisted off the key and handed it to her. "But you're the one who needs the key now, huh?"

"No, you're still – I mean –"

He raised a palm. "S'fine. I have another one. I suppose you'll have to turn over the ledger for the bank appraisal."

She would. "Do you know his banking system? Quickbooks? Excel?"

A barked laugh was the only answer he could give. Hugh didn't trust computers, never had, and had kept everything in that one big book.

"Still?" Adele shook her head. "God, he was stubborn. So what, he's still doing it all by hand?"

"I tried to make him a customer database for the hotel once, just a simple computer form, and I swear he almost fired me over it. He kept talking about selling, so I told him it would be a good idea to pull everything into one place. Easier for everyone involved. But he wouldn't do it." Nate popped open the till's tray and checked to make sure he'd put enough singles in it, even though he knew he had. "I tried, but he said he liked walking to the bank every day."

"Walked to the bank. He was never robbed?"

"This is Darling Bay, not Venice Beach. Besides, you've seen the place. No hotel money, no café money, just the take from the saloon. He would have lost a couple hundred dollars most days. Even our busiest nights don't bring in more than seven, eight hundred. Not a big enough deal to make him go digital. So," Nate folded his arms across his chest, "getting ready to put it up for sale?"

Adele raised her chin. "Yes."

"You'll be pleasantly surprised, I think, to find that I haven't been a complete fuck-up with Hugh's accounts."

She folded in her lips before she spoke. "I wouldn't have thought you had been."

Yeah. That was *not* what her face said. Adele's eyes were saying that she thought maybe he had no clue what to do with a dollar bill. In fact, he'd pay quite a few of his own hard-earned, carefully saved dollars just to watch her face when she went through the Golden Spike's accounts. Closing the café and the hotel had been Hugh's decisions, based on mistakes Hugh had made. There had actually been a time, about two years ago, when Nate had floated Hugh for a month or two while he sold some property he had in Nevada in order to make ends meet. Hugh had paid him back, almost immediately, red-faced about it. Hugh had hated it. He shouldn't have. It had made Nate happy to help.

"Thanks," Adele said into the silence that had fallen taut between them.

"Want a drink?"

"No, thanks."

"You and everyone else around here."

"Really?" Adele looked concerned for a moment. "Yeah, then. I'll have a whiskey and soda."

It wasn't a girly drink. He approved. Not that he would tell her that. He poured and passed. "Here you go."

Idiotically, she tried to slide a ten across the saloon top. "Thanks."

He pushed it back firmly. "It's your whiskey."

"I don't want to . . ."

"It's literally your whiskey."

"Let me pay."

Nate shrugged. "Fine." He gave her the change, and then leaned against the old till, watching her carefully.

She was trying to look calm, but her fingers gave her away. They moved like they were playing the guitar, her left hand making chords at her side, her right doing a strumming pattern that he could almost hear. She reached up to tug on a lock of her hair as if she wished she were wearing a hat that she could pull down.

Damn it, she was *too* good-looking. If only she'd stop biting her lower lip like that. Like it tasted good to her. Those shiny lips – was her gloss the kind some women wore that had sugar in it? Did she taste as sweet as she looked in that plaid shirt? Her breasts were high, just the right size, held up like they were secure but not so pushed up that he suspected major bra mechanics at play. An image, red hot and pornographic, lit his mind – Adele, arched under him, his arm wrapped behind her back, pulling her up so he could trail kisses and bites down her torso, and lower.

Lord have mercy. He couldn't just stand here lusting after her like a thirteen-year-old boy discovering his first dirty magazine. He dug out a clean rag and put disinfectant on it, then he wrung it out and held on, as if it could wipe his brain with it.

Adele bent over the amp onstage and wiggled the cord, sending a squeal of feedback through the room.

Even the oldsters clapped their hands over their ears in protest.

Nate found out he didn't care about the feedback. It didn't even hurt. It practically sounded like a song, as long as she kept herself bent over like that, her sweet little rear round and tight in those dark blue jeans . . .

He put down the rag and rinsed his hands. A few dirty thoughts weren't actually immoral, right? Not yet, anyway. The open mike was going to be a train wreck, and he'd warned her of that. He couldn't stop this particular train from hurtling down the tracks, so instead of trying to, he leaned back against the till again. He crossed his arms.

And then he mentally undressed her, right down to those silly red strappy distracting-as-hell shoes.

CHAPTER EIGHTEEN

I t was a train wreck.

And the worst part was that her turn was still coming. She'd decided to use the pool chalkboard for the list of names. It was a small chalkboard, but only seven people had showed up to perform. "Great!" she'd lied. "If anyone has a second song, feel free to perform that as well! Write your names up here, and we'll get started!" She hadn't wanted to put her name up – this wasn't about her – but the tiny audience had insisted, the cowboys in the back going so far as to chant, "Songbird! Songbird!" until she'd given in and added herself to the end of the still-too-short list.

"Welcome!" The microphone felt strange in her hand, like the memory of a dream. She wrote songs now, and fixed the songs of others. She didn't perform. Why the hell had she given in and said she would sing? "I'm so glad you're here." All, what? Fifteen people? There couldn't be more than twenty at most. When Adele had imagined the night, she'd pictured the saloon full. Two hundred, max capacity. The fire marshal would be summoned to check for safety. People would be packed in, right up to the old wooden beams. Nate would be pouring drinks so fast, working so hard, that he'd sweat. His shirt would be stuck to his skin, and she'd be able to see those muscles flexing, his biceps straining.

Instead, there was a group of senior citizens who seemed both very nice and very reluctant to drink anything but water. A small clutch of women stood near the door, and a few cowboys held up the far end of the bar. Norma was there, her long skirt draped over her bar stool. That was it. Dixie wasn't even there to urge her into bad behavior. (Adele knew she shouldn't feel as disappointed by this as she did.) None of the firefighters who'd been hanging out with Hank the other night were there.

Adele hoped her disappointment didn't show. "All of you! How wonderful you're here. You're in for a real Darling Bay treat tonight, I tell you that. First up, Clois! Come on up!" She put the mike back on the stand and clapped as loudly as she could to make up for the fact that two of the older women appeared to be arguing over a crochet hook.

The woman named Clois had gotten the night started with a bang. She went up with a guitar and a short skirt.

Her guitar playing wasn't the problem. Nor was her singing.

The skirt was the problem.

The stage was about eighteen inches higher than the bar room floor. Because the audience's median age was a hundred and twenty and if they'd been standing they would have just been creaky dominos, ready to fall, they were all seated in the folding chairs. It felt strange to be the only one standing so Adele sat, too.

And from there, Adele could see why the audience looked so gobsmacked.

Clois's underwear was orange. It was the orange of road workers worldwide. No one could miss it, and worse, no one could take their eyes off it.

How did Clois not notice where everyone's eyes were? Every seated woman in the room wriggled miserably, crossing and recrossing their legs, but Clois just kept singing. Adele hoped against hope that she only had one song to sing, but after the first one, Clois just smiled happily at the applause (fervent, heated clapping from the old men) and said, "Oh, thank you! Thanks! I have another for you, a long one that I wrote in the tradition of the folk murder ballad."

Awesome.

By the time the seventeen verses were done and Clois took a bow, Adele felt like her eyes had been burned by the sun. She stood. "Thank you, Clois. That was inspiring, for sure." It was true – she was inspired to wear jeans for the rest of her life, just in case. She looked at the chalkboard. "Benny Simmons?"

Benny was one of the old men in the audience, and Adele was glad to see that he was wearing a full, dark-colored pair of overalls. No chance of wardrobe malfunction. Benny's talent was the harmonica, and it was something else, that was for sure. He did a rip-roaring rendition of "Fur Elise', which Adele hadn't known could be done on a harmonica. When he launched into his second song, "A Boy Named Sue', Adele went to the bar. She'd told Nate she wouldn't need more than one that night, but she'd been wrong.

"Let me guess," said Nate. "You changed your mind."

She didn't bother arguing with him. "I'll take another one. As fast as you can."

"You know he also yodels? You'll be lucky if you get him off the stage with just two songs."

"Make it a double."

The alcohol helped a little bit. Benny did indeed do four songs total, two on the harmonica, two yodeled. Usually Adele could get behind a nice little *yodelay-hee-hooooo* but Benny had the unfortunate musical handicap of looking like he was being stabbed while making his yodeling face. His teeth were bared, his eyes shut tight, and he grimaced painfully. When Adele glanced around, she could see everyone else's faces struggling not to do the same thing.

After Benny came Dorene Hammer, a senior citizen wearing a tight red sequined dress. She did spoken word, and honestly, it wouldn't have been that bad if she hadn't added all the stuff about her loins. Her voice was nice, and she knew where to punch a word out so that it had the most effect.

"My *loins* are girded," she said, her hands outstretched, "But not with fear – they are *girded* with *fury* and *lust* and a moist, damp, *yearning*." Her hands dropped to the loins in question. "Let me tell you *how* my womanhood *feels*, in the morning when you *rise*."

Panicked bubbles tried to break free from Adele's esophagus, but damn, as long as Dorene kept her loins covered up, Adele could keep the laughter inside.

After a man with a singing sawblade (not bad) and a brand-new fiddler (very bad), Adele's was the last name left on the chalkboard. Luckily, the thin crowd had grown even more gaunt – Benny had disappeared claiming a harmonica problem, and Clois had left, citing laundry. Adele visualized orange panties, dozens of them, going around and around in the dryer.

"Adele Darling!" It was one of the young women who'd been too busy flirting with the cowboys to pay attention to Michael Hannah's magic tricks, the one with the low-cut red top (as opposed to her friend in the low-cut black top or her friend in the low-cut white top). "You're up!" She led the room in clapping.

Why? Why had she agreed to put her name up there? She should have remained the organizer. The organizer didn't have to perform. The organizer just organized.

But usually organizers put together things that were successful. She certainly didn't have that going for her, not tonight. She glanced at her wrist even though she didn't wear a watch. "Oh, wow! The time's been filled! We can just –"

She was shouted down by the group of young women and cowboys, whose voices were joined by the seated senior citizens. "No, we're here to listen to you!" Someone yelled, "That why I put up with these clowns!" Laughter rippled through the darkened room.

"You win," she said as sweetly as she could. She stood close to the mike and slung her guitar strap around her neck. "So you might know this one. My sisters and I played it a lot, back in the day."

Across the room, Nate's dark eyes smoldered at her. For a moment, Adele forgot where she was and what she was supposed to do next. Lord, did he always look like that across a dim saloon, like a man about to wander a heath at midnight? No wonder Clois had put her panties on display.

"Um," she went on eloquently, "it's been a long time since I played out in front of real people instead of my microphone at home, so I hope you'll forgive me if I jumble things up." Oh, Lana would be so mad at her for that. You never apologize in advance, her sister always said. Only apologize if you really have to. Even if you've got the flu and can barely talk, never admit it before you start playing.

"So. Here goes. This is called "The Lowdown on Life"."

A rumble of appreciation ran through the group. It had always been one of their most beloved songs. Adele hadn't played it since the last full show. She strummed the opening chords, and something wobbled in her heart.

She sang the first verse, soft and slow. All she could see was Dorene of the Loins nodding her head, mouthing the words before Adele even sang them, so she closed her eyes. What she saw then was harder. Their last full show had been in Nashville, at the Grand Ole Opry. Dad had still been alive. Uncle Hugh had flown out to be there. Adele had stood proudly between Molly and Lana, and her heart had been so big, her hopes so bright, her belief so damn strong.

Funny how things changed.

The chorus had always been hers for this song, so it wasn't like she needed her sisters" harmonies on it to carry the song. But Lord, how empty it sounded without them. She hadn't predicted it. Her throat tightened, and her fingers missed the chord change, slipping for a second. She tried the next line, and – unforgivably – forgot the words.

She forgot the *words*.

She couldn't remember the song that had been a number one hit on the country charts, the song she must have sung a million times. It was one of their father's favorites. She'd *written* it, for Godsake. How did you forget a song you wrote, a song you believed in?

Adele didn't want to open her eyes, didn't want to see tension on the faces in front of her. The worst part of forgetting anything onstage was the moment you looked out and realized that everyone was pulling for you, hoping you didn't fail.

She tried the chord progression again. Maybe if she snuck up on it, the words would come to her.

She felt something behind her, a movement of air. Then, appearing through the darkness was Nate, his guitar in his hands. He played the chord run perfectly, and started singing the harmony to the verse, Molly's usual part. As soon as he sang the first word, the entire verse came back to her.

The lowdown is the slowdown, it's the time of your life

Where your loved ones are your close ones, and there's not any strife . . .

Their voices wrapped around each other like stripes on a barber pole. They wound and blended and shifted and then came back to each other, both of them better by virtue of being together. His voice held a beautiful middle tone, warm and round. His harmony made the hairs on Adele's arms stand up to hear him next to her, and she fought a shiver, although she couldn't tell if that was from his voice or the way he was looking at her.

Because Nate didn't take his gaze from hers. He sang into her eyes, holding the guitar like it weighed nothing, his mouth in a sexy half-smile.

It wasn't like Adele hadn't sung with hot men before. Toby Keith. Once the very young Dierks Bentley had laid a surprise kiss on her at the end of a show, a kiss so hot it had made the cover of the next *Country Singing People* magazine.

It was an act. It was always an act.

Something about the way Nate was looking at her didn't feel like an act. It felt real, like he was singing the words right to her.

The lowdown is the slowdown, it's the time of your life.

Like he'd written them himself.

When their voices fell to silence, the last chords from their guitars stilling into quiet, there was a brief pause. Then applause rose, louder than should have been possible from such a small crowd.

Adele laughed. Wonderful. Making music with someone like him. God, how good it felt.

Nate, though, just smiled briefly, and lifted his guitar from around his neck.

Her hand went out quickly, and she touched his arm. "Thank you."

"It was nothin'." Then he walked back towards the bar as if it had been exactly that.

Nothing.

But it hadn't been. It had been something. Adele watched him walk away, watched the way he threw a tight smile at a woman who asked him for a refill of ice-water.

What that something was, Adele had no idea, but she wasn't leaving Darling Bay until she found out.

CHAPTER NINETEEN

Adele woke early and stretched her toes to the end of the bed. She'd kicked off the sheets sometime during the warm night, and the morning air coming through the screen was cool on her limbs. The window that looked out on the narrow porch and over the roof of the saloon stood open, and from the bed she could see part of the old rose garden that was in front of room one.

Adele's mother had planted those roses. It was so long ago, and Adele had been so young that the memory fragment felt more like a dream, a lovely one that she'd been trying a long time to recapture. Her mother, taking the car to the nursery on Dixon Street. Adele, clinging to her hand, Molly holding the side of the baby carriage little Lana was in. Just the girls on that shopping trip. Adele remembered her mother asking what color she liked better, yellow or red. She'd said yellow (of course yellow, who didn't love yellow best?) and her mother had seated them in the back seat with three small rosebushes, a tight, prickly fit. Those bushes were the first to go in, and they were still out there, overgrown and top heavy – much too tall – but blooming, even though the woman who was responsible for them was long, long gone.

A colder breeze came in through the screen, right off the water, and Adele pulled the sheet over her knees.

She'd been a mama's girl, that was for sure. Molly and Lana had both been more daddy's pets, but Adele had been born devoted to her pretty singing mother. She had thought no woman on the TV came close to being as beautiful as Katie Darling. And no matter who was singing on the radio or on the record player, no one sang prettier than Adele's mother, either.

Katie Darling had been meant to be a star. Everyone knew that. Katie and Adele's father, Tommy, had met in Nashville, both of them working at the same rough-edged bar. Katie was a cocktail waitress, and Tommy did the sound for the little acts that came through town, hoping to be bigger. He heard her sing one night, and that was all it took. "She was a little bird, singing like its heart was going to bust right open." He'd asked her on a date, and she'd said no. When he asked why, she said, *Because I'm going to be a star.*

You don't think I'm good-looking?

You're handsome, but I don't have time for a boyfriend right now.

Tommy had said, quick as a lightning strike, *Do you have time for a husband who could double as your manager?* Katie had laughed at him, but he'd stood there, waiting for her to decide. Remembering it, she'd said, "That's when I knew I couldn't let him go. The way he just stuck there, not cracking a smile, totally serious. I knew he actually wanted to marry me. To be my manager. He wanted to be there when I made it big. How was I supposed to *not* fall in love with him?"

They married. Tommy, full of belief in his new bride, sold his half of the Golden Spike to his brother Hugh in order to put Katie on the road, where she finally got noticed by an indie Nashville label who thought they could make her their star of the year.

Katie, though, got pregnant before she got famous. She couldn't stop throwing up and, five months into the contract, she had to go on bed rest. When she told the label, they dropped her. "It didn't matter, though – having my sweet Adele in my arms was better than cutting any record ever could have been." That had been her mother's line, always. Motherhood was what made her a star, Katie Darling said. Having her little songbirds around her, all of them chirping with her.

It was Adele's earliest memory: all five of them sitting around a Christmas tree in the living room, Daddy with a guitar, Mama singing "O, Come All Ye Faithful" like her heart would break. Adele sang along, mixing up the words as she went, Molly lisping as best she could, Lana still too young to speak but bouncing her legs in time.

Adele had started crying when the song was over – she remembered the tightness in her throat and the way her mother had bundled her into her lap. "What's wrong, baby bird?"

"Nothing," Adele had said. "The song made me so happy. Why am I crying, if I'm happy?"

"Ah, that," said her mother, squeezing her arms around her, holding her in a tight ball in her lap. "That just happens. Sometimes our emotions get all mixed up, don't they? Tears always help. You'll smile soon, my little bluebird of happiness."

"Why is it called that?" Adele asked her mother one morning after she'd made her mother laugh.

"Because it never stops being happy. And you, my birdie, have the eyes to match that bluebird. Sing to me, why don't you?"

So the toddler Adele would sing tuneless songs about birds and worms and sun and leaves, and Katie would smile, and for long minutes at a time, Adele would feel the warmth of making her mother happy. She knew, of course, that it wouldn't last. Her mother always sank back into darkened sadness (*the blues*, her father said, *your mama has the blues again*, but that didn't make sense, since the bluebird was blue and that meant happy – why couldn't grown-ups get these kinds of things straight?).

But for those few minutes while Adele was singing silly songs, Katie's eyes would dance, and her whole being seemed lighter. Adele would make the song sillier – peanut butter and lightning bugs and a tree that sang like Daddy's guitar – and Mama would clap and laugh.

"You fix me, birdie."

It was what Adele was best at, even if it never quite lasted. The depression always came back, sending their mother to a dark bedroom and long days of heavy sleep. Molly could make their mother laugh, and Lana could make their mother spitting mad, another way of bringing her out of the dark. The three of them singing together made something like hope spark in their mother's eyes, even from behind the blankets.

But Adele was the one who could make the light come back into their mother. For Adele, her mother would sometimes dance, swaying in the window, the prettiest smile in the whole world on her face. *You fix me.*

Adele could fix Mama, and if she could do that, she could fix just about anything (after all, it was her conception that had broken their mother, knocking Katie off her trajectory to stardom). Adele owed her. She just had to try hard enough.

The breeze made the curtain flap loudly, and Adele jumped, jerked out of the memory and back into the hotel bed. Emotions. That's all they were.

Were they what had made her feel like crying last night while onstage? She'd thought it was because her sisters weren't with her, because she had sung her song all by herself, not the right way at all. But she'd still felt the tightness in her throat even when Nate had started singing with her. Happy tears, caught in her chest like congestion from a cold.

Her phone rang.

"And?" said Molly, without any intro, as if they'd been speaking just seconds before.

"And what?"

"The open mike! Come on, I've only got like ten minutes before the next shuffleboard competition ends and I get an influx of people who want to know how many calories are in the pomegranate margaritas."

"Do they really do that? Play shuffleboard? Like on *The Love Boat*?"

"Yeah. Except on *The Love Boat*, people were attractive, right?"

"In a late seventies kind of caftan way, sure."

"This boat is full of people who have spent all their considerable assets purchasing food that isn't working well for their health."

"I don't even know why they have a dietician on the boat. Isn't everyone on board just there for the lobster and free cake?"

"And the alcohol. Don't forget the booze. I'm on the boat because they can give me a tiny office and then advertise that I'm there. I make the boat healthier just by being on board. I don't have to *do* anything."

"Oh, good," said Adele, rolling onto her back.

"So, how did it go? Did you revitalize the entire community? Please tell me the whole town was there. That's what I'm imagining. I'm seeing a line down the block, and people jumping up and down at the big window in the front, trying to look over the stage to see inside."

"Oh, it was exactly like that." If by that she meant exactly the opposite.

"Really?" A horn's blast sounded over the cell phone.

"What was that? Are you leaving port?"

"Just getting in. Dude loves to hit that damn horn every chance he gets."

"Where are you?"

"I have *no* idea. I think it's some place with rum, because that's what the stairways smell like after the puke gets cleaned up by the service staff. Now tell me about last night!"

"There were about twenty people there."

"Oh, crap."

"And most of *them* were over the age of ninety."

"Are you serious?"

Adele flexed her toes and then pointed them again. "Would I kid about this? The senior citizens, for the most part, weren't drinking. There were a few cowboys from a local ranch, and they drank, but they weren't there for the open mike – they would have been there anyway. Same with a few waitresses from Caprese."

"So it was a bust."

If you could call singing with a man whose counterpoint voice tangled with hers like her legs were tangled in the sheets, then yeah, it was. "I sang."

"You *did*? I thought you said you weren't going to."

"They made me. I did "The Lowdown on Life". And the bartender sang with me."

"The hot one?"

Adele looked out the window to make sure Nate wasn't in the garden. "I never said he was hot."

"You didn't say he wasn't, remember?"

"I missed you two last night so much it hurt."

Silence filled the space between them, a white static buzz. Then Molly's voice scrambled over the line like sandaled feet on tide pools. "Anyway, I should go. I have a mother–daughter combo that if I don't separate, they're going to pull the whole boat down around our ears, and I don't feel like drowning today –"

"I'm sorry, Molly. I shouldn't have said that. Don't go. Hey, what else do you think I could do? To get people into the saloon?"

Her sister already sounded distracted, halfway out of the conversation. "No, leave that there, I'll be off in a minute. Sorry." The phone made a shifting sound. "Sorry, what?"

"How do I make the saloon a place people want to go to?"

"Hey, love you. Talk soon?" Molly clicked off.

Adele lay on the bed for another minute or two, staring out the window at the roses their mother had planted. The ones their mother had never seen bloom.

Nate. She had to find Nate and *do* something. There were approximately one million things to be done on the property, and the obvious first place to start was Hugh's apartment over the saloon. She could give Nate his room back and figure out what to do next.

An image of him flashed into her mind, Nate standing next to her on the small stage, his body turned to hers. That half-smile that had played at his mouth – oh, those lips. They were as wide and strong-looking as the rest of him. For three seconds (and three seconds only – she timed herself strictly because she couldn't take much more than that) she closed her eyes and imagined kissing him. The feel of those lips on hers. The heat of his hand on her cheek. The strength of his arm pulling her tight against his body . . . and her three seconds were up and then some.

Adele blinked and threw herself off the bed towards the shower. Maybe she'd make it a cold one. She wasn't sure if that actually worked but it was worth a try.

CHAPTER TWENTY

The drainpipe for the bar's dishwasher was clogged. Again. For the hundredth time, it felt like. There were a lot of unpleasant tasks at the saloon, and most of them Nate did with patience. He loved the place as though it were a person. And no one was perfect. He had no problem accepting that. He thought about his mother. He'd loved her completely, and he would have done anything in the whole world for her. That didn't change the fact that she'd been a pretty shitty mom, overall.

You just kept working with what you had.

Like the damn dishwasher. It was old enough that it was practically impossible to get any parts that fit it anymore. The Y-branch tailpiece kept clogging because he invariably missed a cherry or a piece of a lime when he threw glasses into it – the darkness of the saloon when it was busy guaranteed that. And that in turn guaranteed that he would spend part of a day every few months underneath the sink, up to his elbows in slime, swearing at a piece of machinery that hated him as much as he hated it.

"Come *on.*" The wrench slipped out of his hand and whacked him on the brow. Again. "God*dammit.*" He wiped his eyes with the back of his wrist. His other arm was so far into the machine it reminded him of the time he'd seen Travis Dorman pull a stuck calf out of a straining cow. The difference was that the rancher got a cute little baby cow out of the deal. The only thing Nate was going to get was a black clog that would make him swallow hard when it slopped out.

"Whatcha doing?"

The too-sweet, too-chirpy voice could only belong to Adele. Nate tried to yank his arm out so he could sit up but he misjudged the angle and yanked too soon. Pain sliced up the back of his hand.

"*Goddammit.*" He shoved himself sideways on the floor, slamming his legs left, doing his best to avoid kicking over the lower row of overstock bourbon.

"Are you okay?"

"Peachy." He stood, holding up his arm, now dripping blood and grease trap slime to his elbow.

"Oh, Reba!"

Nate twisted towards the sink and hit the faucet before he remembered he'd shut off the water main to the building. "Fuck." The wound was long, from the back of his wrist halfway to his elbow. He must have hit it on the check valve.

"What happened?"

"Does it *matter?*" He was an idiot – that's what happened. He'd done nothing but try to fix the machine he had to fix every damn month of his damn life. He should be able to do it in his sleep. Instead, he was going to get the black plague or something worse from the germs he'd just injected into his bloodstream.

And Adele wasn't helping a damn thing, standing there looking so pretty and *clean*. She wore jeans and a long white tank top that flowed to the top of her thighs. Her arms were bare, and her hair was loose. She wore no make-up and she looked refreshed, as if she'd just woken up from a fifteen-hour sleep. "You need to wash that cut."

"Really? Because I thought I'd just go to the marina and rub some fish scales into the dirt, too." He couldn't keep the growl out of his voice. "I shut off the water main."

"To the hotel, too?"

He jammed a pile of napkins against the wound to staunch the blood. "No."

She turned on her heel – or rather, on her cowboy boot. Her ass looked great in those jeans, and she probably knew it. "Come on," she said.

"I'll be fine." He'd go turn on the water – no, he couldn't, not until he fixed the goddamned beast. Crap. He followed her through the back arbor and up the rock walkway through the rose garden. She stumbled a tiny bit on the uneven gravel, he noticed with too much satisfaction.

Room one smelled like her now, like something sweet, almost sugary, mixed with a tang of citrus. Lord, he could practically chew that smell. How was this fair?

She headed for the closet. "I have a first-aid kit in my suitcase, I think."

"Don't need that. Just need to wash it out." How long would it take to air the place out after she was gone? He could imagine the scent lingering – vanilla in the curtains, orange in the sheets.

He would just leave the doors and windows open for a month if he had to. He headed for the bathroom.

"I'll be right in. Wash it good. I know it'll hurt."

Hugh had always used the hotel's soaps that customers left behind, the slivers that were still good, but Nate hadn't been able to get on board that train, as much as he admired the thriftiness of it. He usually just got a big bar of whatever was cheapest at the drugstore, but the bar he'd left behind wasn't on the edge of the sink. Instead, there was a big pink bottle of something that floofed at him when he pushed the pump.

Crap. This was what the room smelled like. What she smelled like. And he had to rub it into his wound. Literally. He groaned.

"Hurts, huh?" Adele set a roll of gauze and a tube of antiseptic cream on the back of the toilet. "That looks bad. Here, let me."

She reached forward and took hold of his wrist. "Cold water? You don't have to be such a man about it." She adjusted the temperature of the water with her other hand.

Nate tried to pretend she wasn't brushing his upper arm with her breast. He tried like hell.

Turned out it was impossible.

"I can do it myself."

"I'd let you if I thought you could." Her fingers were as warm as the water was, and he caught his breath. "Oh, God," she said. "Sorry. But I've got to get all the gunk out."

"It's fine." He held himself as still as he could. And he prayed she'd lean against him again, just the same way.

Nothing hurt, it turned out. The way she was touching him made him forget that pain was even a thing that existed. The side of her breast pressed against him again, so lightly he almost couldn't feel it. She bit her bottom lip as she rinsed the soap off. It was so quiet when she turned the water off that he held his breath.

She was so close. So close. Her eyelashes were so long he wanted to touch them lightly with the tip of his finger. He could lean forward and kiss her, and . . .

And then what? She'd scream. Jump backward and knock her head on the towel rack. Slap him.

Nate was just being stupid about a pretty girl. And it wasn't the first time that had ever happened. (It was, though, the first time a woman had actually made him feel a little dizzy – it wasn't the sight of blood, either. It was the sight of her. Damn it.)

The hand towel she pressed against his arm was light green.

He jerked his arm back. "You're going to get blood all over that."

"It doesn't matter. Now quit wriggling."

She thought he was wriggly? Nate was using all of his might just to stay still next to her. To keep his free hand from wrapping around the back of her head and pulling her mouth to his. "I'm not."

"Shhh."

She was so close to him he could almost taste the peppermint toothpaste she used.

He pretended he was a statue. A naked statue with a rock-hard – nope, that wasn't working.

He yanked his arm from her hold. "I'll do the rest."

"Let me dress it."

"What, are you a field nurse?"

"Yep." Her nose had a perfect little tilt at the end. A tiny ski slope. "And I'm going to win this battle, so don't fight me on this. Let me fix you up."

He sighed. "Fine. But hurry up."

Adele smoothed antiseptic cream into the long cut which had mostly stopped bleeding now. "It's not deep. I don't think you'll need stitches."

"Wouldn't have gotten them even if I did."

"Ah." She put the top back on the antiseptic tube and then gave him a look that made his insides growl. "Tough guy, huh?"

He stuck out his chin. "Aren't we all?"

"Some of you are worse than others. I mean, tougher than others." Her voice held a wink but her face stayed straight. "I don't think you need a whole bandage, do you? Just a few of these big bandaids should do."

Nate nodded. "Just give them to me. I'll replace them for you later."

She shook her head. "Please." Her gaze shot up and met his.

What would she look like if she said that a different way? In a different place? Under him, specifically? No, no. He grabbed the bandaids out of her hand. "I told you I'd do it."

"Grumpy-pants. What were you doing, anyway?"

He ripped open a bandage with his teeth and spat out the corner. "Fixing the dishwasher. Again."

"It's a problem?"

"It's like a dying possum that's been hit by a car. Refusing to die, but bleeding all over the place."

"What an attractive image."

He winced as the adhesive pulled his skin shut. "You asked."

"Can't you get a new one?"

"Sure." Why wasn't she getting this? "Just as soon as we buy a new water heater and ice machine. Nothing works in the whole damn place and I'm running on the spot just trying to keep the saloon open on the small amount of cash we bring in. If you're bringing any substantive investment to the table, I wish you'd tell me, because if I have to pull the tailpiece one more time, I'll probably slit my wrists on purpose."

"I don't have much." Adele opened another bandaid for him and held it out.

Hating himself, he took it. "Thanks."

"But I have enough to buy a new dishwasher."

Oh, God. "No." He needed her gone, not literally invested.

"We should talk about it."

They didn't need to talk about anything except when she was getting out of town. He slapped on the last one and crumpled the wrappers, then shoved them in his pocket. He moved so that he was closer to the door.

And closer to the bed. Damn it. "Don't you need to be getting back to Nashville? Back home?"

She blinked. "Nah. I have time."

"You don't have . . ." He cleared his throat. "You don't have someone waiting for you?"

Adele laughed. Lord, her laugh was pretty. "No. Remember I said I'd been evicted?"

What kind of jackass would kick out a woman like her? "So where *do* you live?"

She looked around, her eyes still too bright. "I think this is all I've got. And it's not even mine – it's yours and I have to get out so you can have your bed back."

They both looked at the bed. Nate coughed. Why weren't his lungs working the way they normally did? He was a strong guy. He went running with Tox Ellis at least once a week, and sometimes the bastard made them go up into the hills. Nate's capacity for oxygen intake was good, even on a seven-miler with a thousand-foot incline.

But standing near Adele was like standing on top of a twenty-thousand-foot mountain. The air was thin, and he had to actually think about making his lungs work. Okay, that wasn't exactly true. Some bodily reactions were continuing to function just fine without him trying – especially some things downstairs.

If he didn't get out of this room, he was going to kiss her. At least.

Nate threw himself out onto the porch the same way he threw fighters out of the bar – bodily. "I've got to go clean up the mess I left."

"I'll help."

He gripped the edge of the railing and gave himself an immediate splinter. "Don't need help."

"Okay, then let me help with something else." She followed him onto the porch, bringing that sweet smell with her.

"Nah. Thanks for the bandaids." Why had he asked her if anyone was waiting for her in Nashville? He didn't care. Did he? He raised his arm in salute and headed down the old wooden steps. If he hurried, he'd be back in the saloon before she decided to follow him and this time, for once, he'd lock the back door until it was opening time when, by law, the fire exits *had* to be open. Till then, he'd hide from her like the chicken he was.

"Wait." She was right behind him, her boots crunching the gravel.

Nate spun. "What?" His voice was too harsh, but she didn't look surprised.

"You don't have to hate me."

He bit back the groan in his throat. He really, *really* didn't hate her, not right now. "That's not it."

"You're acting like you can't stand to be in the same room with me. I just need to –"

Before she could finish the sentence, Nate grabbed her. Like some Neanderthal, he hauled her against him and kissed her, hard. And like the same Neanderthal, he deserved a smack, but she didn't give it to him. Instead, her lips parted in surprise, but almost as quickly as he'd moved, she kissed him back. She moved her lips against his, her tongue at first tentative, then, seconds later, eager. She tasted rich and heady, like a wine he couldn't really afford to buy for the bar. He was a Two-Buck Chuck kind of guy, and she tasted like top-shelf Scotch, and he should stop kissing her, but he just couldn't do it.

His good arm was strong around her waist, pulling her up against his chest, but her arms were around his neck just as tightly. It felt like gravity, somehow, the way they were pressed against each other. As if they'd both fallen down but were still standing up.

"Oh . . ." she breathed against his mouth, and he grew even harder.

She *had* to feel the effect she was having on him. There was no hiding it, but instead of pulling back in surprise, Adele pressed herself full-length against him. That gravity thing again. Nate slid his hand up into her hair and angled her head back so he could kiss the side of her neck, the spot right under her ear. She made a sound that he couldn't understand as a word, but he knew exactly what it meant.

It meant he should pick her up and carry her up those shallow stairs to his room. Her room. Whatever.

A horn honked from the street, and Nate jumped. No one could see them up here, unless they'd walked in and through the saloon, but it reminded him that this was wrong. He couldn't kiss *Adele Darling*. He pulled back, his hand still at the nape of her neck.

She touched her bottom lip, wet from his mouth. "Yep."

"What?" He'd lost track of what they'd been talking about. If it had been anything at all.

"You're right." She nodded. "This is exactly how I act when I can't stand to be in the same room with someone."

"Adele –"

"No, you're right." She took a teetering step away from him. The front of him, the part of him that had been touching her, felt suddenly cold. "I'm sorry."

She was sorry? He was the ape that had decided to grope her. Shit. "We should probably . . ."

Their eyes met, and Nate forgot that he was going to say they should talk about the saloon, talk about him buying her out. Heat, pure and white, hit his groin. Adele said something with her eyes that he couldn't have put into words even if someone'd had a gun to his head.

Then she spoke out loud. "Hugh." It sounded more like a gasp than a name.

Her uncle. His mentor. The name acted like the slap of cold water he needed. "What about him?"

"His apartment. I'll clear it out. I need to give you back your room so you can get off your boat. Can you give me the key to Uncle Hugh's place, please? I'll just work on that, and work on getting the paperwork together so we can start putting the sale through."

"To me." Nate's chest filled with hope. He'd do anything to help her get out of here faster, leaving him with the deed and the keys and a path forward.

"To you. I just need the names of those guys you said could help me." Her voice was breathy.

If her breathing was as shallow as his was, that would make them *both* in danger of falling over. Breathing was something Nate usually managed to do every day without any extra concentration. Was this heatstroke? Nate looked up at the sun, getting close to being directly overhead. That was probably it. He ignored the fact that it couldn't be more than seventy-two degrees yet. Definitely heatstroke. That or the blood poisoning from the cut had already hit his system. "Post. The Post brothers. Jack and John. I'll write down Jack's number. Stay here." For the love of God, she had to stay right there and *not* follow him into the dim coolness of the storage room, which would be a perfect spot for kissing her more.

She stayed. He looked up the number and wrote it down. When he took it outside to the courtyard, he said, "Jack talks. But John works harder." He held it out. Their fingers touched as she took it, and he swallowed, hard.

Instead of saying anything, she just nodded.

Then she turned and ran up the stairs to his room. She was light and fast and, holy hell, if he didn't want to follow her and never come back.

CHAPTER TWENTY-ONE

W here d'you want us to start?"

Jack Post stood on the deck in front of Uncle Hugh's apartment door. He looked to be in his mid-sixties, salt and pepper at his temples. He was short and slim but had bunched muscle pushing at the edges of his shirtsleeves, as if he slung things around just for fun – logs, or horseshoes. His brother John was taller than Jack, and looked even stronger. He could probably throw a whole tree across the road. For men no longer young, they both gave the impression that they could build a house overnight if the job called for it. Since they'd arrived, John hadn't said a word, but his handshake – which came with an ear-to-ear grin – had been surprisingly friendly. Jack, on the other hand, hadn't stopped talking except to ask this question.

Adele pressed her hands together. "I'm not sure if you've been in there recently, but it's not good."

"Well, your uncle was a man of refined tastes. And by that I mean he liked just about everything. I remember him stopping to pick up soda can tabs like they were fossils, which I guess they kind of are. You know?" It didn't seem like he needed an answer from her. "And books! He couldn't walk past a free-book box at the Friends of the Library sale. Seemed like he just needed all the books, that was all. Adopting them like orphans. So, should we go in?"

Adele unlocked the door. A blast of sour air hit her nose. "I bought masks for all of us."

Jack's eyebrows shot upward. He took one step in, then another one. "You got extras? Because I want to double up on that. How about some Vicks VapoRub?"

"Not on me, no."

"Eucalyptus oil?"

Adele shook her head. "Sorry."

"Maybe you can go get us some while we start. If you put a little bit under your nose, it makes the going easier. Less stinky, right? I have this theory that it actually helps kill the germs, too, before you inhale them. You can inhale germs, right? I'm not getting that mixed up?"

"I think it depends if they're airborne or not." Adele hoped like hell that the men she'd hired wouldn't contract some awful disease while helping her clean the place out. She wasn't sure what kind of insurance Uncle Hugh had carried for contractors (another thing for her to find out) but she doubted if it covered much in the way of environmental hazard safety.

"Huh. Bet you're right." Jack slipped on a pair of blue rubber gloves, the thickest ones Adele could find at the drugstore. He threw another pair at his brother. "This smell here, it don't smell like airborne germs to me. None of them path-oh-gems. This just smells like dirt. And wet paper. Boy, there's a lot of paper in here, huh?"

Adele had hoped that her memory of how bad it was had been wrong, that she'd exaggerated it in her head. But in fact the opposite was true. The kitchen was appalling. If she were Jack or John, she would have backed out and said her thanks, but no thanks.

Instead, the Post brothers pushed in farther. "Okay, shoot me one of them bags, huh?"

Adele gave him an industrial trash bag.

He grinned. "This is going to be fun! I love throwin' things out that don't got no more use anymore. Hey, you know what?" He didn't wait for her to answer. "We can tell you stories while we work. Lots of people like it when we do that. Sometimes," he looked sideways at her, "sometimes we get our lunch bought for us if we do that. You know, talking makes the work go faster. And we tell good stories."

Somehow Adele knew that by "we" Jack meant himself, since John was already silently shoving piles of newspaper off the countertops into a half-full bag. "Pizza okay?"

"Oh, boy. Yeah. We like salami and extra olives. Now, what kind of story you want? Real or fake?"

That was easy. "Real."

"Got it." Jack glanced through a pile of mail that teetered on the edge of what was probably a buried table. "No bills, just junk mail. All in the trash?"

"Recycling. Here, we'll use this bag for that. Can you tell me about people in town? People my uncle would have known?"

"Heck, yeah." Jack said. "Let's start with Cathy, the hostess down at Caprese. Have you ever met her? She's the one with the black hair down to her butt and the lazy eye. Really lazy. Basically, her mama always said her eye went with her personality, but during this one storm, round about ten years ago, she proved that she was anything but lazy by saving four horses and three babies – human ones – from the Singing L Ranch. Give me an extra bag and go get that euc oil. I'll tell you all about that night when you get back."

It took three hours, thirty trash bags, and two extra-large pizzas for Adele to work up the nerve to ask the question she'd wanted to ask when Jack had started his storytelling. "So, what about Nate?"

"Oh!" Jack looked upward, his slice of pizza hanging in front of him like it was about to be lifted out of his hands. "About Jackie Hammstein, I think I forgot to say! Did I mention that she had six toes on one foot? Like, that's the whole point of the swimming hole story, because without that freak show of a foot, she would have never gotten married in the first place, you know?"

Adele had already lost track of who Jackie was and what had happened at the swimming hole. "Ah. What about Nate Houston? The bartender?"

Jack laughed and slid another piece of pizza towards his brother. "You say that like I don't know who he is! I know Nate! You're asking for a Nate story?" He craned his neck to peer down the stairs as if the man in question might be climbing them to the upper porch where they sat. "Because I got some good ones." Jack paused and tilted his head, as if listening to something Adele couldn't hear. "What do you want to know?"

"Does Nate . . ." Why did this take bravery? "So, does he date much?"

"You want to know about his girlfriend?"

Her stomach dropped. Maybe she'd had enough pizza.

"Um. It's none of my business. Never mind."

Jack perched a stack of what looked like religious pamphlets, the kind that get shoved under doors, on the edge of the sink and propped his elbow on the top ones. "Well now, it's none of our business, either, but it sure is fun to watch. See, John and me, we're confirmed bachelors. That's what we say, and I don't mind admitting to you that it's just a thing men say when they can't get the girls no more or never liked 'em in the first place. But we liked 'em, and we sure like to think about the days of old when we could still lock and load. We never married because none of 'em ever caught us, and maybe that's why we like to watch old Nate. Yep. That could be it."

Adele felt as if she were only catching half Jack's words. They were a waterfall, some were soaking her, and some were just running into the stream. "So he's never been married?"

"Nah. Not him. Likes to be single. A loner."

Something inappropriately hopeful propped itself up in Adele's heart. "Really?"

"Yep. Well, if by loner you mean always with a new girl. And I kind of mean that. Constant one-night stands, one after another, those can just make a guy sad, you know?"

"Ah."

Jack bent forward and slapped his knee. "Lord, girl, you should see your face right now. I'm just playing. He ain't a creep. He had a girlfriend last year, Christie? Christine? Something like that. She left, though, got another job in another town."

"Ah." She shouldn't ask, but she did anyway. "What did she do?"

"Nurse. Some specialty kind. Pediatrics, maybe? Always busy off saving kids. She was too busy for him, really. That was probably the last nail in that there homemade coffin. Pretty little thing, though. Kind of looked like you, actually, with that dark hair and blue eyes, but you're bigger at the hips."

John looked up from the bag he was filling and cleared his throat with urgency.

Jack straightened, as if he were about to snap a salute at Adele. "Not that you have big hips! Because you don't! She was too skinny, that one. That's what we thought, right, John? Not that what we thought mattered because we always thought he should go for someone local, someone more likely to actually stick around." He looked appraisingly at Adele. "What about you? You're going to stick around? Not that I'm asking about Nate. I wouldn't want to meddle in his life, not even a little bit. No, sir. But you're clearing out this place like you might want to set yourself down some roots?"

Mildly, Adele said, "Roots are good."

"Well, yeah. Me and John were born at home, didya know that? Just a mile and a half down the road. At home, 'cause our mom was a hippie before they had a word for what she was. Where were you born?"

"Nashville."

"But you're from here originally. Your family named the town – you can't get much more local than that, I think. And your sister Lana was born in town."

Adele had forgotten how much of her family history was held by the locals here. It had always been something that soothed her, and at the same time made her skin itch. Or maybe that was just the dust mites they were surely stirring up by the bucketful.

"You should date Nate," said John – the first words he'd spoken.

A huge cloud of dust flew up from the box Adele was poking through, choking her.

Jack said, "Yeah! He's lonely. I can see that. I got my brother and all, and we watch Netflix at night. If you ain't got romance, family's the next best thing – am I right? Nate, he's got no family no more. Even Hugh's gone. Not that they were family, but they kind of were. And anyway, he's got that look."

Adele didn't want to ask which look he meant, scared he might tell her she wore it, too. She decided to move to a quieter place. "I'm going to go into the beer can room. Let me know if you need more bags."

Jack called out, "Okay, but let me know if you need more stories! Because I got a funny one about when that nurse of his got stuck on a rock when the tide came in too fast."

The story probably involved either Nate saving the pretty little nurse's life, or the nurse saving a drowning baby herself on her way in, so no, Adele was just fine not hearing it. Thank God for hard work. Maybe if she kept dragging bag after bag of trash out of the apartment and down the stairs to the dumpster, maybe if she completely exhausted herself, mind and body, she'd manage to stop reliving the feeling of Nate's lips on hers. The heat of them. Maybe she'd forget the way her whole body had reacted as if it had been plugged into an electrical socket, only hotter.

She rolled her sleeves up higher and tied the kerchief more tightly on her head. Then she dove in again.

CHAPTER TWENTY-TWO

N ate was growling again. He could hear it, he could feel it, and he couldn't stop doing it. "Freaking piece of foreign-made *crap*. Gah!"

Dixie wasn't helping by laughing at him. "Maybe if you quit swearing at it, it would act better for you."

"You call that swearing?"

"Not your last few sentences, no. But when I got here, the wallpaper was peeling off the walls from your blue streak."

"It's a coffee machine. It doesn't mind being cussed at. Needs it, in fact."

"Just buy a new one."

Nate sighed and slumped to a bar stool. He rubbed his face with his hands, cursing again when he remembered he'd had jalapeño on them from the burger Dixie had brought him. He stuck his whole head under the bar sink, opening and closing his eyes under the water until the burn stopped making him want to claw them out.

Dixie just laughed some more as he wiped his face on a pile of cocktail napkins. "I love it when you're grumpy."

"Sadist."

"It's just that you're so good at it."

He was. Even Nate could admit that. It was maybe one of the things he was best at. "It's nice to know I have a specialty."

There was a thump and then a dragging noise at the back of the saloon, outside.

Dixie jumped. "That scares me every time." She looked at her watch. "It's almost seven. Isn't that past quitting time?"

"She never stops."

"Has she let you help yet?"

Nate narrowed his eyes and pulled off the back of the coffee machine with a yank. It gave a louder crack than it should have, and he suspected he'd just bought himself a new machine even though he'd been determined to fix it one more time.

"Ah. The answer is no."

"Every time I go up there, she says she's fine."

"Even when the Post brothers aren't there?"

Especially then. The last time he'd clomped up the stairs, he'd heard her footsteps inside the apartment, light and quick, running for the front door. When he reached the porch, he'd been right in time to hear the lock click in the door.

"Go, then."

"I just said that she doesn't want me up there."

"So?"

He gave Dixie the look that usually shut up the most belligerent drunk in the saloon. "So I'm not usually the kind of guy who ignores a woman's wishes."

"Well, yeah. That would make you just an enormo-jerkwad."

"Attractive phrase." It wasn't like he didn't *want* to help. He did. Desperately. Watching Adele heave things up and down the stairs, watching her haul the huge bags to the dumpster – it was killing him. She and the Post brothers had been working for three days already. He'd gone from being annoyed at hearing their tramping overhead to it making him almost mental. Adele was working so *hard*. The stairs to Hugh's apartment went right in front of the side window of the saloon, and he couldn't help looking up every time she passed by it. She'd started every one of the last three days looking fresh. Clean. By the end of the day, her ponytail was frizzed, and her clothes were filthy. Usually her face was streaked with grime and sweat. Yesterday she'd looked on the verge of tears as she hauled up a mop bucket she must have found in the hotel maid's closet.

It was killing him, not helping.

But she didn't want him to. And if she failed, maybe she'd leave.

That was the whole point. She needed to leave. It was too bad he was having such a hard time remembering that.

"My point is that you're *not* a enormo-jerkwad. Try one more time."

"Enormo-jerkwad. Me." Nate pointed at his own chest. "You're buying me a new coffee machine if she kicks me in the junk."

"You got a deal." Dixie flapped a rag at him. "Go. There's like five people here. I got this."

Nate went.

Adele was in the middle of dropping huge contractor bags over the railing to the gravel parking lot below. Three had already hit, and one had split open. She threw another one over and it came so close to hitting him, he could hear the air whistling as it fell.

"Oh my God! Be careful down there!"

"Me? You should look where you're throwing that stuff! You want to hit a customer?" Without asking whether or not she wanted him to, he dragged the last bag to the dumpster and heaved it in. The trash company had already been out once to empty it, and they were going to have to come out and do it again. He wondered how much the extra trip was going to cost him. No, he had to remember – it would cost *her*.

"You don't have to do that!"

He didn't answer, just started shoving the glass floats back into the bag that had started splitting. Of course it had ripped – shards of glass were now all over the parking lot. "You had to throw this over the side?"

"You try lifting that!" Adele leaned over the railing and glared at him. She had two dark streaks of grime running up her cheeks, and the sleeve of her green shirt was ripped. She looked exhausted – he didn't think the dark circles under her eyes were dirt.

"Drop me another bag to double it, and I will!"

She dropped it – hurled it, really – down to him.

When he was done carefully picking up the shards and sweeping the lot, he went up the stairs. Heavily. So she could hear him coming and bar the door if she needed to.

But she didn't. She was sitting at the picnic table, her shoulders rounded with what looked like sheer fatigue. "Hey."

"Hey." Nate didn't have a follow-up line. He wished he did.

"What can I help you with?" She lifted her head, and the sadness he saw on her face twisted something in his chest, something he'd forgotten he could feel.

"You look like you could use a beer."

"Yeah, well. I dug out the refrigerator and cleaned it. I think it took a couple of years off my life, but when I plugged it in, it worked. But that was just a couple of hours ago. Very sadly, there is no beer in it. There was, though." She tugged on her ponytail, tightening it. "Did you know beer expires? The cans in there had actually caved in on themselves. They were mostly empty, even though they'd never been opened. And they were the cleanest things I found in that fridge." She shuddered, even though the air was warm.

"Well, you're in luck then, that a bartender came to check on you."

"Nope." She shook her head. "I thought about it, but I can't go down there without a good wash and I want to finish cleaning the shower in there so I can do that, and therefore I'm stuck. Sitting here. Until I figure out how to solve this problem."

Was she almost ready to cry? Something about the shape of her mouth, the tight, miserable way she held it, made him think it was a possibility.

"Well, just sit there, then." He turned and started down the stairs. "I'll be right back."

"Nate. You don't have to."

But he did. He had to do *something* to ease that tightness behind her eyes, to make that spot between her shoulder blades drop.

In the saloon, Dixie shot him a loaded look. "Ah. Yes, I'm a genius. Don't bother denying it."

"Don't speak." He put two glasses under the Boont tap.

"Hey, why don't you take the rest of the night off, boss?"

"Hey, why don't you mind your own business?"

Dixie held up her hands. "I'm just saying. If you don't come back down here by one forty-five, I'm closing up," she winked, "and asking no questions."

Nate didn't bother to dignify her suggestion with a response. He grabbed a round tray and put two bags of mesquite barbecue chips next to the pints. At the last minute, he added a couple of lime-flavored jerky strips.

"Classy."

Nate shot Dixie a look that should have killed her dead on the spot. She should be a smoking pile of ash. Instead, she just giggled and waved her fingers at him. "Don't do anything I wouldn't do. So basically, don't chew any lead paint. Beyond that, go for it."

He took the stairs slowly, keeping his eyes on the level of the pint glasses.

Adele was still in the same place. She still looked defeated.

That very fact, the simplicity of it, should have thrilled him.

And it didn't.

CHAPTER TWENTY-THREE

Something inside Nate lit and started crackling like a firecracker landing in dry weeds. "Here. It's not much, but it's the best I could rustle up with short notice."

He set down the tray and sat next to her, their backs to the open door of the apartment. In front of them, on the other side of the parking lot below, the enormous old oak tree spread its arms. The ocean's blue curve could just be seen through the leaves. As the fog crept in with nightfall, the blue of the water was getting darker. The air smelled of dust and, faintly, lighter fluid, as if someone close by was heating up their grill.

"Thank you." Her voice was so clenched it sounded like someone had strung her vocal cords too tightly, like a guitar string about to break.

They sat together.

He didn't try to fill the air with words, just watched the oak tree's limbs sway in the breeze.

At first, the space between them felt as tightly strung as her voice had. Then it eased. This high porch had that effect on people. How many times had he ranted about his mother to Hugh up here? He remembered a time he'd been so angry his hands had been shaking. His mother had been sober for almost three months. Long enough for Nate to get his hopes up again.

Then, of course, she'd flamed out in a big way. She'd drunk a fifth of vodka and chased it with some pills she couldn't even name she'd scored off a guy who had been staying in room three. That guy had gone one step further and accused Donna of trying to rob him after sleeping with him.

Nate had sat right there, his hand wrapped around his lighter. He'd flicked it on, then let the flame die, over and over. "That guy basically said my mother's a whore."

Hugh had kept his eyes on the bowl of his pipe. "Nah. He didn't."

"I should kill him." Nate had looked at his empty hand, wondering if it were strong enough to hurt the man who threw his mother out of recovery.

"If you think about it, he's actually saying the opposite." Hugh had puffed lightly, sending the smoke up towards the oak's limbs. "He said he slept with her and then she *took* money from him. He didn't give it to her."

"Well, shit. What am I supposed to do?" The anger had been so strong, the disappointment so sharp that Nate wanted to leave, to get in his truck and drive away from Darling Bay and every single person who *needed* something from him. Donna needed him to help her stay sober. Hugh needed him to run the bar. The patrons needed him to take care of them. It was his job, yeah, and he was good at it. He liked helping. But his mother falling off the wagon was one too many times. How was he supposed to help her up again?

If he left town, he could start over. Start new. Start by not taking care of anyone but himself.

Hugh had said, "What you're supposed to do is just let your mother do what she's gonna do. And love her if you can. If she'll let you. If she won't, that's not your problem."

Hugh had that much faith in Donna. And in him.

Now, sitting on the porch next to Adele, Nate said, "Your uncle was the best friend I ever had."

Adele sipped her beer and kept her eyes forward. "Why?"

Well, he didn't want to answer *that*. He shouldn't have said anything.

But she was waiting now. She wasn't looking at him, but he could feel her focus on him as clearly as if she'd touched him. Heat slid up his neck. "What do you mean, why?"

"What did Hugh do for you? I guess – I haven't put that piece of the puzzle together yet."

He spoke into his beer. "Just . . . he believed in me."

"Oh." Adele looked into her own glass. "He was good at that. One of the best."

Nate's mother had always thought he wouldn't graduate high school, let alone college. She'd been too drunk to come to either graduation. And he'd never even known who his father was – Donna always got confused when she was asked about that time in her life.

"What were you doing before you came to Darling Bay?"

Before a then-stranger named Hugh Darling called to tell him his mother was in the hospital for yet another alcohol overdose? "Working. Saving. I was out of college, trying to make a go of it."

Adele nodded. "What did you major in?"

"Social work." Nate missed it sometimes. The simplicity of working the suicide hotline. It had been stressful and sad sometimes, sure. But mostly, people called to talk. He was good at listening, always had been. Way better at listening than talking, that was for damn sure. As long as he was putting cards on the picnic table in front of them, he might as well lay a couple more out. "And Hugh always made it clear that if I worked for him long enough, and kept saving my money, that he'd sell the place to me. I mean, if you girls didn't come home."

Adele remained quiet. She didn't meet his eyes.

So Nate went on. "I was just a stray, you know? But Hugh took me in." Good old Hugh, the only man who fully accepted Donna as she was – a drunk who never wanted to stop but who needed a job, a purpose. Being behind the bar gave her an excuse to put off drinking till closer to the end of the night, and that was a small mercy in and of itself.

Nate hadn't understood this, not at the beginning. That first call he'd gotten from Hugh, a stranger to him: "Your mother's in the hospital."

"Where?"

"Darling Bay."

"Where the *hell* is that?"

"Five hours north of you, son."

He'd gotten there from Fresno in four hours flat, driving north on the winding, narrow two-lane highway that led to the ocean and then north some more, till there were wind-scoured rocks to his left, and high stands of redwood and eucalyptus on his right. Darling Bay was barely a bump in the road, a tourist trap, a place to buy ice-cream and kites on the family's road trip.

His mother had been pale and skinny in the white hospital bed. *You shouldn't be here.* They were her first words to him in three years. But she'd clutched his hand and held it tighter than he'd ever seen her hold a bottle.

In the Darling Bay hospital hallway, he'd yelled at Hugh Darling. "You gave her a *job*? In a *bar*? You did notice she's an alcoholic, right?"

Hugh had shrugged his bear-like shoulders. "That means she's gonna drink."

"Oh, right. You own the place. You just keep them around to make money off of, huh? You know she doesn't have money, right? Never has, never will."

"I give her money, because she works for me. Does a good job, too."

"You give her money to drink." Nate thought he might punch the man, right there, just smash him in the middle of the face. "You *pay* her to keep drinking."

Hugh had swatted at his eyebrow as if it itched. As if Nate were an irritating fly. "I pay her 'cause I care about her. She's good people. And if she's gonna be in the bar – and we both know she is – then there should be someone who cares about her close by to get her to the damn hospital when she needs to go."

Nate opened his mouth, wanting to swear or yell, but he found he had no words. No one had cared about Donna Houston in a really long time – no one but Nate – and Nate hadn't ever been able to help her, anyway.

"Now," said Hugh, rubbing his back against a doorjamb, "you want to get a sandwich? The cafeteria has pastrami, but it's like rubber. I do *not* recommend it. I swear by their peanut butter and blackberry sandwich, though. Got a place you can stay if you want to hang out in town with her a while."

Nate never left. He quit his job at the counseling hotline over the phone and had a moving company box up his apartment for him. He stayed at the Spike until he bought the boat where he lived until he'd gotten so close to buying the property he could taste it. He'd found a home, and a mentor. Hugh had been the only father figure he'd ever had. If only he'd been able to let go of his dream of his Songbirds coming home, if only he'd sold to Nate years ago. All this time, Nate could have been using his own money to fix up the place, rather than having to keep his dollars safe in the bank, ready for the purchase that still hadn't come.

"Yeah, that sounds like him." Adele looked over her shoulder at the apartment door. "I think that's where he got all that stuff that filled his apartment. Strays. Orphans. He never could stand to see someone leave a magazine on a bus stop, you know? He had to take it. He had to read it and make it feel wanted." She paused. "It got worse, though. So much worse. When we didn't come home." Her voice trailed off.

Nate opened a bag of the chips, but he didn't feel hungry. "You should let me help you. It'll go faster."

She straightened, visibly rallying herself. "It was fine. The Post brothers were great."

He hadn't been needed – that's what she was saying. "You're not done already, are you?"

"Almost totally done. I was going to hire a cleaning crew to come in, but Jack said he and John were as good at cleaning as any maid service, and he was right. I bought the supplies. I did most of the kitchen, but they did the rest."

"You're kidding." They'd only been working, what, three days? Total?

"We even pulled up the carpet in the bedrooms and the parlor. That was how the dumpster got filled yesterday." Her eyes closed as if suppressing a shudder. "I've never smelled something like that. It was awful. But the floors underneath are hardwood, and with a couple more moppings and a final polish, they'll be gorgeous. There's a problem in the bathroom with the showerhead, but it shouldn't be a big fix."

"Can I see?"

She blinked. "Of course."

They left their pints behind. She went in first, and then spun, spreading out her arms. "Isn't it amazing?"

And God help him, even as dirty as she was, covered head to toe in grime, as she turned in place, giving him that delighted smile, he wanted to kiss her again so badly that he had to shove his hands into his pockets to keep from reaching for her.

He barely looked around at the apartment. All Nate could see was her. "Amazing," he agreed, his voice rough. "Fucking amazing."

CHAPTER TWENTY-FOUR

I t was a good answer, and she was happy to hear it, even though Nate didn't even seem to be looking around.

"I mean, no one could have lived in this place just days ago. Right?"

Nate shook his head as if either agreeing with her or trying to clear it. "Well . . ."

"Does it still stink like bleach in here? Because I think I've become immune to the smell of it. I may have burned off the inside lining of my nose. I'm not sure." She knew she was babbling. "I guess I shouldn't say that no one could have stayed here. I know Uncle Hugh did, but a sleeping bag in a corner of the parlor doesn't really count." She deliberately ignored the fact that Nate had allowed Hugh to live in a place like that. It was obvious Nate had done his hellfire best. No one had ever been more stubborn than Uncle Hugh. "And I'm not ready to trust the mattresses – I have someone coming to pick them up tomorrow. We didn't find many bugs, mercifully, but just thinking about everything that was piled on those beds makes me feel itchy." Beds. She was talking about beds to Nate. "Speaking of itchy, I think working with Jack Post has infected me. I'm talking like him. Do you think I'm talking like him?"

Nate shrugged. A smile slid halfway onto his face. "You haven't thrown in enough non sequiturs. When you start jumping topics from pencil erasers to shrubbery, then you'll sound like him."

"Lion tamers on the television?"

"There you go. Now you've got it."

Seeing Nate's full-on smile, Adele almost felt giddy. It was probably just the half-beer doing it. She ignored the heat she felt in her face. "Come see the parlor."

Always her favorite room in the building, the parlor's clean-out was her proudest achievement of the last few days. When they were kids, she and her sisters had liked to lie on the floor, pressing their ears to hear the music from the saloon below. On busy nights, they'd hear the yips of the dancing cowboys, hear the high, trilling laughter of their dates. When they couldn't see into the saloon, when they could just imagine it, it was full of turn-of-the-century dancers and gamblers. Uncle Hugh had promoted this flight of fancy. He'd come up and tell them tall tales of the gunslingers below, how they'd tied up their horses at the hitching post out back. "No, sugar, it's too dark to go out there. Besides, you wouldn't want to get in a gunslinger's way, would you? They're quick to the trigger, and old Doc Ramsey is out of town birthing another Ingalls baby." To Adele, who worshipped the Little House on the Prairie books, his words were good as gospel. And when Molly and Lana stood out on the small porch that hung over the street, singing along to "Achy Breaky Heart," she would put her fingers in her ears and hum "The Streets of Laredo," the only song she thought a cowboy might know.

The old spinet piano had been the first thing she'd uncovered. Her mother had loved that thing. Uncle Hugh had known it and back then he'd kept it polished just for her. When they came into town, he'd have a vase of fresh wildflowers sitting on top. Adele's father had teased him for having a crush on his wife, and Uncle Hugh had always pleaded somewhat guilty. "You got the best one. Why would I bother looking for someone when she was already taken?"

So many memories in this old room. Once she'd gotten the carpet out and all the books were sitting in boxes outside, once the furniture was visible again, Adele could almost hear her sisters laughing in the back bedroom. Soon they would run in, soon her mother would come in singing, soon her father would thump indoors, pretending to grump when his girls launched themselves at his knees. Earlier, after the Post brothers had left, Adele had been unable to stop herself from crying. She'd lain on the low sofa which had always been their father's favorite place to nap. The crying jag had left her cheeks sticky and the backs of her legs covered with sofa dust, her heart just as empty.

God, she missed them. All of them.

Their mother, gone to cancer, so long now. Adele had been only sixteen when she'd died. Their father, gone to the heart attack. Her sisters, gone to the fight that had followed their father's death, the one that ripped the band apart and sent them to different corners of the world. Sure, she talked to Molly, but she hadn't been in the same room with her for more than three years. She hadn't even talked to Lana since the break-up. So long ago now.

And Uncle Hugh, the glue that had brought them back to Dad's hometown, year after year of their childhood, was dead.

Adele was the only Darling left in Darling Bay. It didn't feel right.

Her eyes still burned from crying, but if Nate said anything about how red they were, she'd blame the bleach and the dust.

"This is the way it used to look." Nate blinked and turned to look behind him. "I'd forgotten all of these." He leaned forward to the black-and-white photos hanging on the wall. The biggest one, in a cracked walnut frame, was a picture of Adele's great-grandfather Riley, back at the turn of the century. He stood in front of the saloon, a shovel in one hand, as if to symbolize the fact that he'd dug the very foundation of the building. His clothes were dark, as was his hat and the dirt of the ground at his feet, but the wall of the saloon behind him was bright in the photo – obviously newly whitewashed. His face was proud. Next to him hung a framed photo of the hotel, also brightly white, and the café, with its black-and-white striped awning clean and new.

Nate pointed to the one next to those. "Your great-granddad, right?"

"Yep. Riley Darling." She'd never known him. She barely remembered his son, her grandfather Charles – he'd died and left the property to the brothers before she was even five.

"He built the place."

She nodded, feeling pride in the accomplishment of a long-dead man. Strange, how family worked. "A saloon went up in the gold rush, but it had burned down by the time ol' Riley got here. The town was almost dead when he built the Golden Spike. Gold was played out, and the miners were a dying breed. But then came the fishing and the logging boom and it turned out he was in the right place at the right time."

Nate nodded and moved to look at another picture. "And here's Hugh and your dad."

"I love that one." In an obvious replication of her great-grandfather's pose, they both stood in front of the saloon holding shovels. Their faces were straight, like the original photo, but Adele could see the laughter almost ready to burst out of them.

"And these. I haven't seen these in years." Nate paused in front of the first official Darling Songbird band photo. They'd been dressed in vintage Old West women's wear, wide hoop skirts and beribboned hats. Luckily, they hadn't kept that up, being happier in western shirts and jeans than the vintage dresses their mother had put them in for their first few gigs. The photo was black and white, to match the rest of the framed photos, but Adele could almost feel the blue of the sky above them, could almost hear their father's whoop of delighted laughter as the professional photographer (their first) clicked his camera.

"Yeah. I should get them digitized. Send them to my sisters." She said it like she'd know where to send them mail. She didn't.

The tired ache started again behind her eyes.

Nate straightened, sticking his thumbs into the front of his jeans pockets. He looked relaxed here, like he fit. Adele realized he'd probably spent more time at the Golden Spike, cumulatively, than she ever had.

"What else needs to be done, besides getting new mattresses?"

God, why did it seem like he was asking her a different kind of question? Heat hit her belly as his gaze tangled with hers. What else needed to be done? So much. Why couldn't she think of a damn thing?

"Um."

"You said the bathroom?"

"Yes! The water runs into the bathtub, but I think the shower might be broken somehow."

He rocked back on his heels slightly. "You want me to take a look at it?"

"I'm pretty good with pipes, actually." She was. She'd found out a long time ago that you could learn how to fix almost anything by looking it up on YouTube.

He nodded. "Didn't mean to imply you're not. Just offering. In case you want another pair of eyes on it."

His eyes, he meant. Those changeable eyes (they were slate right now); those eyes that were doing things to her spinal column, making it feel all melty, like chocolate left in the sun.

"Sure. Give it a shot."

The bathroom was big and egregiously pink. Hugh had painted it when the girls were young, when they'd begged him to. They'd never thought he would do it, but one summer they'd returned to find the room transformed – pink walls and ceilings, a candy-bright shower curtain hanging in the enormous pink claw foot tub. He'd even made pink curtains by hand using old sailcloth dyed with Kool-Aid.

They'd loved this bathroom as girls. Adele still did. She looked out the window over the tub – the night sky was streaked with clouds so pink they could have floated in and been at home on the bathroom ceiling.

"I can't believe what you did in here." Nate glanced around. "This is crazy."

"Almost a real apartment again. It wasn't as dirty as it looked, honestly. It wasn't *Hoarders*-level bad. We found a dead mouse in a kitchen cupboard, but that was the only deceased critter, and it probably would have happened anyway." She caught sight of herself in the mirror. "Okay, I take that back. It was dirty. And it all landed on me, apparently." She was disgusting. How was she even talking to another human being looking like this? And why did that human being have to be someone as naturally hot as Nate? It wasn't fair. He probably woke up hot. She looked like she'd been wearing the same clothes for a week.

Nate did all the things she'd done to the pipes, pushing and pulling the same levers. "This is the one I think is broken. Here, take a gander."

She peeked over his shoulder. "Yeah, that's what I thought. I was going to turn the water off and then pull that out. It's loose if you wiggle it. Like a tooth."

Nate wiggled it.

And a wide jet of water shot straight out the hole at them.

Adele screamed. Nate jumped backward and then forward again, all the way into the tub, pressing his hands against the now-exposed pipe in the wall. "Go turn off the water main!"

"I don't know where it is! I just said I hadn't tried turning it off yet!"

"Get in here." Nate jerked his head. "Cover the water, and I'll go turn it off."

She clambered over the bubblegum-pink cast-iron rim. "Move over." There wasn't room for both of them to kneel in the tub, and her wet body was pressed against the side of his. She crouched as close as she could get to the faucet.

"Here. You have to push hard. It's going to get us as soon as we make the switch, but okay, go, go!"

Nate was right, the water shot out again, soaking them further. Adele made another sound that was part-laugh, part-scream. "Go! Go! Hurry! I got it!"

He stood and swung his leg out of the tub, putting both of his wide hands on top of her shoulders as he did so. "I'll be fast. Hang on."

For a ridiculous moment, she wanted him to stay just like that, pressing his weight against her.

Then he was out of the bathroom, and the coldness of the water soaked through to her skin, and she came back to her senses. Another minute later, the pipe clunked under her hand as the pressure was cut off. She slid backward, still in the tub, and took a deep breath.

Footsteps slammed up the stairs. "Did it work? Are you okay?"

She could only laugh.

Nate entered. "Good, we got it. I didn't know you meant it was *that* loose. I can help you fix it tomorrow."

Adele laughed harder. She was chilled, the cold water turning the layer of dirt on her skin to mud.

Nate's expression did something between a grimace and a grin. "Here. Let me help you out."

He took her hands in his, and pulled. She stood, and then, with his help, stepped out of the tub. She dripped onto the hardwood floor. She hiccuped around another laugh, and then her teeth started chattering.

"You're freezing."

She wasn't. She was cold, but that wasn't why her teeth were clacking against each other. Adele was a bundle of nerves all of a sudden, her arms and legs shaking. It was a combination of exhaustion mixed with the tension of being so close to the man in front of her.

He didn't let go of her hands. "We need to get you out of these clothes."

His voice. That's what did it. Not the darkening of his eyes, the way his face looked over hers. Not the way he held her hands, tightly, like he'd catch her if she fell. It was his voice, that roughened, weather-beaten voice. *We need to get you out of these clothes.*

And Adele made a decision that was instant and probably very, very wrong in the long term. But this minute, the one that stretched out taut in front of her, was the short term. That was all. Embracing the moment. Molly would applaud her.

"Will you help me?" she asked.

CHAPTER TWENTY-FIVE

N ate just assumed he'd misunderstood her. "With the pipes? Yeah. Of course."

A blush lit her cheeks and she closed her eyes for a brief second. Then she opened them, and she looked at him. She gazed *into* him. Her voice was soft, almost worried. "I meant, with my clothes." She stared down at herself. "Oh, ever-loving Patsy Cline. What am I doing?" She pulled back her hands and rubbed at a particularly large patch of wet dirt right over the soft swell of her belly.

"Adele –"

"I'm disgusting."

She was anything but. Even covered in dirt, she was gorgeous. Her wet green shirt clung to her breasts, showing tightly budded nipples under her thin bra. Her hair was a wild, dripping tangle. There wasn't a more beautiful sight in the state; he would wager every cent of his savings on that.

Then she gave that laugh again, the one that made him feel like he was drinking champagne. Fizzed, happy bubbles. "I need a shower."

He looked at the tub with confusion. "Well, that's not going to be easy."

"My room has water." She said the words fast and then covered her face with her hands.

"Oh." His IQ had just lowered into single digits.

She parted her fingers, peeking at his reaction. "Race you."

Then she darted around him, running for the door.

It was a dare.

And damn, he'd always loved a dare.

Her feet were light on the porch, pattering down the staircase. It was fully dark now, only a dull red glow from the setting sun at the water's edge, and the only lights were the white ones twinkling upward from the arbor below. More strands of the lights lit their way through the rose walkway to the hotel, but Nate would bet both of them could run this path wearing blindfolds.

He'd never run it with his heart pounding this hard, though.

This was a bad idea. This *had* to be a bad idea. He couldn't sleep with Adele Darling. He needed to get her out of town. This was the wrong way to do it, not to mention the fact that she was grieving. It would be taking advantage of her, pretty much the opposite of what he usually aimed to do for a woman.

Still, he chased her laughter through the dark.

By the time he reached the door that had been his for years, she was inside. The door to the bathroom stood open.

Her laughter had stopped, abruptly.

He took three more wide steps forward. She would be changing her mind. Of course.

What the hell were they doing?

"It's okay," he started to say. "We can just –"

But then he could see her. Adele stood in the middle of the small bathroom, the side of her face lit only by the moonlight coming through the open window. Her fingers rested lightly on the waistband of her jeans. Her voice was serious. "Is this a bad idea?"

Nate shook his head once. "No." Then he nodded. "Definitely."

That same small sideways smile crept across her face. She kicked off her shoes, sending them flying past him, one at a time. "I agree." She undid the button on the fly of her jeans. "So I'm just going to get in that shower. You can either leave, watch, or join. Your pick."

Well, there was only one answer to that. Nate shucked his boots and stepped forward. The bathroom had been small enough when he'd been the only one taking showers in it. "You know I'm an environmentalist, right?" He pulled off his shirt and then tugged the bottom of hers upward. She gasped as the cold, wet fabric moved against her skin.

"You are?"

"Sure. I'm a very concerned citizen." Nate pulled the shirt over her head. The bra that he'd been able to make out through the cloth turned out to be cream-colored lace, a shade lighter than her skin. He shivered, and it wasn't because of the cold. "El Niño aside, there is a *severe* drought in California. Every drop counts."

"Oh." She reached behind her back to unclasp the bra. "Yes, you're right."

"Conservation is key."

"Conversation, yes. I mean, *conservation*. Key." She dropped the bra, and Nate felt his brain stutter and then stall. Her breasts were full and round, larger than they looked in her clothes. Her nipples were dark and tight. She had goosebumps all over her skin, and he saw the same shiver he'd just felt rock through her. He put an arm around her, pulling her hard against him. She expected him to kiss her, he could tell by the way she angled her head, but instead, he moved his mouth down, bending her back so that his arm was supporting her, so that his mouth was right over that perfect left breast.

He breathed out. All of the warmth in his lungs, he gave to her nipple. He did it again. Three times. Above him, tilted backward, her own breathing quickened. Then he took another breath and did the same to the other one. He didn't lick – he didn't touch. He held her and he warmed her.

Adele gave a little moan and gripped his head with her hands. "Please. Shower. Not clean."

It was funny. She wasn't clean, that was true. Her skin smelled like soap, and her hair smelled like sweet alyssum, but she also smelled like hard work. Sweat. Metal and grime. She smelled like a woman who could roll up her sleeves and work hard as hell to do something difficult, and he'd never smelled anything as sexy before.

But she was cold. Nate straightened slowly, bringing her up with him. He kept his mouth an inch from hers and reached around her to turn on the shower. Her breathing was shallow. So was his. He could almost – almost – taste her. And it made him move even slower. He wanted to prolong the moment, wanted to keep from kissing her as long as he could. It felt like a test.

A test he wasn't going to mind failing.

The shower water heated. Their breath still commingled, he slid his hands down between them and finished undoing her fly. Then he undid his own. Still very carefully not kissing her, he pushed down her jeans, then his. Their underwear next.

He was so hard he was almost scared to touch her. He was so ready that if she'd wrapped a leg around him, he would lose his damn mind and maybe several other things, and what kind of a jerk-off would that make him? No, this woman deserved a really good warm-up.

Literally. Her teeth were chattering again.

Stepping around her, Nate adjusted the faucets so the water was piping hot. Then, holding both her hands, he backed through the water until he was against the cold tile on the other side and she was right under the showerhead. Adele stood in the rush of the water, her eyes closed, her mouth open. Her hair was dark and long, slicked to her breasts. Completely unable to help himself, he reached forward to touch a nipple, slicking the water from it. He would control himself. His body was ravenous, desperate for her. But he could hold himself back. They could go at her pace.

Adele's eyes opened.

Then she leaned forward and her water-sleek lips kissed his, hard, and Nate lost the second-to-last shred of control he had.

CHAPTER TWENTY-SIX

Adele couldn't decide which was hotter, the feeling of his mouth against hers or the heat of his cock against her stomach, hard as rock and slippery with the soap on her skin. While his mouth ravaged hers, his tongue against hers, his teeth tugging at her lips, his hands ran the bar of lavender soap over her skin. It was an excuse; that's all the soap was. She was past the point of caring whether or not she was clean. But when he turned her around, keeping his mouth on her neck, so that he could soap her back and her ass and then all the way down her legs and back up, when he teased her with the soap, getting a finger's width away from the vee between her legs, she threw her head so far back she inhaled a mouthful of water.

And that made her laugh.

And her laughing made *him* laugh, and the sound of him, that rumbling low quaking that poured into her via the kiss that she didn't ever want to break, was like nothing she'd ever heard. If she could put *that* sound into a love song, it would be the last love song anyone ever had to write.

He felt perfect, and it scared her. His arms fit around her, and he knew how to kiss her so thoroughly she forgot which way was up. If the shower hadn't been pounding down on her, she would have floated up, right to the ceiling.

But the shower wasn't the pounding she needed.

"You missed a spot," she whispered in his ear.

"Mmm." It was both an acknowledgement and a threat. He slid the soap down between her breasts and then rubbed it between his hands. He put the soap on the ledge of the tub, and then slicked his hands against the swollen part of her. Quickly and efficiently – devastatingly – he washed her. She was shaking by the time he said, "Now you're all nice and clean."

I don't want to be nice. Or clean. But she couldn't say it. Just the very act of telling him he could join (or watch) her in the shower had freaked her out enough for one day. Adele was normally brave enough in matters of sex, but this felt bigger somehow.

Well, damn it, *he* felt bigger, anyway. She wrapped her hand around his cock, softly, sliding her fingers down to its base. Nate put his head back against the tiles and groaned.

"I have a better idea." She trailed kisses down his chest, the water beating against her shoulders and back. She took the tip of his shaft into her mouth. His hands rested lightly on the top of her head and this time his groan sounded almost pained. She placed the flat of her hands against the backs of his thighs and tasted him with long slow strokes of her tongue. He pulsed in her mouth, and pressed his hips forward. She took him as deeply as she could, then backed off, and then took him deep again.

"Adele," Nate warned, his voice tight, "you have to stop."

She took his cock out of her mouth, her hands still wrapped around the shaft and peered up at him, blinking rapidly through the water. "Or what?"

"Oh, God." Nate hit the shower handle. "*Out.* Where's your towel?"

He sounded so panicked Adele laughed, a bubble of joy at the top of her lungs. "Right there, on the rack. But now I'm curious as to where *you* keep them."

Nate grabbed the towel so fast the rack rattled. He dragged it harshly and haphazardly across her body, then his.

"You're not really very good at this whole drying thing," she teased. She saw his jaw clench. Knowing she was the cause of his tension was a delicious, heady feeling.

"Oh, yeah?" Nate kissed her then, hard. She leaned into him, pushing her hips against his. They gasped against each other. "I'd better show you what I'm good at, huh?"

"Big words."

"From a big man." His voice was teasingly echoing her tone, but there was nothing wrong about his statement. His cock, like his shoulders and thighs and jawline, was wide and long. It was so hot it almost burned to her touch.

Bed. In her bed, now. God, no, it was *his* bed. The thought was a confused jumble in her mind, and she didn't care. She needed him in her, as strong a need as she'd ever had in her life.

"Protection," she muttered, diving for her purse and digging through it. Surely she had an old condom in the pocket where she kept her headphones and spare pencils.

"I have one here," he said, popping open the Martin's case. "Jackpot!" From under a capo and a tuner, he pulled a small cardboard box.

"Guitar players," Adele said. And she laughed again. That was surprising her the most – usually when she had sex with someone for the first time, she was nervous. She wanted to get things right. And with Nate God knew she didn't want to get things *wrong*. But she wasn't worried.

This was just plain fun. Maybe it was because she was exhausted. Maybe it was because she'd spent the last three days doing nothing but hard, backbreaking work and she needed something pleasurable. Maybe it was because Nate's stubbled cheek was the sexiest thing she'd ever seen, but being with him was just *fun*, plain and simple.

She took the condom from him, and unwrapped it. She went to her knees again, this time on carpet, and rolled it onto him. Carefully. Slowly. His left hand had a slight tremor now, she noticed, and it felt like she'd won a prize at the fair. She grinned up at him. "There. Now. You were going to show me something."

With a noise that was more roar than any word she could identify, Nate came at her as if she'd unleashed him. He lifted her off the ground, his mouth claiming hers. He dropped her on her back on the bed and then moved to put himself between her legs. Adele lifted her hips, but he shook his head and moved himself away. "My speed now," he said.

She whimpered as he moved down her body, grazing her skin with his teeth, with his tongue. When he reached her center, he unfolded her with his fingers, blowing gently, following the air kiss with a real one. She gave a sharp cry as he slid a single finger inside her and let his tongue lap her clit.

"Please," she said, but she wasn't sure what she was asking for or if he could give it to her.

He didn't stop, and he didn't slow. If anything, his tongue picked up speed, and he pressed another finger into her wetness. Adele's teeth started chattering again, lightly. Her whole body shook. He raised her higher and higher, and then, right when she was on the very edge of coming, he slid yet another finger inside her and curled his hand, keeping his tongue striking, beating against her. She came so hard and so fast it felt like something broke inside her, crashing to the ground. Unexpected tears came to her eyes. "Oh," she said when she could breathe again. "Oh."

Nate slid up her body, keeping his hand in contact with her, skimming her hips, her stomach, her breast, her neck. He stayed on his side, his fingers touching her jaw gently, then her nose. "Are you okay? Shit, are you crying? Adele . . ."

"I'm fine," she said. She was. She was so fine.

But she was in no way done.

Adele kissed him.

She could taste herself on his lips, and the mixture of salt and sweet went right to her head. He tried to say something, but the twisted noise only came halfway out of his mouth.

Then, because she couldn't help herself, and wouldn't have been able to even if she'd wanted to, she swung her leg over his body. She planted the flats of both her hands on his chest.

"Are you –"

She didn't know how he planned to end the sentence. *Are you sure? Are you ready?*

It didn't matter. She wanted him. He wanted her. And instead of being tangled up in her own thoughts, she could only think of one thing, and it was him.

Just him.

She kissed him again. "Yes." It was a whisper against his mouth. He blinked once, slowly. Then he lifted his hips against her as she pushed down. Her slickness took the entirety of his length into her body in one hard thrust. She stilled – *full*. So full. "Wait," she gasped. "Just give me a minute."

One minute, to adjust to this feeling of – what was it? He was so big that he stretched her, but that wasn't what she needed a second to process.

Adele needed to push back the tears that were starting again. It felt like . . .

It felt like coming home.

And she hadn't done that in a really long time.

Nate raised a hand to her cheek, cupping it. She could tell by the way the muscles in his neck were corded that he wasn't breathing any better than she was. "We can stop. We can do whatever you want." She felt his thumb brush the top of her cheekbone. "Do you want to stop?"

That was the *last* thing she wanted. She shook her head, hard. One teardrop fell to his chest, a tear she barely understood.

"This." She moved against him. "This."

Nate's eyes stayed on hers. She moved, slowly at first. And honestly, it would have been fine if his gaze had drifted lower, to her breasts, to what her body was doing, where their bodies were meeting with such heat and wetness and intensity. But his eyes stayed fixed to hers, and nothing had ever made her feel as sexy, ever.

Faster, then. She sat all the way up, and his hands gripped her hips, lifting her, drawing her back down. The heat rose, red flames flashing up through her till she thought the top of her head might catch fire. *Faster, more, harder.*

He was pumping into her now as much as she was riding him. She lost her balance, dizzy with lust, with heat, and fell forward onto his chest. Instead of repositioning her back up on him, Nate locked her mouth into a kiss – plundering her mouth with his tongue as they moved. He wrapped his arm around her low back and rolled, staying inside her.

"Oh, God." He filled her so much she could barely breathe. *"Please."*

Even faster now. She locked her legs around his back and barely had to move to meet his thrusts.

And still his eyes were on hers, as if he was inside her mind as much as he was inside her body.

As if it was more than just simple sex. It was as if he was making *love* to her.

And with that, Adele's second climax rose inside her. With every one of his strokes, his pubic bone hit her clit. She writhed harder, the flame rising so high in her chest that she forgot to breathe at all, which was fine, since there was no need for oxygen, not for something as perfect as this – they needed nothing but each other, but this, she needed only him.

She came, with a low scream, her head tilting back, finally breaking eye contact with him. His pace slowed, as if he was holding himself back, waiting. Waves of pleasure rocked through her, and she kept her hips in tight contact with his. Unable to help herself, she gave a laugh of sheer delight. She lifted her head and opened her eyes again. His eyes were still locked on her face, and as she watched – as she fell into his gaze – he speeded his thrusts, and then, with one sharp shout, he came. She felt his cock jerk inside her, and a deep, river-wide satisfaction filled her. He blinked hard, his mouth still wet from hers, but never looked away from her.

Adele had never felt so seen. "Oh, Kitty *Wells*."

He laughed, collapsing against her, rolling sideways. His arms wrapped around her, drawing her close.

"Well, yeah," he finally said, the laughter still thick in his throat. "Kitty something, for damn sure."

Joy rose in Adele's sternum, surprising her with how light it felt in contrast to her limbs, which were heavy as river rocks. After sex, Adele was usually the kind of person who bounded out of bed. Normally she would offer her partner a snack, or some water. She'd shower, cut up strawberries, or even do the dishes. In the past, sex had started something up inside her that the actual climax wouldn't finish. She would usually at least start a conversation. Pillow talk, with a purpose – you were either getting to know someone more, or you were cementing a relationship.

But here, in his arms, she just felt finished. And safe.

Adele let her heavy lids close. She was conscious – though barely – that Nate's arms were going to catch her as she fell into sleep.

So she fell.

CHAPTER TWENTY-SEVEN

A dele was the perfect weight in his arms.

It was enough to perturb a man.

Nate had never felt anything like it before – the way the shape of her body fit his. It was normal for two people *not* to be comfortable while lying naked in bed together for the first time. Bodies were weird things, and that was fine – that made life interesting.

But Adele fit him. He didn't have to shift because the weight of her head made his arm fall asleep. His legs didn't get cramped, no charley horse attacked his calf muscle. When she blew out a puff of breath in her sleep and rolled to her side, he followed, wrapping his body against hers. He'd never even understood the term "spooning" before. He usually thought of resting in bed with someone as more like a couple of forks tossed haphazardly in a drawer. But Adele just fit there, too. A perfect smaller spoon to his bigger one.

Nate tightened his arm around her waist. The scent of night jasmine snuck in through the dark, parted curtains. Adele snuggled back against him with a sigh. He'd learned in the last hour as she slept against him that she made the most adorable little sleep noises. She was like a kitten, except she had curves for days and skin like silk.

Kitty Wells. He snorted softly.

Adele murmured something that he couldn't quite hear.

"What was that, darlin'?" He realized he'd just called her by her last name, and was immediately glad she wasn't awake to be annoyed with him for it. That must happen to her with every man she dated. And that small thought, of the other men in her life, lit something in him like a cold flame. He didn't want to think about her with another man.

Not that he was jealous. He'd never been jealous in his life. Not once.

But hell, if this was what it felt like, no wonder everyone wrote songs about it. It felt like a sickness deep in his guts. Not pleasant. He shook off the thought.

"Home," Adele whispered. She turned in his arms so that she was curled on her side, now facing him. Nate put a hand on the side of her head, brushing the lock of hair out of her face.

"What about it?"

Her eyelids fluttered and then opened, slowly. She didn't jump, exactly, but she did have a moment of looking very surprised. And then very pleased. A smile spread across her face. "Hi."

"Hi." He brushed her eyebrow with his thumb. "What about home?"

"What? How long was I asleep?"

"I think we've been dozing an hour or two. You said *home.*"

"I did?" She blinked, and even though she didn't move a muscle – he would have felt it if she had – she got further away from him.

He realized he didn't know exactly what she counted as home. Darling Bay? Nashville? "Where's home for you?"

She pulled her hands up into a ball in front of her, as if she were praying. She was still lying on her side facing him, still shin to shin, forehead to forehead. He held her top hand loosely.

"Where's *your* home?" she countered.

"Here." This very property.

"But where did you come from?"

"A little inland farming town on the edge of Fresno. Known for nothing but its football team, circa 1996, and the amount of meth produced per capita. It was a good place to leave."

"When did Darling Bay start to be home for you?"

Nate still wanted to know why she'd said the word in her sleep, but he'd let her sidle around the edge of the answer if she wanted to. "When I got here. Well, it wasn't instant."

"Of course."

"I expect it took at least a day or two for it to sink in."

"How did you know?"

Nate moved his hand to her side, where her waist curved in. Her skin was warm, almost hot to the touch. If he had to leave his hand in one place for the rest of his life, he would choose to leave it right here, with her face only inches from his, her breath mixed with his. "Honestly? When I met Hugh."

"What did he say to make you feel like that?"

"It was the way he took care of – of Donna, the bartender. I saw the way he looked at her, even when she was falling down drunk. You could tell a block away he was a good man. A man who took care of other people. Then he tried to take care of me, too."

Adele smiled. "He would. Did you let him?"

He paused. "Of course I did."

"Because you never saw it coming."

Nate remembered the way Hugh had suckered him into helping him on the property. *Just a few minutes of raking in the back – do you mind helping an old man with a back to match?* The way he'd made Nate feel like he'd done the best raking job anyone had ever done before. Nate had reacted like a five-year-old being praised for picking up his toys instead of the twenty-four-year-old he was.

Hugh had made him feel like a son, immediately. And Nate had never been a son to anyone. Not to his dad, whom he'd never known, not really even to his own mother. He'd had to take care of her for so long. That didn't leave time to look up to anyone. "You're right."

"Did he call you kiddo?"

Surprised, Nate pulled back. "Yeah."

"Yep. The way he said that, huh?"

Nate nodded. Shortly after helping Hugh rake, still deciding if he should stick around this small town where his mother was being so well taken care of, Nate had changed the oil on Hugh's old Bonneville. And Hugh had just jerked his head in a nod and said, *Thanks, kiddo.* That had been the moment Nate had decided he wanted to stay forever in this town where an old guy was willing not only to give his mom a shot, but to give him one, too. "He made me feel like I was really someone."

"Yeah. He could do that to a person." Adele stopped and covered her lower lip with her fingers.

It felt like she needed a minute, maybe to herself. Nate closed his eyes and just lay there with her, his hand still on the swell of her hip.

Finally, after he'd counted three cars out on the road (and they didn't come by that often after dark), she spoke. "You'd think home for me would be Nashville. That's where we grew up, after all. My mom's grandmother lived on the edge of town, and we all lived with her off and on, when the money was bad. But we always moved so much – anywhere Daddy could get a job doing sound, anywhere Mama could get a gig. We'd move towns even if the gig was only for a month. Chattanooga, Gatlinburg, Franklin, Pigeon Forge."

"She was a singer." Nate thought he'd heard that in Darling Bay gossip, something that was always in fashion in the saloon when one of the girls" albums was playing on the jukebox. "The very first Darling Songbird." The one who didn't make it.

"She was the one with all the dreams, but then I came along and ruined them."

"I'm sure you didn't do that."

Adele ignored him. "She was the reason we formed into our little band. Even when we were so young we practically didn't know how to read music, she wanted her Songbirds to sing to her. We came here to Darling Bay every summer and every Christmas because Daddy wanted to be with his brother, and Mama didn't have any family left in Nashville after her mom died. Uncle Hugh was as bad as she was, putting us on the little stage in the saloon. I remember that at our first show, we had to stand Lana up on an apple box just so she could reach the microphone. When Mama died –" Adele's voice went husky, but her eyes stayed clear, and stayed on his.

He stroked her shoulder gently.

"When she died, that's when we got serious about the band. We *owed* it to her." Her voice dropped. "Especially me."

"Adele –"

"We'd tried to make her happy in life, and it – it hadn't worked. So we tried after she died." She cleared her throat. "Then we got known a little bit, and we just started moving around more. I guess I just never felt like I had any kind of home. I love Nashville, and it's been good to me. But it never . . . wait. How did we get on this topic again?" She reached her head forward to kiss him, and the sweetness of her lips, the quick, light heat of them, made Nate want to forget what they were talking about. He stirred again, just thinking about how she had felt underneath him. And on top of him.

Damn.

Okay, there would (hopefully) be time for that. He pulled back. "But why did you say *home*?"

"Mmm. It was a dream. A quick, five-second one. I barely remember it."

"What was it?"

"I was lost." Her hands balled into fists.

"Where?"

"I don't know. A city I didn't know. I knew that if I could find the right street, I'd find my way home, but every time I was getting close to it, it changed, and I was going the wrong way again."

He rubbed his thumb along the strong tendons in the back of her wrist. "What did home look like?"

Adele's eyes widened and she rolled onto her back, away from him. Her voice, when she spoke, was surprised. "This. I mean, not *this*." Adele waved her fingers in the air. Did she mean the fact that they were stark raving naked in his bed? Because he hadn't expected that either, least of all the way she fit in his arms.

She went on. "I mean Darling Bay. I guess it's always been the only home I've ever known. Oh, my God. That's it. That's what I was trying to find. I can see it now. The street I was trying to find led to Route 119, and then here."

Route 119 was a small back road that locals took to get to the main highway. It was the fastest way to Darling Bay. Locals routinely pulled the signs down, to discourage extra looky-loos on the Pacific Coast Highway. There were plenty of Darlingites who thought their town was better off unfound and unspoiled.

Nate rolled onto his back, too, and followed her gaze. He should be worried about the fine crack that ran from the wall to the old wooden ceiling fan, but at this point, a crack was the least of his worries when it came to fixing up the place. "Yeah, I never had a dream about trying to find the road into Fresno, that's for sure."

"I was trying to get home. Oh, my God."

A chill hit Nate's skin, as if the fog had just settled low outside and was now pushing under the door, in through the darkened window screen. Something was happening, something he couldn't quite put his finger on. Something that wasn't good. "What?"

"This is home."

The chill intensified. "So you've been saying. But I bet a lot of people could have told you that, Darling girl." It was a title now, not an endearment. "That's not news."

Adele spun upward, pulling the sheet with her. "Nate. This is our *home*. We can't sell you our home."

"Excuse me?" What he wanted to say was much less polite.

It seemed so obvious, now that she'd had the thought in full.

"Darling Bay. Oh, my God. You know what Uncle Hugh said every time he talked to us on the phone? And in every card he ever sent us? *Fly home*. That's what he always told us to do, to fly home, and none of us ever thought a thing about it."

Nate sat straight up. He would have been less surprised if she'd sprouted wings from her shoulder blades. "You wanna run that by me one more time?"

"We can't sell. I'm so sorry. This is as surprising to me as it is to you."

He found himself on his feet, naked, unsure how he got to standing but determined to stay upright.

"Nate –" Adele reached one hand out to him.

But he was already yanking up his jeans, jerking on his boots. He pulled his T-shirt over his head, not caring it was on backward. "Where the hell is my ball cap?" He shoved his hands through his hair, which he knew was sticking up wildly from what her fingertips had done earlier.

"I'll help you – you don't have to –"

"It's fine." His scowl felt a mile deep, his voice a growl. "I'll get it from you tomorrow."

"Nate – don't go. We should talk about this."

"What's there to talk about? You're taking ownership of the Golden Spike."

"We'll keep you on."

He froze, his arms still at his sides. His breathing was heavy. "Mighty good of you, ma'am."

"Don't do this."

"Am I supposed to be *happy* for you?"

"I can't do this without you."

The dead middle of his chest felt frozen, as if his heart had been dipped in deep well water.

"Please stay," she said. "I'd love your help."

And that was, maybe, the worst thing she could have said to him. Because she wasn't talking about needing his help as a man anymore. She wasn't talking about needing him in bed.

She meant she needed his help with the hotel.

The sex had probably just been a bonus.

"I know I'm nothing more than the hired help. I've been that my whole life, and I'm used to it." He finally located his ball cap under the side chair and pulled it on, brim forward. He shaded his eyes as if she were the sun. "But I'll be damned if I play the cabana boy role, too."

He slammed the door so hard the shutter on the window next to it fell off the window and hit the porch with a clatter. And if he could have slammed the door twice, twenty times, till this whole side of the hotel fell down, he would have.

CHAPTER TWENTY-EIGHT

Adele slept hard, her dreams bleak, shot with glimmers of silver. One of her dreams was about a dress she'd had, years and years ago, one of her favorite onstage dresses. It looked matte black when she was still, but shined pewter when she shimmied. She'd lost it somewhere along the way, ripped it irrevocably, probably. The stage was hard on clothing.

When she woke, she felt a warmth ripple through her, a happiness that shone the same silver, brightening the room. She remembered Nate's skin against hers. His mouth, so hot, so giving. So demanding. The warmth of the memory was yellow and bright, the same color as the sunshine leaking through the curtain.

Then – *home*.

Darling Bay was home. For the first time in eleven years. For the first time, she wanted to stay somewhere for more than just a few weeks, and it wasn't about work. It wasn't, by default, Nashville.

Nate's thunderous face, as he slammed the door.

The brightness drained away as she remembered his fury.

But she hadn't done anything wrong. She wanted to take over the Golden Spike. *To fix it.* To make it run. Make it work. She knew she could do it. She was good at running a small business. She *was* her own business, and she'd been working without a manager, without anyone else for years. She could do this.

She'd start with the saloon. It would take time to revamp it into something that would pull in both the locals and the out-of-towners, but she was creative. And it was what her uncle would have wanted, not to mention her father. Dead men, running her life, but they were dead men she'd loved with all her heart.

She would honor her heritage and make them proud.

And maybe if she did it just right, maybe it would bring her sisters home. Hugh's plan, all along. She was playing right into it.

If only she'd done it earlier.

It would take some time to talk them into it, but surely she could – she'd have a real home to lure them with. For a moment, she allowed herself to imagine sitting on one of the picnic benches in the back courtyard, side by side, heads back, looking up at the stars. Molly, soft and warm on her right. Lana, thin and impatient on her left. With her sisters – the most important women in the whole world, the ones who completed her – Adele could do *anything*. She could perform open-heart surgery if Lana held the scalpels for her. She could build a spaceship if Molly told her jokes while she did it. Together, they were more than three people. They were Mama's songbirds.

Adele pulled the sheet up to her chin and thought hard. This could really work.

Molly could come and run the café. She was a nutritionist – that wasn't so far away from meal-planning, was it? It was a similar thing on a different scale. Molly would be so *good* at it. She was a wonderful cook and even better with people. Adele could imagine it now – Molly greeting customers with menus and a huge smile and seating them with a laugh. Barbecued oysters and grass-fed burgers would be brought to beach-tired tourists, like the old days.

And Lana – she was so good with – well, okay, she wasn't that good with people. But she'd done that stint on the stage crew, insisting it was more fun to build their sets than it was to write songs. A whole six months, Lana had been either under the stage, building it for the night, or on top of it, singing her heart out to sold-out crowds. Of all three sisters, Lana was the best at construction. She could tear apart and rebuild the hotel. Couldn't she?

Adele stretched across the bed, feeling her body ache in places it hadn't for a long time. She rolled, her cheeks hot as she remembered the night before, and pressed her face into the pillow. It was the wrong thing to do. She could smell him there. Involuntarily, her fingers clutched the pillowcase.

Nate.

In reaching for her dream (it was new, but it *was* her dream – it felt so familiar to her that maybe she'd always had it and just hadn't known it), she'd be taking Nate's away. Completely.

But that wasn't fair of him, was it? He'd wanted to buy the place, but he'd also known Hugh had hoped the girls would come home. Surely there were other run-down saloons on the coast for sale? (No, there weren't. She knew there weren't. Something else, then?)

Or she could talk him into staying on as bartender.

And then what? Would she continue sleeping with the hired help? Was that fair? Would he leave for good? And why did her body feel so empty and cold at the thought?

Adele rose, her legs shaky below her. She showered, trying to force out the images of the night before. The towel he'd used on both their bodies was still lightly damp. She took two aspirin for her head.

A new chapter. She could hear her mother's voice in her head. *Nothing like a new chapter for stirring up the heart.* Mama had loved a new chapter, whether she'd been reading them *Little Women* or moving to yet another town where she might hit it big.

There were lists to be made. Shopping to be done. Old wood to be ripped out (those awful built-in seats that ran under the front windows of the saloon) and new carpentry to be put in. Paint. A new drinks menu. Entertainment to be hired.

And Adele wasn't done quite with Uncle Hugh's apartment. She'd get the mattresses today, and she could be moved out of Nate's room by tonight.

It was exciting. She should feel nothing but eagerness. Enthusiasm.

Instead, she thought of Nate's mouth against her body, the way his lips and tongue had toppled her, the way his weight had crushed her so sweetly.

Don't think about Nate.

She reached for her cell phone and did her best to ignore the deep dread rolling through her stomach.

Molly answered, thank God. "What's up?"

"I want to keep it."

"Keep what?"

"The Golden Spike. All of it. The saloon, the hotel, the café."

"I thought you wanted to sell it."

"I thought so, too. But now I want to keep it."

There was a silence on the end of the line. "I don't know, Adele. I was kind of counting on that money."

"You're practically itinerant."

"So?"

"You don't *have* bills."

"I have some debt."

Adele knew how close Molly lived to the bone, but she also knew how hard she had worked to stay debt-free. "How much?"

"I don't – I can't talk about this right now. I need the money, Adele. And you already made it sound like a nightmare there."

Adele moved outside and sat. "It's not a nightmare at this exact moment. I'm sitting on the porch swing in front of room one. Remember when Uncle Hugh and Daddy hung it?"

Molly snorted. "Mama kept telling them they were hanging it crooked and they wouldn't listen so Mama made Daddy sleep on it that night."

"He was fixing it by dawn."

"I miss you."

"Then come. Help me."

"I thought you said there were no rooms except the one you stole from Hottie McHotterson."

"There aren't. Not yet. But with your help there could be." Adele could almost see Molly's worried look. "You could have the café! Fix it up! We could do it together."

"Have you even been inside it?"

Adele had been too scared of what she might find to ask Nate for the key. "Not yet. But it can't be that bad."

"An old, crappy restaurant. Closed for years. Think about the size of the rats living inside there now."

Adele pushed with her legs, making the old swing creak. "Mama never proved that was a rat she saw."

"Oh, come on. She knew a rat when she saw one."

"Come home."

Molly laughed again. "Home? What are you smoking over there? Have you gone full-California on me now?"

"Remember how Uncle Hugh always said it?"

Molly ignored her, her words tumbling down the line more quickly. "Just because the locals light up doesn't mean that stuff is safe for a country girl like you."

"Fly home."

"Stop."

"I just realized it last night. That this was home. Nate –"

"The bartender, yes? There's a way more interesting subject. The handsome Nate helped you realize this? Did he do that naked?"

Adele choked but managed to say, "No."

"Liar. I can hear it in your voice. You got super-sexy cuddles from him."

"Stop it."

"Fast cuddles."

"*Molly.*"

"You *did*. You go, girl. How long has it been for you, anyway?"

Indignant, Adele said, "You're forgetting Mitch."

"No, I'm not. You said sleeping with him was like taking a nice warm bath."

"I like baths."

"No one likes baths that much, unless you're putting your coochee right under the stream of water, in which case it turns from relaxing into –"

"Molly."

"I'm just saying. You needed to get some of the good stuff. Was it good?"

Adele folded her lips. She was not going to say this. She could barely even think of the night before without her lower parts tightening, clenching.

"Ah. It *was*. Good girl. Is this the same guy who wanted to buy the Spike, though?"

"Um. Yeah."

"Have you mentioned this harebrained scheme to him?"

Adele stayed quiet, the swing moving gently under her. The ocean's foggy breeze caressed her cheek, and for a second, she could feel Nate's touch on her skin.

"Ah. You did, and it didn't go well."

"If you're just going to guess everything, why do I bother calling you?"

"I *have* been taking fortune-telling lessons from the ship's palm reader. I could read yours, if you want. You could just send me a picture of it. I'm not quite sure if —"

"Fly home."

"Stop saying that."

Adele hated the way tears thickened her throat. "Please come home."

"It's not my home." Molly's words were sharp. "It was a place to go in the summer. You know why we went there?"

"Because it was where Daddy was from."

"Because we never had enough money to stay wherever we spent the school year."

Adele knew that. Did Molly think she didn't know that? "Whatever."

"No Darling has ever been good with money."

Adele wasn't bad at it, actually. "Are you really in debt?"

There was a fumbling sound on the other end of the line. "Look. You know Lana will never agree. Can you just sell to him? It's got to be worth some cash, right?"

"But I think this could be good for us."

"You can't fix us."

The pain was sharp and swift, a blade sunk deep, just under her ribs. "Yes, I can. We can fix it."

"It's too broken."

"No." That couldn't be true. Adele had never accepted it. The fight that broke up the sisters had been a nuclear blast of heat, an impetuous bout of screaming brought on by their father's death and their grief – that was all. Didn't her sisters know that? It was time to fix it. All of it.

There was a long pause. Adele heard a clicking on the line. It made Molly feel even farther away.

"Look –"

Molly interrupted her. "We're not the Darling Songbirds. We never will be, not again."

"But if we came together –"

"I've forgiven you. Mostly. But Lana hasn't. You know that."

The blade twisted. In a moment, it would pierce Adele's lungs. "Oh, good. I'm glad you've forgiven me for just doing my best."

"You pushed us on the stage that night. You know you shouldn't have done that." Molly made a strangled sound. "No, I am *not* going to rehash this with you again. I'm done with it."

"We had to –"

"You thought we had to feel the same way you did. You couldn't see that we were different people from you."

"Doing that show was the way to bring us back together. To be us again."

"You couldn't fix us, Adele, no matter how much you wanted to. You still don't know why we're still hurting, do you?"

"I'm sorry."

"Do you know why?"

"What?"

"You say you're sorry, but I think you're sorry we couldn't make the tour."

"That's not what I mean – but I thought if we could just do that one show –"

"I was too sad to sing. Lana could barely stand up."

"That was the pills, not her legs."

There was another pause, followed by a click – an astonishing, empty, heartbreaking click – as the line went dead.

"Molly?"

But her sister had hung up on her.

"Shit," she whispered.

There was a loud creaking above her. Adele craned her head to look. The noise was coming from where the swing's chain bolted into the beam above.

The swing dropped an inch. She gasped and started to stand but then the whole damn thing crashed to the deck, first on the left side, then the bolts on the right side ripped from the beam, too. Adele was thrown off the porch, and down the two shallow steps. She landed on her right elbow and her left knee, her shoulder knocking into the yellow April Moon rose. Her mother's rose. She was stabbed by at least three thorns, and she felt the blood start, sharp and hot.

She wouldn't cry. Adele stood slowly, shaking out her limbs. Nothing was broken. She was bruised badly, but she would live.

And she would *not* cry.

Instead, she held her breath until she saw black spots dance in front of her eyes like whole notes. When she was a child, she'd had fever dreams that she had broken the whole house. She didn't know how she'd done it, but she'd known she was to blame, and even her mother's cool hands on her forehead hadn't helped.

She knew it was just a porch swing. Just some wood and chain and bolts.

But honestly, it felt like she'd just brought the whole Golden Spike crashing down around her ears.

CHAPTER TWENTY-NINE

N ate held the plastic bag tight in his hands and knocked on the door of Dixie's motorhome. It was early, and a seagull squawked sleepily overhead.

"Go away!"

"I'm not going anywhere until you open this door."

"I'm fine!"

She wasn't fine. The message that Dixie had left on his cell phone, asking if she could have the night off, had not sounded okay. She'd been crying, or not far from it, and she was pretty damn tough.

"Open the door or you're fired!" he yelled. "And I'll tell Phil to shut off your electricity! He owes me one!" Or course, Nate would do neither. He liked the fact that Dixie was parking her motorhome in Phil Martino's mobile home park next to the marina. Phil was nosy enough to keep the whole place (full of elderly snowbirds, mostly) safe and sound.

The flimsy door of the wheeled house slammed open. He only saw half Dixie's arm, and then heard a *floof* as she jumped back onto the sofa. She'd already pulled a blanket over her head by the time he entered.

"What's wrong?"

"Nothing! You have to go open the bar!"

"A few minutes late won't hurt anybody." Let Adele open it. Let her just try. Anger twisted his stomach.

"I'm just going to die under here. Alone. Go away. You can have my guitar, but it's a piece of junk, worse than your Martin. Send my ukulele to my sister in Arkansas, it's not half bad."

"Look, lady. I have a pint of chocolate peanut butter ice-cream, a brand-new unread *People* magazine, and a bag of barbecue chips."

"Chips?" Wild brown curls, then one eyeball showed. "Gimme."

"Tell me what's going on."

"I lost a cat."

"You had a cat? Didn't you say you were allergic?"

"Mildly. I was just helping out a friend. Pet sitting for a couple of days. But it ran under the sink and hid, and then I forgot it was here. I opened the door to go for a walk this morning and it shot out like it was chasing a mouse made of tuna. Took a right and went up the hillside, and I haven't been able to find it."

"So you're hiding instead of looking?" Nate yanked open the bag and passed it over. Then he put the ice-cream in Dixie's mini freezer.

"The cat won't come to me. There's no chance. It has no idea who I am. What am I supposed to do, go yell at an animal that's nothing but scared and lost?"

"Whose cat did you say it was again?"

Dixie's face dissolved into tears.

"Ah," said Nate. "What's her name?"

"Georgia."

"And she is where now?"

"In Hawaii for a week." Dixie cried harder. "She loves that stupid cat."

"Color?"

Dixie frowned and hiccuped. "Huh? Why would that matter?"

"Not Georgia. The *cat*."

"Oh. Black. Small. Young."

Of course. That wouldn't make finding it easy. But if he could get Mrs. Suthers' damn cockapoo back every time he ran off, he could do this. "Name?"

"Taco Sauce."

Nate shook his head. "No. Just nope. I'm not calling for a cat named after a condiment."

"She found it crying next to a taqueria's trash can."

"Oh, my God. Fine. Give me some canned cat food."

It took Nate forever to find the damn thing. He was pretty sure when he got back to the Spike, Norma would be blacked out on the floor, the till empty, ravaged by some opportunist passer-by. But he kept searching. "Taco Sauce! Where are you? C'mere, Taco Sauce!" On the other side of the marina, he could hear Dixie calling, too, but she sounded feeble, as if she'd already given up.

"Taco Sauce! Come on, Little Spicy!" He ignored the fishermen's laughter, giving Terry Dunlap a sturdy middle finger before he scrambled into the crawl space under the marina office.

Three hours later, Nate came back to Dixie's motorhome. He was sweating and covered with sticker burrs. Two slashes ran down his left arm. Dixie sat on the tiny sofa, a spoon dug deeply into the ice-cream.

"You got her."

He released his grip on the squirming, furious little animal, and it sprinted back under the sink. "Do we even know it's a her? No, I take that back. With the amount of trouble she is, she's definitely female."

Dixie launched herself at him, kissing Nate on the forehead with a smack. "Look at your poor arm. Now it matches your other one. Was that the cat?"

"You mean Satan? Yes."

"Want bandages?"

He looked at his other cut, the one he'd gotten from the dishwasher. The cut Adele had patched up, when they'd kissed for the first time in the rose garden. The wound was almost healed now, even though it felt like a lifetime ago, instead of just four days.

He'd gotten that cut before he'd felt Adele slick against him, before he'd been inside her.

Before she'd decided to destroy his dream.

"Nah. I heal fast. I'll just wash it."

"Whatever you say." Dixie took a huge bite of ice-cream and then spoke around it. "Now I can work tonight, by the way. You should take the night off." She winked. "Like you did last night."

He was *not* going to go into the night before. "So. This Georgia. Is she good enough for you?"

Dixie sighed and rubbed his arm a little too hard with the washcloth. "No."

"But you're falling in love anyway?"

"You know what I always say: there's no fun in falling unless you're falling off a cliff."

Nate took a wild guess. "Ah. She's in Hawaii with her girlfriend?"

Dixie's eyes welled again. "She told me she's going to leave her."

"You know, the women you date aren't that much different than men. Why don't you just date one of us instead?"

"Because I find your type *boring*. And obsessed with sex. Speaking of which, how was the songbird?"

He wasn't going to let her twist the conversation, though. "Seriously, Dixie. You're too good for her. Just like you were too good for Elaine and Dari before that. Why do you let them treat you like the hired help?"

"Hey." Dixie was obviously struggling to appear nonchalant. "The hired help get tips, just like at the bar."

"What's your tip going to be for watching her cat?"

Dixie looked down at the washcloth. "She was going to spend the whole night."

"You mean she was going to make up some excuse so that she could get away from her partner and spend a stolen night with you?"

"Stolen nights are like stolen cars. They're called hot for a reason."

"You're worth more than a night or two, sugar." He tapped the end of her nose. "There's a reason Hugh was half in love with you. There's a reason I am."

"It's the ginormous size of my rack. I know. I hear it all the time."

"It doesn't hurt." But Adele's breasts flashed into his mind. The perfect size of them, the way they felt in his hand, the way her nipples had budded under his breath.

"Okay, *spill*."

"What?" He grabbed a spoon out of the small drawer next to the sink. Taco Sauce hissed at him. "Gimme some of that."

Dixie yanked the ice-cream out of his reach. "You don't get to try to fix my love life without at least returning the favor."

"I have no love life to fix." He ignored her fake-surprised look. "I know you don't believe me. But it's true." He had anger. Confusion. A terminal case of lust that had only gotten stronger having had Adele in his arms. But no love life to speak of.

"You didn't come back last night, do I need to point that out? *I* am the one who closed the saloon. *I* am the one who walked Max Fitzgibbon home when he couldn't find his car keys – because I'd hidden them two hours before – and by the way, you owe me for that because he tried to grab my boob. Don't worry, I dodged, and when he was passed out in his comfy chair, I wrote *Don't Grab Boobs* in Sharpie on his forehead."

"Damn," Nate said admiringly. "Really?"

"Yep."

"That's a good one."

"I'm hoping it will sink in through his skin and maybe he'll remember it next time."

"I'll tell him he's not welcome anymore."

Dixie rinsed the cloth and washed her hands. "Are you serious? If you had to toss out all the problems, your saloon would be even emptier than it is. I'd be out of a job."

"Speaking of that . . ."

"Uh-oh."

"I can't guess what's going to happen, but, well, I'm going to be real honest here – if you get another job offer, you might want to think about taking it."

"Shit. Seriously, what *happened* last night with her?"

"I don't know. A lot." That was true. He'd been hit by a truck – that's what had happened. "But whatever it was, it convinced her that she should stay."

"Stay? As in stay-stay? Like, not sell the Golden Spike to you?"

"That's what it sounds like."

"Seriously? But what about you? Hugh promised the place to you."

"He always said I could have it if they didn't come back. Hugh's dead. She and her sisters are very much alive, and this one is back."

"She just doesn't know what she needs."

Nate grabbed and got the ice-cream away from Dixie. "Sure. I'll let her know. Every woman loves to hear that, right?"

"This is just one of those times, my friend."

"What kind of time?"

"When you have to save her from herself." Dixie took the pint back, took a spoonful and held it out towards the cat, who was slinking out from under the sink.

"I have a feeling she doesn't need saving. Just like that cat doesn't need chocolate ice-cream."

"Of course she does. Adele, I mean. Look at her. She showed up from nowhere, left her home of how many years to come sell a property? God, now that I think about it, of course it makes sense. She's running from something. It would have been a whole hell of a lot easier to hire a company, one of those property management thingies? They could have sold it for her. She didn't need to come all the way out here. There's a reason she came out here herself. She's looking to be saved." Dixie sat up excitedly and the spoonful of ice-cream plopped to the tiles.

"Waste of chocolate peanut butter there."

"She just doesn't *know* it. This is just a people problem. You're so good at taking care of people, take care of her! Find out what she needs by keeping the Golden Spike, and figure out how she can get that some other way. That's all."

Nate twisted his hands into fists, pressing the knuckles into the tops of his thighs until it hurt. "I don't know."

"Unless you don't want her to leave."

He shot her a bouncer's scowl. "Don't be stupid."

"I'm many things that are maybe less than ideal, but stupid ain't one of them. You know you won't get her to leave unless you figure out where she's supposed to be going, right?"

"Yeah." He hadn't known that until just then, but damned if he'd admit it to Dixie. "I just don't think I'm the one to do it."

"You're the one who deserves the Golden Spike. *You.* Not Adele, as nice as I think she is." Dixie held up the recently truant cat that now had ice-cream all over its face. She waved the cat's legs at him. "Taco Sauce agrees."

Nate could hear it purring from where he sat. "Damn."

"You can do it."

"Do me a favor."

Dixie smiled. "I owe you *so* big. Name it."

"If Adele calls you today, don't answer."

She blinked. "Okay."

"It's just that –"

"I don't need to know, boss. I won't answer. Now pet the cat. It's good for you."

CHAPTER THIRTY

After she pushed the porch swing against the wall and picked up the fallen bolts, Adele stood on her tiptoes and examined the wood above. She didn't know much about wood or construction, but the beams looked like they were made of corrugated cardboard. What did dry rot look like, exactly?

Tension pulled her nerves taut. Thinking about her sister made her nauseated. Thinking about Nate made her want to come right out of her skin. Her sensitive skin, the skin he'd licked and touched and slid against . . .

God.

Adele looked at her cell phone. Only nine in the morning. It was early enough that Nate shouldn't be at the bar yet.

She didn't know where he was.

He wasn't with her. He'd left. He'd left furious.

But this – staying, keeping the Golden Spike – was the right thing to do. Something iron-like had settled into the base of Adele's spine and for the first time in a long time she knew that there was something she wanted to do that was bigger than just writing and rewriting songs. Songs were important – Lord knew sometimes they were life itself – but even Adele could admit they were ephemeral. At the end of her life, she'd have a pile of invisible words set to music. Nothing she could touch. No building. "No home," she whispered.

This collection of buildings, though, *was* home. It was tangible. Built by her kin, her blood.

This was home.

Adele hadn't been in Hugh's office for eleven years, but as soon as she unlocked the door she felt it again: this was where she belonged.

How had she and her sisters just assumed Nashville was their home, instead of this place?

This room had been Uncle Hugh's sanctuary, a place he loved even more than his upstairs lodging. A tacked-on addition on the south side of the saloon, it had been built by hand by Adele's father and Hugh one summer. Adele had been young, not more than five, but she'd remembered that year as one of her father's happiest. Molly and Lana had been tiny, three and two years old.

Adele remembered how her father had swung her up into his arms, getting her out of her mother's hair by taking her with him to play in the sawdust all day. One of the photos on Hugh's wall showed Adele in a pink sundress and yellow shoes holding a hammer that was almost as big as she had been. That been her favorite accessory that summer. Her mother had even put a loop on her dresses, and every morning, Adele had dropped the hammer through it in the morning. She'd been bad at hammering actual nails, always bending them, but she'd been very good at hammering everything else: the ground, boards, the side of the building. Uncle Hugh had called her his best little helper and she remembered the feeling of her father's hand resting heavily on top of her head in the warm sunshine.

The office smelled of pipe smoke and old paper, a musty mix of something that felt like happiness. Adele turned slowly, taking in the room.

Uncle Hugh had outfitted the small room simply, with a rough-hewn heavy desk and a matching chair that spun. An old wooden filing cabinet stood in the corner. The walls were hard to see under the dozens of calendar pages tacked to them. Charlie's Feed and Seed had always printed the best Darling Bay calendar every year. They were beach scenes *and* product placement, combined – harrows on the sand, tractors on the dunes. Hugh had been sentimental about the photos and never wanted to get rid of the last year's pages, so he'd started tacking them up in 1989, and now they were as much part of the decor as the dust motes dancing in the sun streaming through the window.

Adele peeked through the glass.

Nate's truck still wasn't in the lot, and he probably wouldn't get there until just before opening at eleven. If he showed at all, that was.

He'd been so *angry*.

He would get over it though, right? It was a huge blow she'd dealt him. She knew that.

But they could work it out. Surely they could. Like adults.

Adele sat at the desk, feeling the comforting curve of the wooden seat under her. How many times had she spun in this chair while Uncle Hugh pretended to be grumpy about it?

Even though she hadn't seen Nate since he'd left her room in such a furious hurry that morning, his presence was palpable here. A set of steel strings was on the desktop, new in its package. A couple of spy thrillers were next to the lamp, and she knew Hugh hadn't read the genre, preferring westerns and the occasional romance novel.

Inside the desk's biggest drawer was the ledger she'd come in looking for. And there, on the first page, was Uncle Hugh's handwriting. She would have recognized it anywhere, dark and sharply slanted to the left. The particular way he made his four, with three adjoined legs. The sight of it brought a tightness to her throat she hadn't expected, and she flipped the pages forward, impatient with herself and with Uncle Hugh for never moving to a damn computer system.

And there in the last half of the book, about eight months back, the handwriting changed. Straight up and down numbering in a clean hand. Nate's writing. He'd obviously taken over this part of the running of the Golden Spike a while ago. Why hadn't he mentioned that when she'd asked him for the office key? Had Hugh gotten too tired to do it?

Had he really been that close to selling to Nate?

Adele shook her head, as if she could shake out the emotion that was making her thoughts feel heavy and sluggish. She got out the old plug-in calculator from the bottom drawer and pulled out the stack of bank statements that was in the drawer above it.

Time to get down to business. Adele didn't have entrepreneurial experience except with her own career, but she'd made that work. She filed her own quarterly taxes and knew how to maximize her deductions. A business like this would naturally have – she opened the first envelope with the most recent date – quite a bit more money than her own slim business account.

She reread the amount on the bank statement.

This wasn't right.

There had to be another account. The bank balance in front of her was barely larger than her own personal checking account.

She rummaged through the rest of the desk, opening everything she could, before she realized that no, this was it.

This was all she had to work with. This, and her own cash. No wonder Nate hadn't been able to make any improvements on the property. The Spike had no capital. Just the buildings themselves. It explained the recalcitrant dishwasher and the groaning coffee machine. The cracked skylight. The paint job, sorely needed. The shuttered café, and the defunct hotel.

This could be the biggest gamble she'd ever made. She had no idea what she was doing, and the chance of failure was high. How the hell would she get everything done with no money and no experience? Would Nate stay on to help her? Could she afford him? Did she want to?

She heard Uncle Hugh's voice in her mind. "One day at a time." It wasn't until she was in her early twenties that she'd realized this was an AA slogan, and he'd probably picked it up from the people in his saloon who had slipped off wagons a time or two.

But it helped.

One piece of this puzzle at a time. Fix the saloon (hard but doable). Get her sisters back, tuck all the songbirds in the nest (impossible perhaps but she'd try anyway).

Keep Nate from . . . No, keep herself from – God, she didn't even know how the sentence in her mind should end. She couldn't even form the thought, let alone rate how difficult it might be.

She picked up the ledger again.

By eleven, Adele had touched every piece of paper in the office, and not one of them had made her feel better. The only good news, the only tiny scrap of it, was that there were no liens on the property. At least Uncle Hugh had been too proud to borrow money to fix it up. Or would that have been so bad? A loan on either the café or the hotel would have allowed food to be sold and rooms to be rented. Hard cash coming in was what was missing. The mark-up on alcohol was good, but the only nights the money really flowed were Fridays and Saturdays and even then it seemed to run as reluctantly as a California creek in August.

Adele's phone pinged. She blew her hair out of her eyes, wishing for a hair tie. It was hot and airless in the office, something she hadn't remembered.

FYI, it's my day off.

Adele's face heated. There weren't enough words on the screen to be able to read into them, but she could give it a try. Was this about last night? She rubbed her eyes with the palms of her hand. She was sweating at her hairline. She'd need to buy a fan, or put in another window.

The fan was a lot more affordable.

She tapped back, *Of course.* Would Dixie come in, then? Is that how they worked their schedule since Hugh died? Why hadn't she thought to ask Nate about what they did, concretely, on a day-to-day basis?

As if he could hear her thoughts, another text came in: *Dixie sent me a text – she's sick today.*

It was a plan. One they'd set up, together. They wanted her to panic. Of course they did.

So – even though her heart was racing and sweat was wetting her shirt – she wrote back, *Not a problem. See you tomorrow?*

No response.

She took a moment to imagine him – was he on his boat? She wanted to see it. How big was his bed? A twin? He was so tall – how would he fit something so small? Did boats have beds bigger than that, though? Was he lying there looking at his phone, satisfied with plaguing her? Or was he feeling the same way she was – shaken to the core? Scared?

Did his skin ache, like hers did? She felt as if she were running a fever. The only thing that could cool her was more of him. More of his touch.

And more of his laugh, which was the most distressing part of all. Sex was just a thing. Two bodies, rubbing together, making heat. But the *laughter* they'd shared while in bed together was like nothing she'd ever known. The connection. Sparks from their touch, reflected in their eyes. He'd seen her, the whole package of faults and worries and silliness and excitement. And she'd seen him, the way when he was loving her there was nothing else for him in the whole world, the difficulty he had in letting himself go, letting himself feel pleasure, the way – when he'd given himself over – he'd looked like he could reach up and touch the moon.

Whatever that *thing* was between them, it had been intoxicating and immediately addictive. She wanted – needed – more. Could he possibly know how quiet her brain had gone in those two hours she'd lain in his arms like she'd been meant to be there all her life?

What if his not coming in today was about *that* and not the fact that she was going to keep the bar?

A low ache tugged at the back of her neck – a headache, threatening like a storm. She rummaged in the desk drawers until she found a rubber band. She pulled back her hair so tightly her facial skin felt taut. Moving forward.

This was business. That was all it was.

She could run a damn bar for one damn day. How hard could it possibly be?

CHAPTER THIRTY-ONE

Six and a half hours later, Adele knew the answer to that question.

Unlocking the bar and setting up the till had gone uneventfully at a quarter past eleven. No one was waiting on the doorstep, not even Norma or Parrot Freddy. She scrubbed the bar's single toilet with bleach. She hummed cheerfully as the sun came in the front window. It lit up the dancing dust motes, sure, but they were pretty. She could take care of the problems. One by one, she'd fix this place up. It would be fun. Satisfying.

A beer truck arrived at noon. Adele greeted the driver cheerfully. Time to learn! She waited to watch what the driver did, but apparently it was the guy's first day, and he looked at her with a slack jaw when she asked him to just do whatever the last guy did. She was the one who rolled the kegs into the back room and lifted each one, her arms shaking with the effort of the fifth. He disappeared so fast after the last keg was unloaded she didn't even have time to ask him how they were billed.

Norma came in at one o'clock, but her mood was different. Instead of her normal long blue dress, she was clad head to toe in black. She was quiet, and she drank steadily. When Adele asked if she was okay, she didn't answer. She just pushed her glass over the counter for another martini. Had she gotten a text from Nate, too?

After four martinis, Adele started to worry about her. How were you supposed to know when to cut someone off? Was it based on alcohol tolerance? Size? History? Norma was still quiet even after she ordered her fifth, but was it an explosive quietness? Adele couldn't tell.

Two men came in at three o'clock, followed by two more fifteen minutes later. They all sat at a table and played cards.

It might have been poker.

And it sure as *hell* looked like they were playing with real cash.

The wi-fi went out as Adele brought up a search window on her phone: *Is poker for money legal in California?* She was pretty sure she knew the answer, but before confronting them about it, she wanted the law in her hand, to show them. She searched for the modem to reset it, but couldn't find it anywhere, and this spot on the coast seemed to have no satellite coverage at all. Damn it.

At five o'clock, a family came in: a young mother wearing a green-and-white flowered dress and bedazzled flip-flops, the father dressed in corporate-casual Dockers and a T-shirt that read *Code This*. Three little boys followed them in, raucous ducks bobbing and weaving in their wake. The parents sat at the bar while the boys raced each other from the jukebox to the door and back.

"Two rum and Cokes," the man said without looking at Adele. "Three Rob Roys. And four grilled cheese sandwiches. We'll share."

"Sorry," said Adele. "We don't serve hot food here."

The man dropped his sunglasses an inch to stare past her. "Seriously?"

His wife made a distressed noise.

"It's fine, Maris. We'll just get ice-cream afterward at that place up the road."

"This just a bar, then?" The woman looked scandalized, as if she expected fish-netted prostitutes to ooze out from the storeroom.

"A saloon, yeah."

"The website said the Golden Spike was a hotel, café, and saloon."

"*Was* is the right verb. Currently under renovation."

"Are my children even *allowed* in here?"

Adele had been allowed in the bar as a child. Of course she had.

Though maybe that had just been Uncle Hugh flouting the law. Adele would google it, but the wi-fi was still down. And after an hour of searching, she still hadn't found the modem. Where would Nate have hidden it, for the love of God? Who *knew* if children were allowed in a bar anymore? Adele cast a beseeching glance at Norma – wouldn't she have an opinion on this? But the older woman now had a single track of silent tears running down either side of her face. Her tarot cards stayed in a quiet stack in front of her. Inexplicably, there was a candle holder in front of her now and it . . . it kind of looked like a menorah. In September? And was that a pile of candles in the plastic bag hanging next to her on the coat hook? Adele made a hurried mental note to find the fire-extinguisher. Right after she found out if kids were allowed in a bar.

Not that it mattered. The three children didn't appear to *be* children – they were wildebeests. One had climbed to the top of the jukebox and was straddling it, apparently trying to shake the songs loose with his hips. The middle-sized boy was on the stage, yanking on an amp cord. The smallest was lying on the floor, trying to lick up what looked like an old piece of bubblegum.

"Just the five drinks, then?"

She got an irritated nod from the father, and "Make mine a double', from the mother.

The Rob Roys were easy (Molly's favorite childhood drink) but Adele didn't really know what a double rum and Coke was. It *should* be easy, but the more she thought about it the harder it got. Two shots, right? Instead of one? Or did a single actually have two shots? How much Coke? Did you double that, too, for a double?

Another thing that would have been instantly answered by the MIA internet. She just made both of them stronger than seemed necessary and handed them over. The mother muttered something about Yelping the place, and Adele bit the inside of her lip, hard.

Was there a way to pay to remove bad reviews?

Thirty minutes later, a boy and girl came in who couldn't be more than nineteen. Their IDs, though, looked perfect. "What's your birthday?" Adele asked the girl. The girl recited the date without hesitation, and then, unprompted, added the address listed. "Are you an organ donor?" she asked the boy, noticing the red dot's absence on his ID. "Not yet," he said apologetically. "But I'm totally going to sign up."

"Emmylou Harris," Adele muttered. She made their drinks, two Old-Fashioneds. Within half an hour, they were both in the single washroom, and the walls were making rhythmic noises, audible in the saloon.

Adele put five dollars of her own money in the jukebox (shouldn't there be a key for this?) and hit *Random* but all that came out, song after song, were Darling Songbird tunes. One of the poker players said something about what you got when you crossed a Dixie Chick with a Darling Songbird, but Adele, her cheeks on fire, hurried out the front door with a broom to avoid hearing the answer.

She swept the wooden porch, and then swept the last good porch swing on the property. She reached up and swept the cobwebs out of the high corners, for good measure.

Then she sat. It didn't creak and fall, but it was probably only a matter of time.

Screw the customers. If anyone needed a refill, they'd all seen her go outside. They knew where to find her. She leaned forward, putting her elbows on her knees, covering both her eyes with her hands. She could smell the salt of the ocean, just a block away. Its low murmur was something so integral to Darling Bay she almost never heard it but now it filled her ears, a *shuuuush-shhh*.

It should have been soothing. This was paradise, after all. It *would* have been soothing if she hadn't been freaking *out*.

Adele concentrated on her breathing. In through the nose, out through the mouth. In, out. Repeat.

She had a sudden, visceral memory of her breathing the night before – she'd literally panted for Nate. Her breath had heaved, and his had done the same. His body had covered hers as he'd entered her, both of them slick with sweat. His breathing had started to sound like her own, until she couldn't tell what was his air and what was hers.

"Going that good, huh?"

The swing dipped, the chains creaking, as Nate dropped himself down next to her.

It felt as if she'd conjured him. Feelings rose in her, more potent than any cocktail she could mix: relief, lust, irritation and, most worrisome of all, a heady wave of joy.

Could he see all of it? Was it written on her face? Adele tried to fix a scowl onto her features, but the happiness, the sheer gladness of seeing him next to her, might be radiating through. "Yep."

"Wanna tell me why you look like your teeth are gnashed together?"

"I'm speaking. My teeth can't be gnashed together if I'm talking."

Nate pulled a face, sticking out his lower jaw. "Yeshtheycan."

His face. That damn ball cap, worn backward. His flannel shirt, worn open over a black T-shirt. He was so comfortable in his maleness. God, she wanted to touch his jaw, to run her fingers along that bone that jutted out south of his ear. Light stubble. He must have left her this morning and gone somewhere and shaved. Had he napped? They'd had almost no sleep, but he looked bright. Refreshed. He looked the opposite of how she felt.

Her stomach made a yawning noise and she wondered if she'd eaten anything yet. No wonder she felt a little dizzy.

She stood, feeling awkward. "So."

He stayed seated, his legs splayed comfortably, as if he owned the whole building. "So," he agreed. If he'd been wearing a cowboy hat, he would have touched its brim, she just knew it.

"I thought you weren't coming to work today."

"Oh. I ain't workin'. I just came in for a beer."

Adele sucked in a quick breath. He was trying to get to her. That was fine. He could try all he wanted to; she'd remain calm. "What kind would you like?" *Say something in a can. Say something in a can.*

"How 'bout a black and tan?" His eyes danced.

That was a beer mix, she knew, but she didn't know much more than that. But she said, "You got it." She'd put something black in a glass and then put something tan on top of it. And he would like it, by God.

Adele didn't look to see if he followed her, and she tried to tell herself that it didn't matter one way or the other. But she heard the swing's chain creak as he stood, and she could *feel* his eyes on her backside as she pushed her way through the half-door. She tried to add an extra sway to her hips and instead felt like she was hiccuping from her tailbone. Not a good look.

Behind the bar, she pulled half a glass of Guinness and topped it, still thick with foam, with a light IPA.

"That's a black and tan?"

Nate looked so *satisfied* that she had screwed it up.

"It's the only way to make one. People who say to do it the other way are just plain wrong, I've always said."

He stared into the foaming top and took a slow, careful sip. "Huh."

Adele crossed her arms, daring him to criticize her drink.

Instead, he tipped his head to the side. He was listening to the damn Darling Songbird song that had just started playing. "Ah. A classic."

"Wait Till Your Father Gets Home" was one of the songs that had risen the band to fame. It had been a coincidence entirely – Lana had been reading *Little Women* for the first time when she wrote it – but it happened to come out near September 11. It had become an anthem.

It had been the song playing when Molly went down onstage. The night that ended everything, the night the band and the sisters broke up.

"I swear to God I didn't put this on. I hit the random button."

"Sure you did."

"It's just playing Darling Songbirds. I can't make it do anything else."

"Your uncle wasn't too fond of the random button. Possibly paid the tech to reprogram it so it wasn't really random."

"Sweet Dolly Parton." She sat on the high stool she'd placed behind the bar.

"Nope. Not on random, anyway." Nate's shoulders jumped as a particularly loud *thonk* came from the bathroom area.

"Ignore, please."

"What *is* that?"

"I believe it's two teenagers having sex."

His eyes widened. "Lucky kids. Most of 'em have to do it in the back of pick-up trucks around here. Aren't you nice? You didn't card them?"

Adele willed him to leave, to drain his beer before he noticed everything else wrong around him. But his eyes stayed on hers, light and amused, and his long fingers (oh, those fingers – she'd sucked them, one by one last night, making him groan) stayed wrapped around his glass. Adele squirmed on the stool and then stood. It was just more comfortable to lean her arms on the bar top, anyway. "Their IDs were perfect."

"Signatures and birthdays raised?"

"Sorry?"

"They have good machines, but most of them can't do the raised embossing. You can tell by rubbing your thumb across the card." He reached forward, wrapping his fingers around her wrist. His thumb swept slowly across the skin at her wrist. "Like this."

Adele's mouth lost all moisture. She pulled back her hand quickly. "Well. What am I supposed to do? Bang on the door and ask to see their IDs again?"

"They're under-age. That's a hefty fine."

"How much?"

"A thousand bucks, plus a year in jail if they throw the book at you. Which, this being Darling Bay, they might not, but do you want to gamble on that?"

"You're *kidding*."

"Speaking of fines, what's with the rug rats?" He pointed at the boys with the disgruntled yuppie parents.

One boy was tapping his head against a wooden rail and another was sitting open-mouthed on the floor, his eyes fixed on the air in front of him. The third boy wasn't even visible, but neither parent appeared concerned, both absorbed with their cell phones. Apparently *they* had satellite service.

Adele straightened her shoulders. "They're with their mom and dad."

"Still illegal. We don't serve food. You can't have a kid in a bar unless it serves meals. You like playing chicken with the penal code, huh?"

The door swung open, and a tall, dark-haired man entered.

"And *now* you have real trouble," said Nate.

"Why?"

"That's the sheriff."

"Oh, no. Wait, Colin McMurtry is the sheriff now? Oh, crap."

"Want help with him?"

God, the satisfaction audible in Nate's voice was enough to choke a pelican. Adele would *not* say yes. She couldn't.

But then the sheriff's gaze landed on the poker table.

"Yes," said Adele. "Mother Maybelle *Carter*. Help me."

CHAPTER THIRTY-TWO

It was a little pathetic, maybe, to be so good at this one thing. Nate had felt the occasional pang of remorse that his true life's talent seemed to be keeping a bar running while helping the patrons stay on track, too.

But right now? It felt damn good.

He greeted Sheriff McMurtry with a thump on the shoulder. "Colin. Good to see you, brother. Been a while."

Colin wasn't one for grinning, but he smiled wide enough. "You, too, Nate."

"Let me buy you a beer." They'd been friends a long time. Nate's mother and her frequent jail stays had gotten them acquainted back when Colin was a rookie on the force. Quite a few years had passed since then.

"No, thanks." Colin's gaze raked the room again. "On duty. Got a call about –"

Nate cut him off. "Hey, you two must know each other, right? Local yokels and all?"

Adele all but audibly gulped. "Good to see you again, Colin."

Colin's face softened. "Heard you were back in town, girl."

While Adele came around the end of the saloon to hug the sheriff, Nate swung into action. He grabbed the extra bathroom key. On his way to the back, he swooped to where Lane Thomas and his boys were playing poker. "Put the money away, stat, or you're out on your ear, and I'll tell your wives, too."

He grabbed a boy who looked about nine years old by the back of the shirt. "Are you chewing on that wood? You're not a termite. Hey! Mom and Dad! You can't have your kids in a bar. What kind of parents are you?"

The appalled gasps and squeaks the parents made were righteously satisfying. He hoped they'd threaten to sue. Those were his favorites. Then, ignoring the dad's heated puffings, he hauled ass to the back bathroom, and gave the door three short raps. "Pants up," he called. "I'm coming in."

When he unlocked the door, the boy – Roman Elmwood's son Bruce – was hurriedly struggling with his belt buckle while his girlfriend, the Landrys' youngest, hastily reapplied lipstick.

"We weren't doing anything," said Bruce.

"Don't play a player." Nate held out his hand. "IDs."

"No way." Bruce shook his head.

"IDs or I call your parents and tell them you weren't using a condom."

"But we *did* use one," gasped the girl who only then realized her mistake. "I mean –"

"Now."

"They cost me five hundred bucks," Bruce grumbled, but he put them in Nate's hand. "That was all the money I had."

"Did you get them local?" There'd been a guy at the mobile home park that had an ID-printing rig, but Colin had shut him down last year. It would be worth passing the news on to the sheriff if he'd popped back up.

"Internet."

"So you're stupid as well as broke. And seriously, keep using protection. You're too dumb to be parents yet! You see those idiots out there with their kids? You want to end up like that? Out!" He waved his arms like he was shooing a cow out of a field. "Get out of here!"

They hightailed it.

In the saloon, Colin was still talking to Adele. Her face was bright, and she looked genuinely happy to see the sheriff. Had they ever dated? They were about the same age, weren't they? The space between Nate's shoulder blades was suddenly tight. He imagined Colin's hand against her face, Colin going in for a kiss, and he felt a blast of something hot and shocking in his gut.

Jealousy. The second time he'd felt it in his life, and both times, it was about Adele. He was known for *not* getting jealous, blast it. Past girlfriends had gone so far as to try to make him feel the green-eyed monster, to prove his affection. It had never worked except to tick him off and make him break up with them faster. This feeling, though – this stomach-churning pit of acid in his belly – it just made him sick.

Stupid. He was being an idiot, as dumb as those kids in the john.

Keep it moving, Houston. He brought his bar (no, *her* bar) and its patrons back into focus.

Laney and his boys were gone, a single ace of hearts face up on the floor under Ned Randal's seat. He'd always been a God-awful cheat. Nate raked up the pile of ones they'd left behind and stuck it in the tip jar.

The parents with their hellions were gone.

That only left Norma.

Poor thing.

She sat at the end of the bar, and he could tell by her pallor that she was at least six martinis in, maybe seven. He looked at his phone to confirm it, but he already knew what day it was just by the color of her dress. Thirty years prior, her father had died on the nineteenth of August. Now, every single month on the nineteenth, Norma commemorated his death. For every drink she had Nate made her have a glass of water and light a candle. The man had died on his eightieth birthday. Nate had found a candelabrum online that held each of the eight candles she lit for every decade of his life. It wasn't until he'd unwrapped it that he thought maybe it was a menorah. He'd been a little worried he might get in trouble for using it disrespectfully, if that was the case. On the other hand, the base was decorated with a ring of skulls, so it was possible that he was reading too much into the number.

Norma could get away with eight drinks, but only if she started early, only if she ate something solid – he usually bought her a sandwich from Nell's – and only if she took it slow. It was usually a long, sad day, but he liked that if she was going to be so sad, he was the one who was with her.

"Hey, sweetheart." Nate sat next to her instead of standing opposite her like he usually did.

Norma mumbled something almost inaudible.

"What was that?"

"Lighter. She didn't give me one." Another mumble. "Matches."

"She couldn't find them, huh?"

He grabbed the bag of candles. He stuck in all eight and found a lighter for her. "Here you go. Light 'em up."

"All eight?" Norma looked surprised and glanced out the window. "Already? It's still light out."

Even if she hadn't had eight drinks, the tear tracks meant she was cut off. Adele hadn't noticed her silent crying? "Yep, already. I'll walk you home after you light them and blow them out, okay?"

Norma struggled to insert the first candle, but then again, her hand wasn't steady even when she was sober. While she worked at it, Nate tried to catch his breath.

Anger lit inside him, a blue flame of heat. Adele wouldn't be good at this. Not even with training. This wasn't her world. He wanted to physically heave her onto the sidewalk and lock her out, and with the next breath he wanted to kiss her within an inch of her life. The push and pull of the two feelings was miserable, and he waited for his breath to slow.

Norma had all the candles lit and Colin was saying goodbye to Adele by the time Nate felt it was safe for him to sidle down the bar. "See you soon," he said, clapping Colin's hand in a shake. "Horseshoes? At the Doughertys'?"

"You got it. Hey, you need a hand with her?" Colin jerked his thumb towards Norma.

Adele gasped. "Don't arrest her! If she's too drunk, it's my fault for serving her."

Colin and Nate both laughed. "I meant walking her home," said the sheriff. "I'm happy to do it."

"You read my mind." Nate helped Norma blow out the candles. He hugged her for a long minute as she wept lightly against his chest, then gave her to the safekeeping of Colin. "Thanks, man."

"Anytime."

Then the saloon was empty.

Just the two of them. Nate sat back down on his bar stool on the customer side.

"I owe you a thank you." Adele rubbed the top of the bar with a napkin. She didn't wet it first and it just stuck to the varnish.

Nate waited.

She didn't say anything else.

So Nate said, "So go ahead, then. I'm waiting."

CHAPTER THIRTY-THREE

Nate waited to see what she'd say.

She pulled in her lips – those soft, still-slightly-swollen lips – and looked up at the ceiling. Her breasts were pert and perfectly displayed in the low-cut vee of her T-shirt. Nate dragged his gaze from them and back up to her eyes, those ridiculous, gorgeous blue eyes that reminded him of inland spring mornings when the mist from the crops rose into the clear sky.

"Thank you," Adele finally said. "Now that I realize who the sheriff is, I guess I'm a little less worried about what he would have done, but I'm glad for your help anyway."

"You know, we have to talk about this." *Keep fighting for it, Nate.* He could hear Hugh's voice in his ear. Why had Hugh wanted him to fight the girls for the property?

Was that really what he'd meant? Hadn't he been able to see how that would go? (What if he *had*? What if Hugh had had this in mind the whole time? Getting Nate hooked on one of the girls? He wouldn't have been so cruel, would he?)

Adele looked at the front door as if hoping someone – anyone – would enter. She wanted a distraction, obviously.

So he'd oblige, although he wasn't sure until he spoke whether he'd oblige with a kiss or an argument.

Fight won, though he regretted the lost kiss. "You're not fit to run this place." As openings for important conversations went, this one left something to be desired.

"Just because I was a little off my game doesn't mean I'm not fit," she countered. "It's not like I have any practice at it. And you didn't show up, leaving me to figure out every damn thing myself. I didn't even know where you hid the money until I remembered my uncle's floor safe."

Apparently she'd remembered his combination, too (DB123, not that hard when it came right down to it).

"Did you start the ice machine?"

She looked startled and glanced over her shoulder at the ice beast. "I thought it would just kick on when it got low."

"I bet it's low now."

Adele glared at him. "Do you know how small a thing that is? Learnable, all of those little things."

If she had someone to teach her. He wasn't going to be that guy.

But making her bristle wasn't going to do any good. It was pointless, and if he were her, it would just make him dig in his heels even deeper.

He drew his stool even closer to the bar, four inches closer to her on the other side. He smoothed his features. This was important. It was so important. "Look. You'd be an amazing bartender. I know that. But it's more than that, isn't it?"

Her eyes betrayed skepticism. "What do you mean?"

The jukebox *finally* changed, swinging into Patsy Cline's "Walking After Midnight'.

"What about the money?"

"What about it?" Her chin was up, challenging him.

"If you sell to me, you and your sisters walk away with cash."

"Probably not that much cash. This place is run into the ground."

That was the whole point – that was why he could afford it. "What about your home? Nashville?"

"I told you. This is home."

"What about your apartment?" Belatedly he remembered she'd told him she'd been evicted.

"Homeless. I'm itinerant." She crossed her arms. "That makes this place a whole lot more attractive."

"What about your friends? I'm sure you have some girlfriends you miss like hell."

She picked up a napkin and folded it into a small square. "Of course I do. But they're all either getting married or having babies or both."

"So?"

"It's different for women. Husbands get in the way. Once a woman is married, she says she'll stay in touch with her friends, but when that first baby comes along, she forgets about her babyless friends totally, like nothing existed before she gave birth. All she can talk about are children, and every conversation revolves around her kid." She unfolded the napkin, smoothing it against the top of the bar as if she could get rid of the wrinkles.

He stuck his hand in his pocket and gripped his mother's two-month chip. It was worn smooth from his rubbing it, and warm from being against his body. He kept his voice casual. "You don't want kids?"

"Of course I do." Her smile was a hundred watts. More. "But only when it's right."

The relief he felt was unwelcome. "How are you planning on keeping yourself from turning into one of those women?"

"Oh, I'm not. I plan on going whole-hog baby-crazy. I probably won't even speak to strangers on the street until I've deemed them worthy of hearing my baby stories. I'll be the worst of them all."

"Was your mom like that?" It had started out as a ploy, a plot to convince her to give up the idea of keeping the Golden Spike, but now, for some reason, he had to know what she might be like as a mother. *Nothing like mine.*

"No, actually. She was more shy than she would have liked. It was my dad who was friends with everyone. With the grocer and the big music producers. You know the ones."

He shook his head. "I know the grocers. Not the producers. I play guitar in a band whose biggest crowd was when we played homecoming a few years back."

She flashed him a quick smile. "There's a type of music producer who never marries, and never has kids. He dates women who get progressively younger and prettier, and my mother always said it wasn't their fault. The producers are kind of like gods, and pretty girls are placed on their altars. My point is: Dad was friends with them. Buzz Holden and T. Jones Barclay, they practically lived at our house when they were between girlfriends. They loved my mom, too, but she was a little harder to know. Post-partum never really let her go, I think."

"Does that scare you?" Nate could see her way too clearly, a baby on her hip, opening a screen door to let friends inside. For one second he saw himself in the backyard, firing up the barbecue, putting the beers on ice.

Shit.

This was crazy.

Adele had taken a second to think about it. "No. Mom and I were so different, in so many ways."

"What about your sisters? Do they have kids yet?"

Adele laughed. "No way. Neither of them could afford a baby."

He kept his voice gentle while he went in for the kill. "Wouldn't the money from the sale of the Golden Spike help them? What did they say when you asked?"

She stared over his shoulder but didn't respond.

It was all the answer he needed. "Why would you want to be tied down to this place, anyway? You could always come visit. Keep it as your home base. We could write that into the sale, that all three of you can stay for free whenever you wanted to. If there was someone in the room you wanted, I'd kick them out."

"Just like that." Her voice was small, and something about the way she'd tucked her head made him desperate to chew right through the wood of the bar to get to her, to fold her into his arms.

But he just said, "Yeah. Why tie yourself down? You're young. You could go anywhere. Why strap yourself to this place?"

Adele's head rose and she met his gaze, her eyebrows drawing together. "Wait. Why tie *yourself* down? You've still never told me why this place is so important to you."

"Yeah, I did."

"Uncle Hugh. I know. You said that. But I'm not buying that's all there is to it. There's something more. I can feel it."

She didn't deserve to know about his mother. "I'm just saying, working this place is like being married with none of the benefits. Since Hugh died, I haven't had a day off until today."

"And yet you're here."

"And yet I'm here."

"Why?"

You. You're the damn reason.

He didn't say the words out loud, but it seemed like maybe she heard him, clear enough. Her cheeks went bright pink, and she reached for one of the dirty glasses lined up on the bar waiting to be washed. She started washing it in the sink right in front of him, and every damn time she moved the glass under the running water, she had to lean forward enough that her T-shirt gaped. Just a little. Not like he could even see the top of her bra cup.

Just skin. Just soft, smooth, glorious skin that he could practically taste.

"You're doing it wrong," he rasped.

She narrowed her eyes, but didn't respond.

"No, seriously." He stood and moved – finally – around to the back of the bar, where he belonged, where his feet fit the floor. "This is the wash sink. Fill it like this, and add this soap and disinfectant. This is the rinse sink." He took another glass and dunked it, twisting it, hitting it with the soaped washrag and then pushed it in and out of the rinse water. "Fast. Done. See?"

"I see," she said.

They both froze in place, side to side, both their hands near the soapy water. The heat from the sink rose, practically making wavy lines in the air. Or was the warmth coming from her?

He half-turned, and his knee touched her leg. He waited for her to move away.

She didn't. Only five or six inches separated their torsos.

She had to move away because, God knew, he'd never be able to. It was an actual physical impossibility, like plucking protons from neutrons by hand.

Adele took a quick breath, so short he almost didn't hear it.

"You should let me buy the saloon from you." He moved his hand so that the back of it touched the back of hers. "Please."

Still she didn't answer.

He turned his head. Her cheek was right there. So close he could almost . . .

Then she turned her head, too. Their lips were a breath apart.

And there was nothing in the whole world that could keep him from kissing her.

Fast and hard, he wrapped an arm behind her back and drew her full-length against him. His mouth was hot against hers, and the way she gasped against his lips told him everything he needed to know. He put his other hand behind her neck and pulled her tighter against him. Her tongue was as insistent as his was, and she drove herself forward. Her fingers tangled in his hair and then gripped his shoulders.

"Let me buy the saloon." He would stop kissing her, of course, as soon as she asked him to. As soon as she stopped tugging at his belt. But for now, he kissed her more.

And Lord in heaven, the woman kissed him back.

Finally, he felt her say something against his lips. "Why?"

"Because you feel perfect." Everything about her was perfect, her lips, her breasts, the way her ass fit, cupped in his hands.

She gave a small laugh, and the kiss went carbonated. "Why do you want the bar?"

He honestly couldn't remember. "Because."

"And you get whatever you want."

"Yes." It was a lie, one he wished were true, because right now all he wanted was her.

She looked over her shoulder at the front door. "Anyone could come in."

"Anyone could." Though they probably wouldn't. This time of day there was always a lull between afternoon drinkers and evening socializers. "That *Open* sign says *Closed* on the back, y'know."

Surprise flashed in her eyes. "We couldn't."

"The place is empty. Likely to stay that way. Not like it'll hurt the rock-bottom line if we close up for a minute." He walked to the front, praying to every god there was she wouldn't change her mind. Her gorgeous mind. Which matched every other asset on her. He flipped the sign and shot the front lock.

"Rock-bottom line. That would make a good song title." Her words sounded nervous.

"Inventory." He paced back towards her, step by inevitable step. "In the back room. We should definitely check the stock levels, you think?"

Adele nodded, and bit her bottom lip. She leaned against a bar stool as if she were drunk, and he knew she hadn't had a drop. "Inventory," she said. "It's just good business."

Holy shit, man, you're so far over your head. "Adele –" He kissed her again, and tried to tell her how much he needed her with just that touch.

"Oh, Loretta *Lynn*."

Their kiss never broke as they made their way into the storeroom. Nate closed the door with one hand behind his back as his other hand undid the buttons of her fly. She pulled at his belt, seeming as impatient as he was.

Nate hadn't had sex in a storeroom since he'd lost his virginity to the cashier at the Stop and Shop in Fresno. That time had been fast and fumbled, awkward and apologetic.

This time? With Adele? He was shocked that the heat rising off their half-clothed bodies didn't make the bottles of liquor spontaneously combust. The gin could have exploded, the vodka could have gone up like a propane tank on fire, and they wouldn't have noticed.

"What about –"

He dug in his wallet and pulled out a condom. "A guy doesn't always have his guitar with him."

Gratifyingly, she laughed. Nate thought he could probably fly.

Then the condom was on, and instead of going slowly like they had the last time, just last night, she jumped up and sat on a stack of 7 Up boxes, wrapping a leg around his waist.

"Now," she said and then he was in her, hot and slick and fast, fucking her so hard he had to hold on to the metal shelf behind her, so fast her gasps against his ear sounded like his own, and maybe they shared the same breath. *Now, now, now.* Now was the only time in the world. There were only the two of them. Adele leaned forward and bit his shoulder so sharply he knew she'd leave teeth marks. He repaid her by biting her lower lip and thrusting into her harder.

He pushed his hand between them, pressing his thumb against her clit. She let out a curse, a real one, not a country singer's name, and ground herself against him. She tucked her forehead against the curve of his shoulder and wrapped her arm around his lower back, and Nate realized he'd never needed release more than that moment, and he needed release in her and basically there was probably nothing he'd ever want as much as her, and while she whispered his name in a strangled voice against his skin, he came, and he felt her coming around him, and then he had to wrap his arms around her to keep from falling to the floor. Blood pounded in his ears and black spots danced in the corners of his vision.

"Jesus," he finally said.

And she laughed.

Adele laughed, a peal of delight, and Nate – at that moment, at the pretty bird-like trill of it – fell in love like he'd fallen off a cliff.

CHAPTER THIRTY-FOUR

W hat had she done? Adele lifted her hands to her cheeks and laughed again. She'd just fucked Nate in the storeroom of Uncle Hugh's saloon. Jesus and Reba McEntire.

She'd never felt as bad-girl as she did at that moment.

And she'd certainly never felt as sexy as she did, seeing herself in his eyes.

They should probably at least pull up their jeans. The front door was locked – she'd seen him do it – but then again, there could have been someone out there making margaritas in the blender and she wouldn't have noticed.

"Lord." His voice was low at her ear, and there was a richness to it she hadn't heard before.

Then Nate kissed her.

And it was different. Last night, his kiss had been hot. When they'd launched themselves at the storeroom, their mouths had been an inferno.

This was . . . this kiss was something else.

It was something gorgeous and terrifying and so many million times more disturbing than just a hot kiss.

Adele couldn't be falling for this guy. No way. She was going to be his boss. Technically, she was already. You didn't fall for an employee. For that matter, she had no intention of falling for anyone anytime soon.

Why, then, did it feel like it was too late? Had her heart fallen like a wounded robin plummeting to earth, without giving her any kind of fair warning at all? How was she supposed to fix *this*?

Adele buttoned up her jeans.

She smoothed her hair.

She rubbed her eyes.

The whole time, even while he was snapping his belt buckle back into place with a clank, Nate was looking at her with a heat she couldn't quite name.

Adele just knew one thing for sure. She was in trouble. Big trouble.

"So. That was . . ." How was she supposed to finish that sentence? There wasn't really an adjective that was appropriate. *Fucking amazing* would have worked, but she seemed to have lost the ability to swear again.

"Adele –" Nate started.

"I have to get back out there." She pulled on her shirt, which had somehow landed on the concrete floor and bore the distinct impression of Nate's boot print. "Um. In case. I mean, you're not at work today. It's all me . . ."

"It's all you," he said, but his words made them sound very, very different.

She poked her head out into the main room. Still no one. Thank God. Norma hadn't let herself back in with the key, no one had broken in. She opened the door and the room stood empty, the ocean-scented wind the only thing occupying the bar stools. "We got away with it," she said, the laugh creeping back into her voice. She couldn't quite push down the hiccuping giggles, and she wanted nothing as much as to lock up the saloon for the rest of the night and take Nate back to her room and start everything all over again. And again. And again.

There were still things to talk about, though. Things to talk through. So she walked to the front and flipped the sign back to *Open*.

Then she set herself on a bar stool on the customer side, fitting her hands between her knees. "So." She knew the shape and weight of him. She knew how the underside of his tongue tasted. More than that, she knew how he rested against her, his cheek next to hers, his breath in her ear. How was she supposed to just talk with him?

He sat next to her, his boot heel propped on the lower rung of her stool. "Yep."

"I wonder if that's ever been done back there before," she said before she thought it through. If Nate had done that in the same spot, she honestly didn't want to know.

"Don't answer," she said at the same time as he said, "Not by me."

"What does that mean?"

"Nothing," he said.

"Did my uncle . . . ? No, *please* don't answer that."

"I won't." His grin was as wide as the Pacific.

"Oh, God. That means he did."

"My lips are sealed."

Adele gave a sharp laugh. "Oh, my God. What if it was that bartender of his? Old what's-her-name. Can you imagine?"

Nate's eyes narrowed.

Ignoring the voice that told her not to keep speaking, Adele said, "But he wouldn't, would he? Not someone like her."

"What does that mean?"

"Well, come on. I think my uncle would have had better taste than that. She was nice and all, with that big belly laugh she had. But she probably slept with anyone who would buy her a drink." There had been a sometime-employee at a friend's bar in Nashville – Allison – who'd brought in her boyfriends proudly when she had them. But when Allison was single, she shimmied her crotch against any man that would put up with it, in the hopes of getting a gin and tonic for free. "Uncle Hugh liked to save people, but I don't think even he would stoop to messing around with a boozer like her."

Nate's face twisted as if she'd just insulted a member of his family.

"I'm sorry," she said. "I didn't really know her. I guess you did."

"Whatever." He dropped his hand flat against the top of the bar. A dull thunk. "My beer's warm now. Can you get me another?"

The words felt like a slap, and Adele slipped off the stool. She needed her feet below her, strong on the wooden boards her great-grandfather had put in by hand. "Sure."

"Thanks." His chin jutted forward, and his eyes were clear lakes of frigid anger.

"Are you mad at me now?" What had she missed?

"Nah. Just thirsty."

Adele pulled another pseudo-black and tan and set it carefully on the bar in front of him. He kept his eyes on the old wood, his brows drawn together, his expression stormy.

"I'm sorry. What did I do?"

He snorted.

"Are you *punishing me* for having sex with you? Because screw you if that's it." The words hurt.

"Already did that, now I want the chaser." He took a loud sip. "Yeah, that hits the spot."

Adele's heart quailed. She could have sworn he had just felt – that they'd just had a connection. A real one. "Is this about us selling to you?"

"Well," he drawled insolently, "I knew it would cost me more than a lay. I'm prepared to write the check, too."

"Nate."

"Or will I have to fuck your sisters, too? Is that part of the deal?"

"What the *hell* is wrong with you?" *Her sisters.* Her sisters who were farther away from her than ever.

"You didn't think there was anything wrong with me a few minutes ago, when I was so far inside you that –"

"You're fired." The words were instant, and irrevocable.

He stood then, drawing himself up to his full height.

Adele's heart quickened, and her hands curled into fists.

"You want to run that past me one more time?" His voice was so quiet she almost couldn't hear it under the low whirr of the fan blade overhead.

"You're –" Her voice broke, and she started again. "You're *fired.*" Could a heart break, just like that? A huge part of her – the majority of her body and mind – wanted to apologize, wanted to take it back.

But he apparently thought she owed him something. Was that what this was about? Even worse, maybe he'd thought he *had* to fuck her to make the purchase go through.

She was – what did they call it? – a contingency. Maybe she was a nice one. He certainly hadn't had much problem doing it – the heat was real, she knew that much.

But the motivation, the deeper, scarier, lovely longing she'd thought she'd seen in his eyes, tasted on his breath, felt in his touch, wasn't real. It wasn't even close to real.

"Leave your keys on the counter." She turned her back on him and opened the till, even though she had no reason to do so. She pulled out the ones and started counting them. She lost track completely after seven so she just straightened them, unfolding creased corners and facing them all the same direction. From behind her, she heard keys slam onto the bar top. Then his footstep, heavy, thumping through the bar. The swinging door creaked furiously, and the iron security door banged shut with a thunderclap.

Adele had thought she was just falling – she had thought there was time to arrest her descent. But it seemed like maybe she was too late.

And it turned out there was a place even lower than the bottom.

CHAPTER THIRTY-FIVE

The rest of the night was horrible.

No, that wasn't it. A horrible night in a bar – Adele knew from past experience – was one in which you had to sing in front of people eating dollar hot dogs, too drunk to care about the act on the stage besides yelling lewd and usually-physically-impossible suggestions every once in a while.

Tonight wasn't like that.

She was stone-cold sober, for one thing. She'd seen drunk bartenders before (the old red-haired one jumped to mind) but Adele knew that if she were even a little bit tipsy, she wouldn't be able to do a single thing right, and as it was, she was getting enough wrong already. She'd slung a cherry into a gin martini and an olive into a Tom Collins, one of the beer taps was clogged, and the sink appeared to be backing up.

And if *one* more person asked her where Nate was, she might throw something. There were plenty of good things to choose from. Small shot glasses would hit the floor like a tiny detonation. Bigger rocks glasses would quiet the whole, packed bar.

The *packed* bar. Where had all these people come from?

Adele wasn't naive. This was her town, after all. She knew that a Monday night in September should have been one of the slowest nights in the bar's history. She'd been counting on it. A drinker or two, sure. She'd planned on being professional and then running to the back room to cry before the next one came in.

But the place was freaking packed with bodies.

And she wasn't imagining it – people were staring at her. She knew the weight of that gaze, and she was wilting under it. She'd caught two ranchers openly whispering about whether she was staying in town or out in the new hotel up the highway. She didn't react, topping off their water glasses with what she hoped was a chipper smile.

It felt more chipped than chipper, though.

It wasn't even like she could go hide in the storeroom. She'd be lucky if she was ever able to make herself go into that room again. The space in there was too full to fit her into it – full of the image of him over her, the way his eyes had burned into her own, the way he'd felt inside her. The words she'd thought he'd said with his eyes. She thought they'd been talking about love.

Stupid, stupid Adele.

Donna. That had been the old bartender's name, she finally remembered.

At midnight, the jukebox, which she'd very carefully queued up to play the good stuff – Hank and Dolly and Johnny – suddenly lurched into a Songbird tune.

Wait till your father gets home, just a little longer now.

It was the song that had played earlier, a song that would always break her heart into a million pieces. Earlier, while working with the jukebox's programming, she'd tried to delete the song entirely, but she hadn't been able to figure it out. Why, in a town like Darling Bay, did they have a damn new-fangled digital jukebox? It wasn't right.

I swear to the moon above, he'll be home soon, my love.

The shot of brandy she'd been pouring into Pastor Jacob's glass landed on the top of the bar instead.

"You all right?"

Adele didn't care. "Who put this on?"

No one answered her.

So she raised her voice. "I'm serious. Who put this album on?"

"Shuffle, maybe?" The rancher who answered rubbed a finger alongside his nose.

"No. Someone put this song on *on purpose*." She said it as if it were against the law.

No one, except the startled pastor in front of her, seemed to take her sudden release of emotion seriously. Instead – goddammit – most of them seemed to be singing along. Heads nodded, and a low murmur rose at the chorus. Good God in heaven. They really were singing.

Wait till your father gets home, wait a little longer . . .

For one moment, Adele's heart felt as if it had become a red paper one, carefully cut out for a Valentine's Day gift for someone who wouldn't care, who would take pleasure in ripping it up. The pieces fluttered to the floor, leaving nothing but an empty space in her chest.

That emptiness made it a whole hell of a lot easier to reach behind the jukebox and yank out the cord.

Voices continued for a moment, as if it were an acapella part of the song. But they stopped, one by one, when they caught sight of Adele's face.

She climbed up to kneel on the bar stool that leaned drunkenly against the jukebox. "Closing time! Sorry, y'all!"

A man who'd been drinking doubles all night slurred, "Last callsh what you mean, honey. You don't just getta close."

Adele stared at him. Then she channeled Hugh on a grumpy night, and jumped down from the stool. She stalked to the man who stank of bourbon and nicotine from the cigarettes he'd been smoking on the front porch between drinks. She picked up his glass, still half full.

"Hey, I paid for that, honey." He pawed comically in the air, nowhere near the glass.

"Yeah. You did." Adele pushed open the half-door motioning him outside. "Why don't you have another smoke?"

"Well!" The man wobbled, then patted his shirt pocket, digging out his cigarettes with a hooked finger. "Good idear."

Adele tossed the liquid out so far that it half-landed on the edge of the porch and the rest wetted the parking spot in front. "There's your drink. Enjoy."

"You little – why, I oughta –" The man bobbed a bit, his knees doing a slow but repetitive buckle.

Adele turned to face him. The guy had been a jerk all night, hadn't left even a single dollar for a tip. She'd relish the chance to call the cops on him for drunk and disorderly. Carefully placing her hands on her hips, she faced him. "You ought to what?"

"I . . . I . . ."

"Get the hell out of my bar." It felt good. It felt right. And Lord, she missed Uncle Hugh.

The man lurched sideways, aiming his footsteps off the porch and right into the traffic lanes. Luckily it was Monday night at midnight in Darling Bay, and the street was empty.

"Not very hospitchable." Adele could almost see him coming up with his next thrown barb. "I'm gonna – I'm gonna tell *Nate* on you when he's back! He'll show *you* what's what, all right!" Finally back on the sidewalk, the drunk tilted southward, stumbling as he went.

Nate.

Nate wouldn't be back.

A spike of something horrible and cold shot up her spine. She could *feel* the other customers clustered at the window and the door, and sure enough, she had to push her way through to get back inside. "Show's over," she said. "Everyone *out*."

This time no one argued with her.

And no one met her eye as they shuffled out the front door.

That was the worst part of all. Most of the people leaving weren't impaired. They weren't over the limit. They'd just been hanging out with friends, spending time in the bar because this was Darling Bay and a new bartender firing the old one was – literally – the most interesting thing to happen since the library had gotten a new card catalogue system.

As the half-door swung closed behind the last, silent person, Adele pulled the iron door shut. The click was unsatisfying and she shot the deadbolt home, trying hard not to remember when Nate had bolted it earlier in the day, just for those few stolen minutes.

She went into the middle of the wooden dance floor. She sat, cross-legged. Then she flopped backward and looked up into the rafters. Even more cobwebs up there. With her luck, they were strung by brown recluses and black widows.

And even though she'd unplugged the jukebox, the song kept playing in her head, as clearly as if she were in the recording booth. As her sisters" remembered voices filled her ears, she cried the way she'd wanted to since Nate had left.

I swear to the moon above, he'll be home soon, my love.

When Adele was young, she and her sisters had ridden bikes all over Darling Bay, up the hills and into Radiant Valley on the other side. The best ride had been straight up Devil's Mound. (It felt like a mountain to them – now Adele realized it was barely a hill.) The path had been rocky, strewn with blackberry that threatened to choke closed the narrower parts of the path. Every single time, one or more of the girls got a flat tire. Adele loved it when they did. Such an easy fix, so simple and satisfying. While whichever sister it was sat on the side of the dirt path, making a necklace out of pine needles or daisy stems, complaining because of the heat or the wind or the fog, Adele got to work with her patch kit. She'd gotten so good she could patch a tire and reinflate it in under three minutes. It had been like a game.

Now, sitting on the dance floor under the cobwebs, tears leaked from her eyes like the patch she'd applied hadn't held. There was no glue strong enough to stick her back together. Things that were simple when they were children weren't simple anymore. Okay, that wasn't totally true, she thought on a hiccup. She bet she could still patch a tire if not in three minutes, then pretty dang quickly.

But the rest of it.

No sisters.

No Nate.

Nothing but this falling-down shell of a building. The hotel and café that needed to be gutted.

Which was exactly the way she felt.

Adele gave one last hollow sob as the song ended in her mind. Then she stood, slowly. She did the closing things that made sense to her to do. She washed everything. She mopped. She counted the money, all six hundred dollars of it. Whatever she'd forgotten, she could do in the morning. For now, she'd satisfy herself by turning out the lights and locking the door behind her.

She turned off the white lights in the courtyard, and without the way they lit the fog, the back porch just looked sad. Lonely.

Then, without asking herself why she did it, she peeked into each room. Rooms three, four and five all smelled like they should be opened up and aired out. For weeks. Maybe years. Rooms six, seven, and eight were so damp that she knew they'd need to tear open the walls. Rooms nine, ten and eleven were as open as they could be to the elements, covered only by the flapping blue tarps overhead.

It was overwhelming. Completely and utterly. And what was she looking for, anyway? Ghosts? Vagrants? Old western haunts, having one last romp at the old hotel?

No.

Nate.

She was looking for him. And damn it, the realization pissed her off.

But Adele wouldn't cry. That time of the night was over and she was firmly committed now to being strong.

Totally strong. She could do this. She *had* this.

It lasted until she opened the door of room twelve.

Inside, the ceiling still stood open to the stars, waiting on a new roof. But there was something new: a sleeping bag carefully laid out on a mat. One pillow.

And Nate's guitar, the one he'd played onstage eleven days before.

Nothing else.

"Nate?" Her heart in her throat, she flipped the light switch and was surprised – ridiculously so – when nothing happened. "Are you in here?"

Of course he wasn't.

But he had been. He'd been sleeping here.

It didn't make sense. Adele's brain felt like she'd been on board a boat all day – wobbly and confused to be standing on land. Her legs shook. But *he* was the one who was supposed to be on a boat. Right? Living on board? That's what he'd told her when he'd given her his room.

She backed out slowly, pulling the door all the way shut, and ran to her room as quietly as she could. One more night in it, one more night before Hugh's apartment was livable.

Maybe, if she stayed flat on her back and faced the ceiling all night, maybe then she wouldn't risk smelling him in the sheets. Maybe then she could keep herself from falling apart.

CHAPTER THIRTY-SIX

I need a job."

In the small white room which passed for the sheriff's office, Colin McMurtry looked more amused than anything else. Nate kind of felt like wiping the smirk off his face. Screw the fact that they were friends.

"What about the bar?"

"I quit."

"You quit?" The tone of the sheriff's voice implied he knew the difference between quitting and getting fired, and he knew which one had happened to Nate.

"Whatever. Yeah. I'm out of that place. I can't work for her."

"Who?" Colin was acting dumb, something Nate couldn't stand anyone doing, let alone one of his best friends.

"Shut it. Just tell me how I start."

Colin laughed and sat behind the big wooden desk which took up most of the small space. He pointed at the red plastic chair on the other side of it. "Sit down. I won't bust your ass anymore. What's going on?"

"Nothing." Nate bent his neck sideways in a stretch. He'd stayed on Dixie's tiny couch last night, and there was no sleeping platform more uncomfortable in the whole wide world, he'd bet. He just hadn't been able to stomach the idea of staying (hiding, really) on the Golden Spike property. Not for a minute longer. "It's just, I've got – I guess I've got basically nothing left." The admission surprised him as much as it hurt.

Kindness flickered in Colin's eyes. "The bar?"

"Is hers. Theirs. Definitely not mine."

"So you quit."

It was kind of him to say that. "Yeah."

"So what are you going to do now?"

"Are you even listening to me? That's why I'm here. I need a job."

"Nate –"

"Don't tell me I'm not qualified. I have a bachelor's degree in social work, which is about four more years" education than any of your other deputies have."

"You want to be a *deputy*? I thought you meant, like, a clerk or something."

Nate settled his feet firmly on the floor. "Why the surprise?"

"It's just –"

"It's a good job. Probably pays a lot more than bartending, if John Sinclair's new house means anything."

"His mother owns the lumber mill."

"Still."

"Nate."

Nate closed his eyes and drew air in through his nose. Soon this part would be over and he could just move forward with his life.

His Adele-free life.

"What?"

"This is not the job for you."

"How would you know that?"

"I know." Colin leaned forward and picked up a pen. Without looking down, he doodled small, perfect squares on his calendar blotter. "Look, you think you want to help people."

Nate felt his cheeks heat as he watched the small squares, as if hypnotized.

He wouldn't have said it out loud, not just like that, not to Colin, but yeah. If he couldn't take care of people at the bar, he'd damn well take care of them some other way. Being a police officer would let him do it, right? Helping old ladies cross the street (and there were a lot of old ladies in Darling Bay), occasionally saving a woman's life from a shithead who wanted to hurt her. That would be just fine. He imagined a scowling scumbag towering over Adele in the bar, and anger lit the fuse that seemed to be perma-curled at the base of his neck. Adele should take a self-defense class if she was going to be at the bar late. Samantha Rowe taught some ass-kicking ones. Nate had never had a gun behind the bar, but maybe he should get her one. Tell her it was Hugh's. Make her learn to use it.

As if she would even talk to him.

"I do want to help people." Yeah, it sounded cheesy said aloud, too.

"*Definitely* not the right job for you, then."

"Damn it, man, stop messing with me." Nate's temper was frayed and getting thinner by the second. The knot in his throat wasn't helping anything.

Colin drew a circle and then another one, connecting them with an arrow before he responded. "You want my job, then?"

"Okay, any job. Put me on the desk. How about meter maid? Put me in one of those three-wheeled car things, I'll write tickets all day until you promote me to officer."

"Go be a firefighter."

Nate gave a hollow laugh. "And run into burning buildings? I may want to help people but I'm not crazy."

"Police don't help people."

"Come off it. I'm serious." Nate's annoyance meter crept into the red again.

And so, it seemed, did Colin's. He flung the pen to the right, not even blinking when it hit the wall. "You know how much I hate this job sometimes?"

Nate folded his arms over his chest. "You can't tell me you don't help people."

"Sure I do. Sometimes. Most of the time, though, I'm just reacting to something that I can't do a damn thing about. I'm trying to protect a little boy from his grandma who verbally abuses him so bad he's going to need therapy by eighteen. Old people, living in filth, refusing all offers of help." His knuckles went white on the pen. "Or I'm going out yet again to the home of a woman who keeps bringing the guy who beats her back inside. Those guys kill their women eventually, or they smother their spirits forever. And the women don't listen." Colin gave a heavy sigh that made him sound older than his mid-thirties.

"I can do that."

"You can what?"

"Make them listen. Keep them from going back to the bad guys."

Colin snorted. "You don't actually believe that."

"Why not?"

"How did talking your mom out of drinking go?"

Nate narrowed his eyes. "Low blow, you ass. Alcoholism is a disease."

"It's exactly the same. It's you wanting a different outcome for someone else."

"What's *wrong* with that?"

"Oh, my God." Colin sounded honestly shocked. "You really don't get it, do you?"

Nate felt his neck get hotter. "I can be talked down to at most other places in this town, you know."

Colin leaned forward. "You can't change anyone."

Nate took off his ball cap. He punched into it, as if it were a baseball mitt he was breaking in. "I know."

"No, you *don't*. You really thought you could save your mom, I knew that. I thought she was your blind spot. But seems like she was just a symptom, huh? For a greater problem." Colin nodded in what seemed like satisfaction. "And *that's* why you stay at the bar. I finally get it. But you have to listen to me: you can't change one damn person. *Ever*. All you can do is be there to help pick up the pieces sometimes. That's about the best we get in this life. It turns out I like picking up those pieces, and I like tossing assholes who break things – and people – into jail and watching them wish they could change what they did. Occasionally I hear an apology that matters, that means something. But besides that, we just have to let people do what they want to do."

"You really believe that?" Nate resisted the urge to kick the waste basket next to the door. He shoved his hat back onto his head.

"I do."

"If you believe that, then why would you try to change *my* mind on the topic?"

Colin had the grace to look surprised. "Guess you're right. Are you okay?"

"Yeah," lied Nate. "I'll see you around." He turned, hitting his elbow on the doorframe in his haste. From the front office he heard Sweetie Swensen say something to someone about a warrant. Somewhere a window slammed shut.

"Hey, Nate." The sheriff's voice rose behind him. "Your degree. Go see Peggy at APS."

Nate just wanted out. "What?"

"Peggy Simon. She works for the city. Runs our Adult Protective Services."

Surprise was a dull thud. "We have that? In Darling Bay? We *need* that?"

"You'd be surprised."

Nate took a moment and mentally collated the elderly he personally kept an eye on. There had to be ten of them. Maybe eleven.

Colin shook his head. "You're not taking care of all of them, buddy. It might feel like you are, but you're not. You're barely scraping the surface. There are plenty of elderly who can't get out of their houses even to get into their gardens, let alone make it to the bar to socialize. Go talk to Peggy. Tell her I sent you."

"Fine." If moods could be seen, his would be blacker than sin, with dark red anger radiating at the edges. But Colin was trying, Nate could tell. "Thanks. I guess."

"And remember. You can't save anyone. Not even her."

Everyone. He could at least *try* to save everyone. And he refused to admit that he knew who Colin was talking about. Because he wasn't thinking about Adele. Not for one second.

"No one," reiterated Colin. "No matter how pretty she is or how blue her eyes are. You can help 'em, sure. If they want it, and if they're willing to accept your help. But that's it."

The starkness of it was terrifying, and Nate hated it. Hell if he'd show Colin that, though. "You're a pain in the ass. And you're wrong."

"Just think about it."

"Screw you."

Colin laughed. "Yeah. Well. What are friends for?"

Nate, walking out into the sunshine in front of the police department, was so irritated it felt like he could pull his own skin off. The saloon had been the only place he'd ever imagined himself helping people. He'd found his way there, and he hadn't planned on leaving it. He hadn't ever thought about where he would go, what he would do without the bar, without the patrons he took care of.

But maybe Colin was right, maybe there was a place in the world he could do more. A place he could do *better*.

The image of Adele's face, bright with laughter and hope, filled his mind.

Maybe he'd hidden behind that swinging half-door for too long.

CHAPTER THIRTY-SEVEN

Adele spent the morning fixing the porch swing in front of room one. It was a minor job, handled by an hour's worth of work, the use of Uncle Hugh's toolbox, and thirty bucks spent at the hardware store. When the swing's chains were rehung into a beam that looked ten times more solid that the one it had thunked out of, she was covered in sweat and had regained the smallest feeling of control.

She sat, dialed her sister, and promptly lost that feeling.

"What?"

"Don't hang up."

Adele could hear the groan that Molly stifled. "I don't have time for this."

"You're on a cruise ship. You have time."

"*They* have time. The customers have time. I have a *job*. Something you forget, constantly."

She did. Nerves swam in the pit of her stomach, and her mouth went dry. "I'm sorry."

"I know. You always say that."

"And it's not enough."

"Seriously, Adele, I do *not* have the bandwidth for this today."

Adele kicked her legs too hard and the swing gave a massive groan. Wind riffled the edges of the rose petals, stripping some into the air. Fall was almost here. "You were right. You were always right."

Molly's voice was guarded. "What?"

"I shouldn't have made us go up onstage that night. I shouldn't have finished singing. I shouldn't have apologized to the crowd."

"Adele –"

"Your reaction was the right one."

"I fainted. I hit my head and came up bleeding. It was not a good reaction."

"And I kept singing."

"You've apologized before. I know you're sorry."

"I was sorry for the wrong thing. I said I was sorry it happened. I was sorry that we didn't finish the tour. That you hit your head. But I never said you were right. And that I was wrong, and I'm sorry that I thought I knew better than both of you. I can't imagine how painful that was."

There was a pause, full and heavy. Adele held her breath.

"I – yeah, it was painful."

"I'm sorry," said Adele again. She'd keep saying it. She'd keep meaning it.

"I thought you'd never figure out why we were so hurt. We needed to be alone. Together, the three of us. Instead you put us in front of the whole world."

"I don't know why it took me so long."

"Well. Damn." Molly sounded exhausted. "It was a long time ago. We've all moved on."

"That's the problem." The words felt jagged. "Moving on is good. It's what we needed to do. But I miss my sisters."

Another long pause. "Well . . ."

"What?"

"I think I'm about to get fired."

"What happened?"

"The cruise line changed hands. Rumor is they're letting everyone go and picking up new crew in Indonesia."

Hope beat frantically inside Adele's chest. The biggest, yellowest rose nodded in the wind in front of her. "*Fly home.*"

"Adele."

"Please."

Everything hung on the space between them, the line pulled so tight it almost felt like a cord. "I'll think about it."

"Oh, God. Yes. *Please* think about it." It would do for now.

"How's the bartender?"

The words tumbled out in a jumble, with small plastic clicks, like the Sorry! pieces made against each other on the game board. "I'm in love with him." She touched the blue piece, the broken one, that she put in her pocket every day.

"Oh, honey."

"And I hurt him really badly." She'd taken his bar away.

"Well, did he hurt you?"

The question surprised her. "Yes." He'd thought so little of her that he'd hoped a roll in the hay would be part of a business transaction.

"So apologize. Move on."

"It's not that easy."

Molly's voice was so soft Adele could almost not hear her. "Sometimes it is. It can be. Just accept him." *Like you should have done with us.*

Adele cleared her throat, suddenly thick with emotion. "Do you have Lana's address?"

"Um."

"Come on."

"She told me not to give it to you."

"I promise you I won't hound her. I just found something here I want to send her." She touched the Sorry! piece. Dot Rillo would have wrapping paper at the post office.

What was Nate doing? How had the man gotten so firmly into her blood that he felt like a need, as essential as water or air?

She shook her head. First things first. She would take the photo she'd found to the art supply store, see if they could blow it up. Rush order. She'd buy a frame for the picture, and then she'd hang it where all could see.

She'd buy wrapping paper for the Sorry! piece. She would focus on that. She'd only need a little bit of paper, a stamp and an envelope.

And a whole lot of hope.

CHAPTER THIRTY-EIGHT

Adele had been worried Dixie would be hard to find but it turned out there was only one mobile home park in Darling Bay. All she had to do was ask Dot Rillo at the post office, and she had her fill of not only directions, but a whole litany of what the postal worker thought about Dixie. "You know, she's not a local. Not like you are, dear. But she's just fine, in spite of that. In the Christmas town pageant last year, she played a sheep for all she was worth. She had the best *baaaas* of anyone."

Adele and her sisters had spent at least four or five Christmases in town when they were young. "Isn't that a kid's part?"

Dot looked at her in surprise. "The children need a good role model, of course. How else would they know how to be a sheep?"

"Okay then." Adele waved the map Dot had drawn on a change-of-address form. "Thank you for this."

"Any time. Tell her I have a box from Amazon here and I think it feels like candles."

"All right."

"And tell her to order the bayberry-scented ones next time. I'm allergic to vanilla. It's been making me sneeze."

At the mobile home park, sure enough, there was only one pink-and-silver trailer in the whole place. And instead of appearing tawdry, the place looked adorable. Two tall plastic flamingos were stuck into a potted palm, and wind chimes danced. In every window, bits of color shone. The postmaster had mentioned Dixie was a stained-glass artist, and here was the evidence of that.

Dixie popped out the door at the knock. "Madge, I told you – oh, crap." She gave a puny cough. "Sorry. Excuse me." She rubbed her throat and pulled at the front of her yellow banana-printed pajamas. "This cold, you know."

"You're not in trouble."

Dixie came all the way out and stood with Adele on the small circle of fake green grass. "Are you sure?"

Adele nodded. "Sure."

"Because it wasn't really . . ." Dixie clammed up.

"Your idea? I know. It was his. He's why I'm here." Adele couldn't quite bring herself to say his name. *Nate.*

"Coffee?" Dixie looked up at the sky. "Look at that. I'm up before noon."

"I wouldn't say no."

"Sit." Dixie gestured to a pink plastic table with matching chairs under a palm frond awning. "I'll be right out."

The coffee Dixie made was hot and strong. It reminded Adele of the coffee Molly made. They used to tease her about her coffee being able to strip paint and clean silver. The back of Adele's throat ached. Maybe she was catching Dixie's nonexistent cold.

"So. What do you need to know?"

Adele took another sip. "*Great* coffee."

"Thank you. And I know this isn't a social call. What's up?"

"It could be a social call."

Dixie nodded slowly, suspicion in her eyes. "Sure. Most of my friends call or text before they come over, though. When they just drop out of the sky at the crack of dawn –"

"It's after nine!"

"Oh, God, it's *that* early? I just went to bed." Dixie held her ceramic mug like she wanted to hug it. "So if you're not here to fire me, too, then –"

"You heard?"

"That you fired Nate? Of course I did."

"Oh, God."

"Come on. You know there's no one in town who doesn't know."

"The postmaster didn't seem to know."

Dixie's eyes widened. "She tweeted about it."

"Dot Rillo put it on *Twitter*?"

"Of course."

"Does Nate know that?"

Dixie shook her head, and her short curls bounced. "I doubt Nate even knows what Twitter is."

Just the sound of his name made something hurt in Adele's chest. Was she too young to have a heart attack? It ran in the family, after all. Wasn't this the way they started? With a dull ache in the chest, followed by a foggy feeling of confusion? A deep well of sadness? That was totally medical. She knew it. "Can you tell me where he docks his boat?"

"Sorry?" Dixie blinked and stirred her coffee lazily.

"His boat. The one he's been living on. Is it at the main marina? What's it called?" She would go find it and – and then she'd come up with a plan.

"He doesn't have a boat."

"Yes, he does." Adele heard the ludicrousness of her words. As if she knew more about Nate than Dixie did. "He told me he's been staying on it while I'm in his room."

"Yeah, well, he lied to you."

"He never had a boat?"

"Oh, sure." Dixie smiled. "He had one. He loved that thing. But the bank turned him down the last time he applied for a preapproved loan, saying it was too old a boat to be counted as security. It was just a liability. So he sold it to Ruthann, and she put it in dry dock. She lives on it with her dog. If you want to see it, it's just over there, on the other side of the gazebo. That big white yacht is mostly hiding it, but it's right behind it."

A seagull swooped down and perched on the edge of the pink table, making it rock. Adele's coffee spilled.

"Oh, sorry. Shoo, you vile thing."

And even though Adele knew Dixie was talking to the bird, for a moment, she really did feel vile.

"When?"

"When did he sell the boat? Oh, maybe five months ago? Yeah. The loan got preapproved just before summer. I remember, because we were hanging new white lights in the arbor, taking down the strands that committed suicide over the winter."

"So he was never staying there."

Dixie tilted her head. "Probably not."

"He lied."

"To make you feel better, he probably did. He does that."

Adele rubbed her hands against each other. The sunlight was warm on her shoulders, but she felt chilled to the bone. "Well, he shouldn't."

"Yeah, well. He takes care of people. If it hadn't been you he put in his room, it would have been someone else. Heck, he put me in there when we first met. Though back then he *was* still sleeping on his boat."

"Why does he do it?"

"Put people in his room at the hotel? Because he could, I guess. Probably goes back to his mother."

"What do you mean?" Something prickled at the back of Adele's neck.

"You know. Him taking care of her for so long."

"His mother?"

"You knew her, didn't you?"

Adele shook her head. "I don't think so. How would I have known her? He's from Fresno, right? Somewhere around there?"

"Donna."

The inside of Adele's brain went quiet. "Who?"

"The bartender. You knew that was his mom, right?"

Adele covered her mouth with her fingers. "Oh, God."

"A lot of people didn't know that, but I thought you would have."

"Why wouldn't he tell me?"

Dixie shrugged. "He didn't really tell anyone."

"He was embarrassed."

"No, that's the weird thing. Hugh told me Donna made him swear not to tell people. Not till she was sober."

"But . . ."

Dixie raised her mug as if in salute. "And she never got sober. She went a couple of months a few times, I think. Hugh said she had a whole six-month plan. That if she could stay dry for half a year, she'd believe she'd really done it and then Nate could brag to everyone who she was. She wanted to have a big party. She said she needed to make them believe in her. But she was wrong about that."

"You don't think Nate believed she'd quit?"

"No. The opposite. She had two people who totally believed in her – both Nate and Hugh."

"I don't understand. Family is family. I don't understand how he could keep that a secret."

"Donna wanted him to be proud of her, and she was even more stubborn than he is. It was her plan." Dixie kicked her feet up on an empty chair. "And she wouldn't budge from it."

"How did *you* know, then? He told you?"

"Nah. I overheard Hugh talking to him one night."

"He believed that she would quit drinking." Adele remembered that she'd never seen a woman pack away more alcohol and stay on her feet. She remembered how Donna had smelled the next morning, when she came wobbling in to work and Uncle Hugh sent her up to his place for a nap and a shower. "Why? Why on *earth* would he believe that would ever happen?"

"Because Nate believes in people. That's what he does."

"I told him she probably slept with men for drinks."

Dixie's mouth formed a perfect, shocked O.

Adele put her forehead briefly on top of the pink plastic tabletop. "I know," she mumbled to her shoes. "And then I fired him."

"Hoo, boy. That's a shitstorm, right there. How are you doing?"

It was how Dixie said it that made Adele lift her head. Dixie's voice was kind. Soft.

She was listening.

It felt so good to be listened to by someone who looked as if she cared. Adele couldn't have stopped the words from tumbling out of her mouth if she'd tried. "I'm so *mad* at him."

"What did he do?"

"It's . . ." It didn't feel hard to admit the truth to Dixie. "He thought, because I slept with him, that meant I'd sell to him. Or that I was thinking about it, that he would get me to reconsider."

Dixie laughed. "With the power of his cock! Oh! That's good."

"You can't laugh at that!"

It seemed to make Dixie laugh more. "Oh, yes, I can. That's hilarious."

"*How* is it funny?"

"Because I've always said that sex ruins everything. Especially business. And trust me, I have experience with this. So he thought y'all were going to be celebrating the close of the deal?"

"I think so. Maybe. Yes."

"He's always been damn sure he'd end up owning the place."

"He never had the right! Where did he get that from?"

"You know, honey. Just sheer hope. The Golden Spike was the one place his mother loved. He took care of her when she couldn't take care of the bar. And then he took care of the bar, too, when Hugh got too old to do it. Like I said. It's what he does. Hugh said he could have the place if y'all didn't come home, and he was close to believing you never would."

Adele felt like she'd tuned in to a station that wasn't coming in clearly. If she moved her head, maybe it would get clearer. She shifted in her seat. Nope. Still static. "And then I came to town. And worse, I went and goddamn fell in love with him."

Dixie leaned forward, a small smile at her mouth. "I know."

"No, you didn't."

"Honestly, who wouldn't fall in love with that man? I like women, and I'm half in love with him myself."

Adele gave a laugh that felt more like a sob. "What do I do now?"

"Oh, honey. I'm so bad at relationships I live in a trailer so I won't accidentally let someone move in."

"Really?"

"Kind of. The one I want to move in is already living with someone else."

Adele nodded and perched her elbows on the table. "So we're both doomed."

"Yep."

"I have to apologize to him."

"Um . . ." Dixie, for the first time, looked unsure.

"What?"

"Didn't you say you called his mother, like . . . a whore?"

Adele felt her face go red. "I didn't say that. I just – oh, God. I did. That's exactly what I said. How am I supposed to fix this?"

"And didn't you say that you thought he slept with you to get the bar from you?"

"I don't know." Adele hit her knee on the underside of the table. "I don't feel like I know anything except that I want to fix it."

"Maybe you can't." Dixie looked into her tilted mug as if she'd find more coffee at the bottom of it.

"Oh, no. That's my superpower. I can always fix things. Always."

Dixie shook her head. "And Nate always thinks he can keep things safe. Sometimes –"

"Don't say it."

"You're both wrong a lot, that's all I'm saying."

Adele dug her heels into the Astroturf, making an almost inaudible sound. "I can fix it."

"Okay, then. Good luck."

"I can." She straightened and tried to believe herself. "I *will* fix it. All of it."

She had to.

CHAPTER THIRTY-NINE

N ate entered the bar at the very last minute. He went straight to the stage without looking towards the cash register. He didn't want to see either one of them – Dixie, because she'd probably laugh at him or something, and there was nothing funny in the whole world.

Or Adele.

Because he'd gone and gotten twisted up over that woman, as twisted as old, rusted barbed wire. Good for nothing but making people bleed and snapping under any weight at all.

"You're here!" Mack looked happy, if happiness could be judged when the guy never took off his sunglasses. "I thought you'd chicken out."

"You didn't leave me much choice, did you?"

"Hey, we can't play without a guitarist."

"There have to be a hundred in this town."

"None that know our songs."

"Our songs ain't hard."

Scrug looked up from fiddling with a leg on his kick drum. "Hey, don't insult our songs. No one needs more than three chords."

"Hi."

The voice came soft, from behind him. He should have known. She crept up on a man like the flu – you didn't see it coming till you were flat out and done for, almost dead.

"Hey."

"I'm glad you're here."

Why bother pulling punches? "So you can gloat?" Nate finally turned, and immediately wished he hadn't. She was in some light-colored doily-like dress that pulled in at her waist with a red belt, accentuating her high breasts. The skirt was short enough to show enough leg to make a man crazy. Shiny red heels. Red lips to match. She looked a cherry on top of whipped cream, and he'd always been a sucker for sundaes. "Or because Dust & Rusty packs 'em in? Just in it for the money?"

"I'm sorry."

He walked past her. Yeah, he'd made it his life's mission never to drink when he was upset, but he'd never had to play a gig in a bar in front of the woman who'd stomped on his heart *and* stolen his dream. He would help himself to a rum and Coke, God help her if she tried to stop him. This was still his place. In his heart, this was still where he *belonged*. Here, with these people. Norma was sitting at the bar. Was she looking skinnier? Sometimes she forgot to eat protein altogether if he didn't remind her. She was talking to Parrot Freddy, laughing raucously at something he'd said (or maybe it was something the parrot, Ethel, had said). Willie Rayburn and his brother Wagoner were playing dice in their own leather cups (the bar's cups had never been quite sturdy enough for their tastes). Lily Dario was just disappearing out the back door into the courtyard, hand in hand with one of the two Petes. He'd have to ask her about that later.

Or maybe he wouldn't.

He couldn't take care of the whole damn world.

His boots stalled, though, on the threshold of going behind the bar.

It was her place.

She'd fired him.

He wasn't doing real well taking care of anyone, not even himself. He didn't work here, and he couldn't help himself to a damn thing. It would be wrong to push her. And for once, he wished like hell he *was* the type to push a woman, to push her as far as she'd go before she snapped.

But goddammit. He wasn't.

A bag of salt and vinegar chips hit him in the chest. Adele grinned at him. "Want a drink?"

She was too cheeky. Too insouciant. He couldn't play that game tonight – what the hell had he been thinking? He wanted to kiss her, to take her to bed, to yell at her all night, to listen to her yell back. He couldn't play guitar and sing, not in front of her . . .

And then Nate looked up.

Over her head.

"What the hell." It wasn't a question. He knew what it was; he just didn't know how it had gotten there.

"Do you like it?" Adele looked worried, as if his opinion mattered to her.

The huge frame over the mirror held a blown-up photo of Hugh. And Nate's mother. They were grinning at each other, standing at the bar they were now overlooking, expressions of sheer delight in both their faces.

It was a gut punch of emotion that threatened to level him, and that, by God, was *not* okay. "Where did that come from?"

"I found a small version in Hugh's apartment. Also framed. I got it blown up. I'm not sure who the photographer was that day, but isn't it great?"

"I think I took that shot." With his old Nikon. It had been raining outside, he remembered. He'd come in to find them warm and happy behind the bar, and his heart had expanded with love for both of them. That had been a good day.

She looked worried, a small line appearing between her eyebrows. "Is it okay?"

"Not my business." Literally.

"I hoped you would like it. They both look so happy, don't they?"

He nodded. There was no denying that. They looked like they were about to play a practical joke on someone, or just had. His mother was even pretty in the photo, light snapping in her eyes, and Hugh was just as bright.

"Oh, my God."

Her voice was low. "You see it, too."

They'd been in love.

They'd been in *love*? Hugh had loved his mother? Like that? How had he never seen it until he looked at the photo? "I didn't . . . I didn't know."

"I didn't know until I saw this, either. It's nice, I think."

He rubbed his neck, which suddenly ached as much as his stupid heart.

What else was there in the world that he didn't understand? Was it all this obvious? Was he just stupid?

His mother seemed happy in that shot.

Suddenly, the reason why Hugh had taken care of her so long made sense. It was crystal clear.

You're an idiot, Houston. He looked at Adele, let her image sear into his brain so that he wouldn't forget it. *For so many reasons.*

"Can I get a rum and Coke?" He thought for a moment. "Please." The picture hanging over her head made him hand over that courtesy. Grudgingly. He'd give her a thank you and a dollar tip because he was a decent man. He'd play his set, then he'd quit the band, and he'd never set foot in the saloon again as long as he lived.

CHAPTER FORTY

Adele had asked Scrug her question when he arrived. Scrug had asked Mack. Neither of them, because she asked them not to, had asked Nate.

So when they finished the first half of their set, when Nate's back was already turned as he unstrapped his guitar, Adele stepped onto the stage.

Her heart beat so fast it almost hurt. Her breath caught. "Hi," she said into the mike.

The crowd, the biggest one she'd seen in the saloon so far, went silent. Expectant.

Good Lord, she hoped she didn't let them down.

She hoped she didn't let *him* down. She held up his mother's guitar, the old Martin. "Do you mind if I play this?"

Nate looked startled, as if she'd just slapped him across the eye. "You can. You don't want to, though. It won't stay in tune."

"I put new pegs on it. It holds true now."

Nate blinked hard. Then he nodded.

The three men stepped off the stage into the crowd on the dance floor. She lost track of Mack and Scrug almost immediately, but not Nate. Adele felt him there. In the darkness. She couldn't see his face against the spotlight shining in her eyes, but she could see his outline. She could feel his stare against her skin. She overheated, instantly, and felt the sweat start at her hairline. Sexy.

She just needed to do this.

"Okay, then. I wrote this song. It's due to my publisher next week, and I thought it was going to be late, but then it kind of came to me." Her words tumbled over each other like a bird wheeling too fast to the ground. Soon she'd crash. "This is the first time it's been played out. I hope you like it."

Hope was so small a word for what she felt in her chest. A swell, as huge as the ocean's tide, rose inside her, and she strummed the first G chord.

Simple lyrics. Simple chords. She could do this.

"It's called 'My Confession.'"

She sang.

The café's closed, the sink's got mold,
The fridge is warm, and the beer's not cold.

Oysters gone, the fries are too.
But it all tastes right when I'm here with you.

Doors don't lock, and the beds are gone,
Roof is open to the break of dawn,
Hotel can't hold more than one or two
But it's all good when that's me and you.

The room was silent behind her words. They were listening. They were supporting her. Adele remembered this feeling – the way the audience could either tear you down or hold you up. They were holding her now, and thank God they were – her spine was liquid and her hairline damp with sweat. Fear danced through her, and still she could only see his outline in the dark.

She gathered every ounce of bravery she could and kept singing.

This saloon is old, and some wood is broke,
The floor is rough, the air is smoke,
The roof, it leaks, and the door's untrue,
But it's paradise when I'm here with you.

The lights out back, they dip and sway,
You took the stars and you made them stay.
You held this place and you made it new,
And I confess . . .

No.

Adele couldn't sing the last words. She just couldn't. They were ridiculous.

She'd written the song, and she'd thought it would work a miracle. She was so *stupid* for thinking this would be okay, that this would help, that this would do anything but humiliate her in front of a town full of people who seemed to care about her. She'd run – if she just stuck the mike back in the stand and started running –

Then a voice rose out of the dark.

"*And I confess . . .*" His voice. Rich, dark as the bar, and warm.

Clumsily, she strummed the abandoned chord. Then she raised her voice to join Nate's. Together, they sang the words that had been ripped from her soul and hung between them, like the line of stars in the courtyard. They sang the line that was inevitable, the only way the song could end.

"And I confess, I'm in love with you."

Then he was on the stage, the guitar pressed between their bodies, and he was kissing her, and she was kissing him back and laughing and there was clapping from somewhere close by, but really, there was only him, there was only Nate.

"I'm sorry," she started, and she was. "I'm so sorry – I did everything the wrong way. From the very beginning. From the moment I walked in here and didn't see immediately what was important." *Him. Nate was the most important.*

"So did I. Adele –"

"Wait. Can we start over?"

He gave a short laugh. "All the way to the beginning?"

She nodded. "Yes."

"We can try."

Behind them, the jukebox started playing an old Porter Wagoner tune. Adele tugged Nate's hand, pulling him offstage, almost tripping as she went. She felt his other hand at her waist, making sure she stayed steady. She dragged him into an even darker corner, under the broken Coors sign. Then she stuck out her hand. "Hi. I'm Adele Darling."

"Nate Houston. You're sure pretty."

Adele grabbed for breath as his arms went around her waist. Her mouth was inches from his. She would *not* kiss him, not now, even though it was all her body wanted. "Nice to meet you. What I'd really like to find out about the Golden Spike is – well, maybe its financial paperwork . . ."

"Screw this place."

"What?" Adele had a whole plan – to start over, to start honestly.

"I don't give a shit about this place."

"You love it."

"I love you. Everything else, every single thing, is secondary."

If his arms hadn't been around her waist, her legs would have buckled. As it was, she sagged a little. "Oh."

"Oh? That's your response to me telling you I love you?"

"I just . . ." Tears came to her eyes.

"What?"

"I've always been a songbird."

Nate kissed her cheek, catching the tear. "And?"

"But this is the first time I've really been able to fly." She leaned her forehead against his. "I love you. I love you so much I might die of it."

"Oh, God, Adele. I thought you were going to break my heart," he said, moving his lips to her hair, his hand against her cheek. "Isn't that your job?"

"No, no. I don't break things." She smiled at him. "I fix them."

EPILOGUE

O h, my," said Adele.

"What do you think?" Norma spread her arms wide. "The suit was my father's." Instead of Norma's usual flowing skirts, she wore a Santa Claus suit that looked the worse for its years: the enormous and frayed red suit was belted at the midpoint of her girth. She wore a Santa hat that stood so high she'd had to duck as she entered the room, and a fluffy white something perched precariously above her bosom. "My beard!" Norma said and pulled it up for a second. "It's itchy, though." She let it fall again. Four or five necklaces of bells were strung around her neck, and she jingled merrily with each breath.

"Is that – how did you . . . ?"

"Three full strings of outdoor Christmas lights." Norma was lit like a holiday sale at Walmart, all flashing colored lights and twinkles.

"How did you *do* that?"

Norma opened the top of the red jacket to display a dozen wires taped to a tie-dyed T-shirt. "Full battery pack, with a DC converter."

"You look like a mad bomber."

Norma looked pleased. "Thank you! Dixie! A martini! Make it minty and seasonal!"

Adele hurried to the stage, hoping that no epileptics got too close to Norma tonight – if anyone could trigger a seizure, it would be her.

Dixie, already pouring gin into a shaker, called, "You have two more messages from the media."

"No more!" called Adele. "If they want to sing small-town carols, they can just show up like the rest of them." Adele jiggled the amp's plug in the socket and then tested the speakers.

It was going to be a big night at the Golden Spike. Adele had been running since early morning, making sure the soda vendor came (he hadn't last week, and half the bridge club had complained about it – the other half happy enough to drink whiskey). Adele had swept and mopped the floors an extra time, and she'd polished the bar until the wood gleamed. She'd rearranged the storeroom so that they'd have more space for the two extra kegs of pumpkin-flavored beer that should be arriving any minute.

The saloon and its holiday singalong had been written up, and not just in the local paper. Not sure they'd be interested in her little announcement, Adele had sent both the *San Francisco Chronicle* and the *Eureka Times-Standard* a press release anyway. *Holiday Singalong and Hootenanny at the Golden Spike.*

The media loved it. A Darling Songbird, home for the holidays, leading the Christmas carols, with "local favorite" Dust & Rusty backing everyone up. It was delicious small-town flavor and after the papers had run it, two different affiliate TV stations had showed up, antennae sprouting from the vans" roofs. Adele had given three interviews already, and it wasn't even fully dark yet. Every spare room in town was rented, and Adele wished for the millionth time they'd had a chance to fix up even one extra room in the hotel above.

But running the saloon was proving a full-time job. She loved it, but it wasn't easy.

"Hey, Earl Cornejo called and asked if he could kick things off with the bagpipes." Dixie's words were punctuated by the ice clattering in the shaker.

"Of course he can. When's Nate coming?" Adele knew Nate and Dixie had had lunch together that afternoon.

Dixie rattled the shaker harder.

"Hey, Dixie. When's Nate coming in? I think his cell phone is dead. He hasn't answered my texts all afternoon."

Instead of answering the question, Dixie slid the martini to Norma. "Minty fresh, like holiday toothpaste! Now you'll be ready for the mistletoe."

"Dixie?" Adele straightened, wiping her dusty hands on her jeans.

Blinking quickly, Dixie said, "Yeah?"

"What's going on?"

"Nothing." Dixie shook her head hard. "Absolutely nothing! Why?"

"Why aren't you looking at me? What are you hiding?"

Dixie pressed a hand to her chest. "Me? Nothing. Nothing at *all.*"

Norma, too, was staring too hard at the photo of Hugh and Donna above the bar, as if they might start moving in the frame.

"Something's going on, and you both know it. I want to know what it is."

Dixie leaned forward, her hands flat on the bar. She spoke in a stage whisper. "Nate has a little surprise for you. But don't you *dare* let on that I said anything."

"What is it?"

"Are you kidding me? He may not be my boss anymore, but I'm still not risking his wrath."

"Wait. I *am* your boss. I order you to tell me."

"No way."

"Well, then, you're fired."

"Again? You're so trigger-happy." Unconcerned, Dixie turned the overhead TV to the Yule log channel. "Here we go."

"Fine. Don't tell me." A shiver of excitement slid up Adele's spine. She couldn't imagine what the surprise might be, but whatever it was, she knew it would be good. One night, Nate had gotten a serious look on his face that had both thrilled and terrified her, and then he'd fastened a chain around her neck. The pendant was his mother's two-month sobriety chip.

There was no present he could give her that would ever mean more to her than that.

"Did he go back to work after your lunch?" She couldn't remember what he'd said his schedule was today, but if it was like other days, it would be grueling. Nate came home exhausted from his long days of work with Adult Protective Services, and he sometimes had haunted shadows behind his eyes from what he'd seen. He would lie with Adele on the old parlor sofa and together they'd listen to the quiet noises of the street below. She would kiss his temple and listen to him, and then she'd tell him what she'd accomplished at the Spike that day (always less than she wanted to – there was still so much to do). Then he'd kiss her, really, truly kiss her, and the whole world melted away.

Adele wrapped her fingers around her necklace. The jukebox, as if warming up for the night to come, swung into a country version of "O, Come All Ye Faithful." Norma laughed at something Dixie had said, and Parrot

Freddy came in, both birds on his shoulders. He said they sometimes sang along to "Jingle Bells", and Adele was hoping to hear their version at some point in the evening.

But sweet Patsy Cline, what was the surprise?

Adele stood at the edge of the stage and tucked one more strand of tinsel around the extra microphone stands. She heard the swinging door slap open, then closed.

"Come on now, this place doesn't look so bad."

The voice came from behind her. Everything in Adele's body stilled. Her brain replayed the words once, and then once again.

She turned slowly. The hope – if she was wrong – would kill her. And if she was right, the happiness might do exactly the same.

"Hi," said Molly.

It was Molly, *her* Molly. She looked tired, dark circles under her eyes. Her black shirt-dress hung on her, as if she'd recently lost weight.

Adele launched herself at her sister, almost knocking her down with the force of her hug. "You, you, *you*. You came. You came home."

Then Adele didn't know who was crying harder: her, or Molly, or Norma, who was wiping away her tears with her Santa beard. "How did you get here? How long are you staying? Have you met Nate?"

Because Nate was there, standing behind Molly, with the most *satisfied* look on his face.

"We met," said Molly, sniffing hard. "He got me here. It's been hell trying to keep it a secret."

"I can't believe –" Adele swallowed the sob in her throat. "Thank you." She met his eye. *Thank you.* She'd tell him more, so much more, later. If he'd scrambled up a ladder to steal her the moon, he couldn't have brought her anything that could make her happier.

"We're singing tonight," Adele said, and even headier joy filled her – if she drank all the liquor in the bar, she couldn't be drunker on happiness. "We're *singing.* Together."

Molly nodded. "I got here in time, then."

"Will you stay for Christmas? Please stay. *Please* stay."

Molly bit her lower lip and then nodded. "Yes. But don't push. Okay? One step at a time."

Adele held up her hands. "Promise." Then her hand fell and she clutched the chip at her throat. "Oh, *Molly.*"

Her sister turned in place. "You'll have to show me everything. The wreckage. All of it."

"I will. I will."

"And introduce me to everyone."

Nate laughed. "You don't have to worry about that. Every single resident will be in here trying to catch a glance of you tonight. Word's already spread." He looked suspiciously at Adele. "You really didn't know?"

Adele leaned against him, grateful for his bulk, for his solidity. "Not a clue."

"Hey, that isn't the old jukebox," said Molly. She moved forward to look at it.

Nate dropped a kiss on the top of Adele's head. "Happy?"

"It would be impossible for me to be happier. It would probably be illegal." *Unless Lana was here.* It was an ungrateful thought, and Adele banished it. This, right here, was all she needed. She wrapped her arm around Nate's waist. "How am I going to thank you?"

Molly moved to the middle of the floor and looked out the side window, towards the shuttered café.

Nate said, "You were standing right there when I first saw you."

"And you hated me."

"I loved you. I think I've always loved you, even when I didn't know it."

Joy made Adele's heart soar. She was opening her mouth to respond when Norma, still seated at the bar, gave a screech.

"Lord have mercy! Would you look at this?" She gave another shrill cry. "Look!" Norma jabbed her finger at the tarot cards. "A wedding is on the horizon!" She looked up from her cards, peeking at Dixie and then over her shoulder at Adele and Nate. "And I see a baby here! A baby coming!"

Adele blinked, hard. Next to her, she could hear Nate swallow.

"And I also see plenty of drinks on the house! I can see it in the cards! Right here, look!"

ABOUT THE AUTHOR

Rachael Herron is the bestselling author of the novels *The Ones Who Matter Most*, *Splinters of Light*, and *Pack Up the Moon* (Penguin), the five-book Cypress Hollow series, and the memoir, *A Life in Stitches* (Chronicle). She received her MFA in writing from Mills College, Oakland. She teaches writing extension workshops at both UC Berkeley and Stanford and is a proud member of the NaNoWriMo Writer's Board. She's a New Zealand citizen as well as an American.

Rachael *loves* to hear from readers:
Website: rachaelherron.com
Facebook: Rachael.Herron.Author
Twitter: RachaelHerron
Email: yarnagogo@gmail.com

CPSIA information can be obtained
at www.ICGtesting.com
Printed in the USA
BVOW06s2133091117
500024BV00007B/180/P